Darcy Dates

Jena Kingsley

Darcy Dates is a work of fiction.
It is based on the 2010-2011 blog of the same name, Darcy Dates.
Names, characters, places, and incidents are products of the author's imagination and are used fictitiously. Any resemblance to actual events, locales, or persons, living or dead is just coincidental.
Copyright © 2025 by Jena Kingsley
All rights reserved.
Printed and distributed in the United States by IngramSpark.
No part of this publication may be reproduced, distributed, or transmitted in any form or by any means, including photocopying, recording, or other electronic or mechanical methods, without the prior written permission of the publisher, except as permitted by U.S. copyright law. For permission requests, contact info@jenakingsley.com.
1st edition 2025
ISBN 979-8-218-61824-7 (paperback)
ISBN 979-8-9985864-0-8 (hardcover)
ISBN 979-8-218-65371-2 (ebook)
ISBN 979-8-9985864-1-5 (audio)
Printed in the United States of America on acid-free paper.

1.0

I started writing Darcy Dates six months after my father died. Darcy Dates is dedicated to my father, who told me I was funny. Really funny. And one day the whole world would know.

And for James. Always James.

CONTENTS

Darcy Dates   ix

   Prologue   1
1. Darcy Dates   3
2. Your Vagina Has Cancer   5
3. Can You Be Friends After a Defriend?   9
4. Supermarket Aisles and Charity Work   14
5. Jonathan, 40, is Really 47   18
6. Wink Not, Want Not   23
7. JDon't 101   27
8. The Bait and Switch   28
9. Hello, Old Friend   33
10. As Long As You Are Happy   37
11. Real Texts From Real Men   38
12. Do Not Touch   40
13. He Will Boil Your Bunny   41
14. Cinco De Mayo   44
15. Real Texts From Real Men   47
16. Townie-rific   48
17. Yankees V. Red Sox   53
18. Can You Hear Me Now?   57
19. Jonathan, 47, Really Had A Girlfriend   59
20. GayDate   62
21. Real Texts From Real Men   66
22. Real Texts From Real Men   67
23. House Arrest   68
24. Real Voice Mail From Real Men   72
25. Ghost of Risotto Past   73
26. Real Phone Calls From Real Men   78
27. Single Man Drought   81
28. Scenes From A Night Out   82
29. The Robbie Report   85
30. Step Away From The Blackberry   88
31. No Gifts Please   89
32. Full Disclosure   91

33. Channeling Demi	93
34. When you Least Expect It	100
35. The Pious Life	105
36. Real Texts From Real Men	110
37. Breaking The Rules	112
38. Real Texts From My Mom	118
39. Needing Space	120
40. Darcy Plus Party	123
41. Real Texts From Real Men	127
42. He Shoots, He Scores	128
43. The Third Date	130
44. He's Baaack	133
45. My GPS Can Suck It	134
46. Advice From My Ex-Husband	137
47. Interpret This	138
48. Robbie Reunion	142
49. Mr. Wrong Right Now	145
50. Dear Date From Last Night	147
51. Bridal Skeletons In My Closet	149
52. Snooki Said It	153
53. The List	154
54. The Prankster	156
55. Thank you? I Think?	159
56. My Date With Robbie	160
57. It's Not Me, It's You	164
58. Online D(egr)ating	166
59. Dear CVS Management	169
60. It's Not Rocket Science	171
61. Pretension Is A Four Letter Word	172
62. The Doctor Won't See You Now	177
63. Forget Paris	180
64. Dating Detox	184
65. Anatomically Correct	188
66. Real Texts From Robbie	189
67. Spray And Wash	191
68. When Life Gives You Citrus...Don't Make A Collar	193
69. Driving With My Mom	194
70. Breaking The Fast	197
71. Real Texts From Real Men	200
72. It's Complicated	202

73. Meet Robbie's Family	204
74. Under My Umbrella	214
75. Don't Ask, Don't Tell	217
76. More On My Vagina…	221
77. Deal Breakers	222
78. Hey Jealousy…	225
79. Take My Ex-Wife. Please	228
80. High Stakes	229
81. Songs About Darcy	232
82. My Mom The Stalker	235
83. I'll Have What He's Having	237
84. Auld Lang Syne	241
85. What's In A Name?	243
86. Wishful Waxing	244
87. Robbie On Housekeeping	245
88. Crossing The Lines	248
89. Nightmare On Boyfriend Street	251
90. Real Phone Calls From Real Men	254
91. A Ring On It	255
92. A Visit From Robbie	256
93. Advice From My Doorman	259
94. Survey Says…	262
95. Lessons From Boys Night	265
96. Dodging Bullets	267
97. Moving and Shaking	271
98. I'm Divorced, You're Divorced…Let's Party?	276
99. A Diamond is Forever. And So is Robbie	278
100. Time To Go	280
101. My Penis Pen Pal	282
102. Matchmaker, Matchmaker Make Me a Match…That is Alive	284
103. Taxi Cab Confessions	285
104. My Wingmidget	288
105. Robbie.com	291
106. Dog Days of Summer	294
107. How To Pick Up A Guy	296
108. Sugar and Spice and All Things…Technological	301
109. I Don't Have To Say I'm Sorry…'Cause I Love You?	303
110. Your Mama	305
111. The Green Thumbs Down	308

112. Family, Party of 2	311
113. My Mother, My Pimp	314
114. There Were Two In The Bed and The Little One Said...	317
115. The Thing About Crushes	318
116. Sometimes...I Stalk Too	325
117. Friday Night Lights	329
118. Kick Off Your Sunday Shoes	332
119. The Most Dramatic Rose Ceremony Yet	333
120. Breaking Bad	338
121. General Hospital	339
122. Having What It Takes	341
123. On Being Discovered	345
124. Mildly My Type	350
125. All His Children	354
126. Eleven Missed Calls	355
127. The Pimp Award	359
128. Robbie Gets Cocky	364
129. The End	365
Acknowledgments	369

Darcy Dates

PROLOGUE

I have always said, the best material writes itself. This was proven one night, late at night, when I started to document my dating stories. Social media was in its earliest stages. The masses were just beginning to use Facebook. People would upload 43 pictures from a night out. Nothing was edited. Nothing was curated. Filters did not exist. There was no algorithm. It was the wild west of blogging days, when people could write about what they wanted, when they wanted. They could do it anonymously. And that is what I did. I took what I had written, and uploaded it to a blog. I called myself Darcy. Darcy Dates.

It was started before the days of Instagram. Before the days of caring what people thought. At least before the days of me caring what people thought. After all, it didn't matter because no one knew who I was. Over time, 5 people shared it with 5 more. Until I had a following. Darcy had a following. Darcy had a community of readers and Hollywood came calling. I...got discovered. That is when it got complicated. Darcy Dates was being developed as a show that didn't work out and then developed once more, until it was shelved.

Years later, I have decided to set it free. Release it as a book that I self published. Free from comment, criticism and the vision of anyone other than myself (and of course, anyone who reads this). It is raw and unedited as it was written in 2010. Keeping it in a setting of 2010 makes this a period piece, when people clung to their Blackberrys and there was no debate about skinny jeans. *Everyone* wore skinny jeans.

Names, locations and any identifying information have been changed to protect the innocent.

For those of you reading this, thank you for giving it life once again. I have always said, if one person likes it, I have done my job.

The world has changed *dramatically* since this was written. So much has changed for me *personally* since this was written. I would update you here, but I do not want to ruin the ending of this book. If people end up reading this, there just might be a sequel.

1

DARCY DATES

APRIL 30, 2010

I GOT MARRIED YOUNG. At the tender age of twenty-three. To a great man. But I was young. And having been so young (in college) when I met my husband, I had never really been on the adult dating scene. Seven years of marriage, one child and one divorce later, I find myself out there dating in New York City. Sometimes my experiences are more insane than a fever dream, and after sharing them with friends I realized what a great story I had to tell. So here it goes. I will write what I can, when I can, so dear friends and strangers, or whoever reads this blog, can enjoy this wonderful crazy journey with me.

My dating stories that pre-date this blog are incredible, and at times unbelievable, and while it is truly a shame they have not been written about, I am starting on this wonderful day, April 30, 2010 where I can only hope to have more dates going forward to write about. For now, I will write bits and pieces of what I have learned from my experiences. Names and locations will often be changed to protect the identity of my dates, who might fare better with the protection of a padded room than a name change on a random blog. But I digress.

2

YOUR VAGINA HAS CANCER

APRIL 30, 2010

IT WAS A BEAUTIFUL SPRING DAY. I had just had lunch with one of my current beaus, a man I am casually dating who I am taking it incredibly slow with. I only see him once every other week or so. On the off weeks, we schedule dates, but I usually cancel. Having texted all morning in between appointments with a new client in the village, he invites me to an impromptu lunch date by my office to where I have just returned.

I picked a nice restaurant, that will remain nameless, which has excellent food, a great atmosphere, but is a bit more low profile than some of the other high-profile lunch haunts on Madison avenue where I can possibly run into someone at any time. Dating as a mom in New York City is funny like that. I don't want to be very public about it, especially since Manhattan (read Manhattan Jews) is such a small world and everyone knows everyone and everyone has gone to camp, college, teen tours, their kids are in the same class, etc, etc, etc. Before you know it, your date is over before it even began because your best friend's cousin dated this guy when they were 20 and he never called her back and has been forever labeled a player and everyone absolutely FORBIDS you to even go for coffee with this terrible man.

I sit down at the table and wait. Some friends are suddenly seated at the very next table. I smile politely and plant my face in the menu, hoping that they don't notice I am meeting...*gasp*...a date. My date shows up and as always it's very "nice." We exchange witty banter, I tell inappropriate stories. He looks at me in admiration as I sprinkle my conversation with the word tits and polish off my glass of Sauvignon Blanc, which is really chardonnay but I didn't want to make a big deal about it (even though I don't love chardonnay). He asks me out for next week. I say yes, knowing inside I may possibly cancel.

He is a bit short for me and when I wear heels he seems exactly my height, if not an inch shorter which is usually a deal breaker for me. I will divulge this early. I am tall and I love to wear heels on a date. I would prefer borderline obese to short when it comes to the men I date, but this is a nice guy, and surprisingly funny. He has an unexpected tattoo on his forearm and for an upper east side money manager that is rare. I am pleasantly surprised to learn this at dinner one night. It makes me like him more since I believe it gives him the edge I think he is missing.

I say goodbye to him outside the restaurant and head down Madison to my next appointment with my new client. I have a spring in my step. Maybe it's the new client, maybe it's the chardonnay. I just had a surprisingly good lunch date with a guy who really likes me and I don't totally dislike. Either way, I am feeling good and nothing can bring me down.

Suddenly a woman walks by me. She is dressed sensibly, in her late forties. She takes two steps back and stops me.

"Excuse me!" she says. "Your aura! It's incredible! I can see it all around you shining bright!"

Now, I am a believer of the supernatural and have nothing against a good psychic reading, so she happened to pick the right girl.

"Really?" I say. Beaming. Maybe things are looking up for me, I think to myself.

"Yes! They are sending me so many messages for you!"

I am not sure who this proverbial "they" is, but I like it just as much. I will take any "they." I will take "they" the doorman's union. I will take "they" the people that play Farmville. I will take it. It sounds positive.

"I am India! What is your name?"

"Darcy!" I say, hoping this will send more messages from the "they."

Before I know it she shuffles me to the side on the sidewalk.

"The messages are so strong! They are sending you messages. I need to get them to you. They said you are here on this earth to do incredible things! They said you are here to break new ground and this world hasn't seen the best of you yet."

I eat each spoonful of crap she feeds me, trying to decipher its meaning, even though deep down I know she's a whack job. Suddenly she reaches into her fanny pack, yes, she had on a fanny pack, which now makes me wonder why I describe her as sensibly dressed, though fanny packs are hands free and in a sense sensible no? She takes out a tiny black bag. I can see where this is going. She pulls out stones, I think psychics call them ruins, but maybe I am confusing psychics with archaeologists at this point. She tells me she is going to give me a quick reading.

"Is this going to cost me money?" I ask.

"Well people pay me, if you want you can." She says with her intense smile and crazy eyes.

"I have no money and I am actually on a way to a meeting. I should get going." At this point I realize this is all a scam and I am trying to extract myself from the steps of the church I am somehow sitting on at this point. I always think I would not get in a van to help a man try to find his puppy, but maybe I am *that* girl.

"That's okay," she pleads, "I will walk you to the nearest ATM machine."

Is this woman kidding me? We have gone from Madison Avenue to Deliverance in 40 seconds flat.

"No, I am fine, you aren't walking me to an ATM machine."

Suddenly India goes from the dear lady you would like as your nanny to crazy grifter with a fanny pack in a flash.

She screams to me with desperation, "They are sending me messages you need to hear, you have an infection inside that is turning into cancer in your vagina! I can't believe they did this to you."

"Listen up!" I say, "This started off very positive and is suddenly more creepy than carneys. I am walking away and don't want you to say another word."

"This is positive. I am telling you how to cure yourself of the cancer in your vagina."

She keeps screaming to me about my cancerous vagina as I walk away as quickly as possible, knowing she is crazy but thinking I need to call my gyno asap.

Fitting I think to myself. It's all fun and games til someone tells you your vagina has cancer. And as I heard many times before, the SNL theme song of Debbie Downer plays in my head. Wah wahhhh.

3

CAN YOU BE FRIENDS AFTER A DEFRIEND?

APRIL 30, 2010

DATING in a world with so many mediums is tough. If you have seen the movie *He's Just Not That Into You,* you will remember the scene when Drew Barrymore is explaining that there are so many complicated ways to figure out if you are getting dissed; you have to check your email, your texts, your voicemail, your Facebook, your twitter… and it's true. In a world with so many new and exciting ways to keep in touch, comes major trouble for dating.

Let's look at the facts. You meet a great guy. He sends you a Facebook friend request. You look at his pictures. He's cute! You realize you have friends in common. He can't be that bad! He is randomly friends with your best friend from 3rd grade. He has to be a good guy. She was nice. She let you play with her cabbage patch kid because they were sold out everywhere. He has pictures with his nieces and nephews and it looks like he is being nice to them. Aw. *So cute.* His status updates are witty. He is funny AND smart. To be witty you have to be smart. He is a freakin' genius. Did he actually just quote Tribe Called Quest? He is cool too! You could love him. You could one day have your facebook status set to "Darcy is In a Relationship with New Facebook Guy".

Suddenly he adds a new Facebook friend. It's a girl. She is cute. Who is she? Why weren't they friends last week? How did he find her? Do they have friends in common? When he said he was going out to dinner with his grandma last night was he really having drinks with his new Facebook friend? Suddenly someone tags him in a picture. He is at that new place in the meatpacking district that has a list. How did he get on that list? Is he cooler than you thought? Maybe he is too cool for you. He is sitting with girls in the picture. Who are they? *What*? One of them just planted an apple tree on his farm on Farmville. Are they moving in together? Why are they milking each other's Farmville cows? Wait! He just responded to an event next Thursday. It is in an art gallery and 114 people are attending. Guess you aren't seeing him next Thursday. Who are the 245 people that haven't responded yet? Why weren't you invited??? And so on and so on and so on.

Let's call him Andre. He just moved back to the city from Texas. Southern guys are nice right? Gentleman? We have our first date on Valentine's day. I send him a text before the date:

"I know it's Valentine's day, but please don't propose. It will be awkward and I am not ready for the commitment."

"But I love you," He responds. He gets my humor so the date won't be a total disaster. We meet for margaritas. Tequila always makes me fall in love, or at least in like. On our first date we plan our wedding in Vegas and name our unborn children. I like him. Not enough to actually marry him, but I will go out with him again.

Andre really likes me. He emails the friend that set him up that it was basically the best setup he's ever had. We set another date. Dinner and Jay Z at MSG. It's fun, but I realize he isn't for me. He seems stubborn and controlling. We go out a few more times, as he is funny and I am bored. He even brings me to dinner with his mother. A lovely woman. Something shifts. Now I am starting to like him. He seems like a really nice guy. He is patient with my crazy schedule. I tell myself this is who I should be dating. A nice guy. From the south. Who likes Obama even though he is from Texas. He thinks I am beautiful and funny. He tells me I am one of the smartest girls he has ever met. I know he is dead wrong but nod and agree. When he picks me up for our dates he smells a bit like liquor which strikes me as odd and a bit alcoholic, but I tell myself that is what Texans do. He introduces me to all his friends, and constantly complains to me that he thinks he likes me so much more than I like him. I decided this must be what it's like dating a girl.

A month and a half into dating Andre, we go to dinner. On the way to the restaurant I wrote something funny about Andre's facebook status on his wall. Andre and I are best facebook friends. We might even tag each other in a picture soon.

My cousin calls. I answer at the table. Andre yells at me and tells me I am rude for taking a call during dinner. It creeps me out that he got so angry but the Martinis are numbing the fear. Soon we are sharing a sea bass and gang up on the next table. We made up. I decided to see his house for the first time. After he plays me every song he has ever loved, I pass out. In the middle of the night I am awoken by Andre doing things around the house. Fully dressed. I glance at the clock and it's 4 am. *Where is my phone*? I need my phone. I always sleep with it next to me in case of an emergency. I went into his living room and looked next to my bag and coat. No phone. I know for 100% certainty I left it there. I ask Andre to call my phone cause I can't find it anywhere. He tells me he will find it. He returns holding the phone and tells me it was on his kitchen counter. I know for 100% certainty I had never stepped foot in his kitchen.

I look at my phone. I noticed some emails were opened that I didn't read. I think my mind is playing tricks on me and I had possibly had more to drink than I realized. Andre tells me to get back into bed and gives me his favorite blanket. I fall asleep and wake up at 7 am. Andre is already awake and on his computer.

"Good morning gorgeous, you look so beautiful. Can I make you coffee? Breakfast? I will make you whatever breakfast you want." I am proud of myself for sticking with Andre. Finally I chose a nice guy. I agree to a cup of coffee that turns into two. Andre gives me the paper and asks me to hang out. I realize I have to run. I need to get to work.

Less than a half hour later I am home and on the phone with one of my best friends. I tell her I just spent the night at Andre's house. I told her he yelled at me about using the phone at dinner but other than that he was a total gentleman. I tell her I will email her a picture of him. I log on to facebook and go to his page so I can screenshot a picture from his profile.

It gives me the option of adding Andre as a friend. *Huh?* He is my friend. I just got back from his house 10 minutes ago. Confused, I refresh the page. It is staring at me mockingly. "ADD AS FRIEND." I text Andre : "Defriended?? Ouch."

Andre explains he gets the sense he likes me much more than I like him and that I don't take him seriously. I am confused beyond belief. What about the blueberry pancakes he was just offering to make me? What about my second cup of coffee he was squeezing out of a french press? "What are you talking about?" I ask. He tells me it's how he "feels." I realize Andre might be watching more Oprah than he leads on.

I don't hear from Andre for 24 hours when I finally ask him if we are on for the concert that night we are supposed to attend. He tells me he is tired and going to watch basketball with his friend. I am knocked off my feet. *BUT ANDRE, YOU WERE CRAZY ABOUT ME?!* I scream. In my head. There is more to this story but I don't know what it is yet.

After two days of not hearing from Andre he sends me a drunk text at 1 am. He confessed to me that he went through my phone when I was sleeping (*I KNEW I HADN'T LEFT IT IN THE KITCHEN*), and that he saw some risqué texts between me and a guy, we will call Adam. Little does he know Adam is a very old dear friend with whom I have never even come close to an inappropriate encounter with, we just share the same raunchy humor. Andre had taken my *text* out of *context* and ruined everything. Gone was our farm, gone were our tagged facebook photos, gone was our "friend"-ship. He wrote me some apology manifesto emails. I told him for the first time in 6 years since owning a blackberry, I now had a password on it. And the password was Andre. Four Weeks later Andre was listed as being "In a Relationship" on his Facebook page, which by the way, he never realized was public.

4

SUPERMARKET AISLES AND CHARITY WORK

M<small>AY 1, 2010</small>

W<small>HEN YOU ARE SINGLE</small>, they always say you will meet someone fabulous walking through aisles of a supermarket. They claim if you join a group of some kind, do some type of charitable work, possibly plant a tree in some sort of community garden, he will be there. Your soulmate. He will approach you in a parking lot (creepy), you will meet him in a bookstore (lurking behind a shelf somewhere), you will lock eyes in a coffee shop somewhere and he will approach your table...the people that give this dating advice have never been to New York. Okay, okay, so it *does* happen. Sometimes. People meet people in public places. In fact, it happened to my mother, but it is rare.

It happened one time early on after my divorce. Out to dinner with my family for my sister's birthday I locked eyes with a very handsome stranger. He was very cute. After a virtual staring contest and 2 Appletinis later, I summoned up the courage, with the encouragement (albeit inappropriate) from my sister to send this handsome stranger a drink. The waitress informed us he ordered a beer and when we asked if he was cute she told us he had a thick accent like he was not from the city (I believe redneck was the exact term she used), and she had assessed there was some type of missing tooth. Figures.

Minutes later he approached our table. He said he was not from New York City but was here for work.

"What type of work do you do?" I asked this toothless hick stranger.

"I play hockey for a team in Pittsburgh, we are in town to play the Rangers." *Are you kidding me? A Penguin? It explains the missing teeth!* He asked for my number and asked if I wanted to come to the game tomorrow. I told him I would be cheering for the Rangers, but I would go. As I left the restaurant an hour later he and his teammate suddenly had a posse of groupies or prostitutes of some kind surrounding their table. I waved awkwardly and he said he would call me, which he did, at 12 midnight and asked me to hang out. What? Was this real? I was getting booty called by an NHL hockey player? I said no thanks, but was a bit flattered and quickly erased him from my mind. Three months later I read in the paper that he got married. Engaged no doubt when he called me. I guess the stereotypes regarding pro athletes were obviously true!

Well, it happened again. The dating unicorn, as I like to call it. An urban myth if you will, when a man and woman meet by coincidence in a public place. Where drunken bar talk is not involved and you lock eyes and everything falls into place, whether it be while picking cereal in the cereal aisle, working in a soup kitchen, or praying in some type of religious establishment. Only this time it was at a swank restaurant on the Upper East side.

I had met a male friend for dinner and went to the back of the restaurant to use the bathroom. As I was returning to my table the hostess was escorting two men to their table when I locked eyes with one of them. He was insanely handsome and I flashed my greatest Darcy smile at him without even realizing I was doing it. He stopped in his tracks and smiled back. It was exactly as you picture it to be, only better, because it was real. I quickly prayed he wasn't married, promised to go to services on the high holidays this year if he wasn't and returned to my table. An hour or so later he was leaving the restaurant and had to walk past my table to exit. Again, I began to summon my inner light and shot him my most dazzling smile. Quickly eyeing my dinner date he asked if we knew each other.

"I don't know. Do we?" I asked coyly, knowing that we did not, but hoping we would soon.

"I'm Jonathan," he said, again eyeing my male dinner partner with suspicion.

"I'm Darcy. Do you know me?"

He smirked and said he wasn't sure.

"Did we date?" I asked, knowing that we didn't, but at this point I couldn't control my shameless flirting.

"I don't know, did we?" he said.

"For six months, I think." I giggled at my own joke.

It was shameful. I had to suppress the voice in my head that was screaming "thank you, thank you very much, I'll be here all night."

But like every other New York story where boy smiles at girl, girl smiles back, boy gets off the subway and it becomes nothing more than a craigslist missed connection, he said to have a good dinner and I watched him walk out of the restaurant.

Just like in *Back To The Future*, when people's faces start to disappear from the pictures as history starts to change, the same thing happened with our imagined relationship. Sigh. Back to my sushi and my dinner date.

My dinner date's cell phone rang. "It's my girlfriend, be right back" He stepped out of the restaurant to talk to her in a quiet place, when suddenly the hostess appeared at our table.

"Are you Darcy?" she asked. She couldn't be a stitch past 24 and not a wrinkle in sight.

"Yes?" I said, not sure where this was going.

"You have a phone call."

I didn't know what to make of this. Who knew where I was. Was my child okay? Oh my goodness. My child. Is there some type of emergency? It quickly dawned on me that if there was an emergency they would try my cell phone first and not some random restaurant no one even knew I was at.

I followed the hostess to her stand and she handed me the phone. "Hello?" I said.

"Darcy? It's Jonathan, from 5 minutes ago".

Was this really happening? Was I really the star of my own private romantic comedy? These things only happened in Julia Roberts movies. I could not even fathom this to be real.

"Oh yes, hi Jonathan."

Yeah, hi Jonathan, like I had already forgotten who he was.

"Hi, listen, I wanted to ask you to dinner, but I wasn't sure if you were there on a date with that guy. If you weren't and you would like to have dinner with me, I'd love to take you out. I couldn't let this night pass without trying everything I could to see you again"

"Sure, that would be great," is really all I remember saying at first. But then it happened. Barbara Walters invaded my body and a barrage of questioning ensued right from the hostess stand's telephone. "Are you married? How old are you? 40? Oh, divorced. Do you have children? No? Oh, I do, yes. One. Yes. What do you do? Investment Banking? Huh. Where are you from? I see. What is your last name? Oh! You're Jewish?!" Like any diligent woman, I was collecting my facts and assessed that Jonathan, 40, Jewish, investment banker, divorced with no children would be a suitable dinner date. I gave him my number and walked back to my table feeling like the hottest girl in town. I was sure it was the new belt I had been bullied into buying at Intermix only a week earlier. I never owned a belt, but it had to be good luck, or a good look for me. It was definitely the belt. I couldn't remember Jonathan's last name, so I was not able to do my run of the mill google-facebook–peoplepages–ecourts extravaganza. But he texted me, and just like that, we had a date for Thursday.

5

JONATHAN, 40, IS REALLY 47

May 1, 2010

It has happened to all of us at one point or another. We want to believe something is as good as it seems, even if there is information telling us otherwise. Sometimes when we see red flags, we ignore them, for one reason or another. We have all been there, and have made excuses for things we know deep down are clearly bad news. I myself have been guilty of ignoring them. At times I have not only ignored flags, I have ignored banners, bonfires, forest fires, and volcanos. One time, and I have never shared this with anyone, I had men in hazmat suits come to rescue me in an emergency vehicle, yet I waved them away. "I am fine!" I screamed, as they looked on in horror. I have clung onto ships sinking faster than the Titanic, and I have gone down trails with avalanche warning signs during avalanche season. It's been me, it's been you. It's been all of us.

In this case it was me. Jonathan, 40, investment banker shows up to meet me for our Thursday night date. I am waiting at the bar when he walks in the restaurant. In the light (or at least a *more* bright restaurant than where I had first met him), he looks older than when we met. However, our first meeting was so romantic that he was built up so much in my mind even George Clooney may have been a disappointment. We say hello and I immediately ask him the burning question.

"So. You're 40?"

"Actually I'm 47."

Awkward silence.

"I thought you said you were 40."

"I know. That was the first time I have ever lied about my age."

Suddenly the tiny referee on my shoulder raised his first red flag.

"I don't know why I did that", Jonathan continues, "I have never ever done that and couldn't believe I did!" He says, trying his best to convince me, although it seemed like he was working harder to convince himself.

We walked to our table and just like that, I ignored my first red flag.

Something about Jonathan seemed feminine. I couldn't put my finger on it. Maybe it was his affected accent that was a cross between queens english and gayness, but whatever it was it earned him the moniker, GBF for Gay Boyfriend. Oh yea, flag number two.

We sat down and I asked Jonathan what he does for a living. Actually, I now thought Jonathan had ruined his credibility, so I was cross checking his new answers against his original ones. He mentions he is a very high level exec (he doesn't use these words, he uses the actual title, but for privacy reasons I will keep it to myself) for a very very large bank. I am actually shocked. He then continues that he was on the board of directors of another large, very public company. Huh. What I was impressed with is how subtle the references were and if you weren't knowledgeable about Wall Street careers, you might have even missed it. This impressed me. I have dated a lot of men who like to pepper the conversation with references to their private planes, their drivers, how powerful and successful they are, stories about their lunches with Don (Donald

Trump) and so on and so forth. Jonathan did none of these things. I liked that. It impressed me more than his career and the fact that he was obviously incredibly bright.

I asked Jonathan how long he was married for. He said two years in his early 20's. I did the math. He was 47 and not yet again married. Super handsome, super successful, seemed very kind. Suddenly an entire strand of flags unfurled from my mind and the restaurant looked like a grand opening for a used car dealer. I couldn't control myself. Don't ask Darcy. I could not help it. I turned to him.

"Are you gay?"

"What?"

"Gay? Are you gay?"

"No I'm not gay!"

I didn't let it go.

"Do you ever get asked that?"

"I have been asked that before," he admits, "But I am definitely not gay."

It wasn't comforting that I wasn't the first to ask this.

He tells me he was engaged again in his early 40's but called off that engagement. I didn't know how I felt about this whole thing. But the oysters came and for the time being I was occupied.

Jonathan was clearly incredibly well read, and had a socially awkward habit of quoting books and poems and random things that I knew nothing about, other than they were probably famous. Many of the references were lost on me and made me cringe a bit. I am a freshman in poetry, but I have a PhD in rap.

Fifteen minutes into dinner, Jonathan asked if he could kiss me. I said no. I found this request odd. We hadn't even gotten half way through our first drink and the restaurant was not dark AND I had already asked if he was gay. It seemed that Jonathan was not good at picking up social cues. Of course I looked past this too. I would have made an excellent WASP the way I just sweep things under the rug and look the other way. That, or a great mafia wife of some kind.

As dinner continued I found myself liking Jonathan. He was still cute, a little gay, but seemed like a gentle soul. Jonathan told me he thought the date was great and asked me out for the very next day. I said I could not go then and set a date for a week later.

Our next date was great. We had dinner at 8 and closed out the restaurant at 11:45, not before dancing the hustle together (don't ask- long story- involving a drunk restaurant manager with an excellent playlist). Jonathan seemed straight, more laid back than I had originally assessed and we had fun. Jonathan dropped me off at home and sent me a text that basically said he was excited about the prospect of someday having children with me. It was crazy I thought, but he was a little crazy so I just chalked it up to eccentric and crazy (read ignored more red flags), and smiled myself to sleep. We set a date for the following week. He was headed to LA for a long weekend.

I thought it was odd I didn't hear from Jonathan for a few days. For someone that wanted to have children with me, he certainly didn't want to speak to me. On our next date I asked him about it. It didn't take much for Jonathan to come clean that he was visiting a woman in LA, but he broke up with her, because he would rather date me. Because I could give him children and I was what he was looking for. I could give him children? Was Jonathan mistaking me for a cow?

My mother called me when I was out to dinner. Jonathan took the phone from me and told her he was sorry he had lied to me (again) and he hoped someday she would be his mother-in-law.

Jonathan asked me to come home with him that night. I told him his penis had had too much action that week and no thanks.

Jonathan now tried to woo me even harder. The next day he delivered flowers. He also messengered over a book he bought me. It was a serious book by a serious author with small print and big words. A topic he knew I would find interesting (if it was a movie). I panicked. UGH. I have to *read* this now. Oh, but no. Jonathan informed me that he wanted to read it to me. Oh boy. Help me. That could be worse than having to read it myself.

The next day Jonathan called me. "Do you have a minute?"

"Sure, hi."

"OK, I am going to read to you for a bit."

"What? Now? On the phone?"

"Yes, I bought the same copy of the book I bought for you. I can read it to you. Do you have the time?"

"Um, hi? How are you? How was your day? Please don't read to me."

"Come on, just for a minute."

I put the phone on speaker and began to do things around my apartment as Jonathan read this book. He read with a monotone voice. He could have at least done the character voices with some inflection, I thought to myself. After basically cleaning my whole room and possibly shaving my legs I heard a lull in the reading.

"Is that the end of the first chapter?" I asked.

"NO! It's only the end of the second page!" he laughed.

"Listen, this is really sweet and cute, but please don't read me another page. I am distracted."

"By what?" He asked.

"By every single thing that comes into my line of vision!" I said.

Jonathan let me off the hook and was a sport about it, but told me that he was going to be reading to me soon. *Yay*, I thought.

Over time I discovered that Jonathan had been engaged a couple of more times and called each one off. He was a classic commitment phobe. Peter pan syndrome maybe. I also discovered that he didn't sleep with his bed in his bedroom, his bed was in his living room so he could sleep in front of the fireplace. His apartment was littered with classic literature and Audrey Hepburn DVDs which I found incredibly disconcerting. Oh, I should also mention that he told me he still had feelings for his girlfriend Roberta in LA. One of my best friends was sure Roberta was really Robert.

This was a perfect example of ignoring flags, which I say I will not do anymore. Jury is still out.

6

WINK NOT, WANT NOT

MAY 2, 2010

HE WAS TALL. It's really all that mattered to me from the get go. He also had a cool interesting job that wasn't the typical wall street, lawyer, executive job. It was cool. It's something you wanted to tell people about. It was a blind a date.

We met at a cool restaurant in the Meatpacking District. I love the Meatpacking District just as much as any bridge and tunneler does. For one, it is not my neighborhood, so it seems like a vacation from the mundane. I remember years ago, when I was in high school, all that was there other than prostitutes and meat carcasses hanging on steel hooks was my very first nightclub I had ever been to. Mars. But now the neighborhood is a completely different place.

I met Craig for our date. He was as tall and cute, if you looked past the hair gel. He was a little too "outfitted" for me, and spared no mention that his "outfit" was from John Varvatos. I didn't want to know that much about what he was wearing, other than, I was hoping he would remove his jacket, which he didn't, because apparently it was part of the "outfit."

The moment we sat at our table, the DJ started to increase the volume of the music. Craig informed me that he wanted to "kick the guys ass" and "shove his headphones down his throat." I was taken aback. Is Craig trying to be funny and falling flat? Or does Craig have an anger problem? Craig was very twitchy and I casually asked if he dabbled in any recreational drugs. He assured me he didn't.

"Good. Drugs are a deal breaker for me." I said.

Craig was also divorced, but had no children. Craig and his wife lived apart for work reasons a year into their marriage and Craig's wife picked up a new beau. Craig was still angry about this, even though he pretended not to be. Craig quickly bragged that he got to keep all his money and got the ring back. These were things that I felt he should keep to himself. It made me a bit uncomfortable.

Soon a large party was seated next to us. One of the guys at the table went to take off his coat and Craig got pissed that the guy took his coat off so close to our table.

"HE HAD TO TAKE HIS COAT OFF RIGHT NEXT TO OUR TABLE? What the hell?" Craig said in a huff.

Ah, anger problem, not trying to be funny, I thought. My next thought was I wish Craig would take his jacket off too.

Craig then tells me we will be going to another hot spot in the Meatpacking District for dessert. Craig knows every word to every song the DJ is playing. He sings along to every song and breakdances with his upper body. I find it very uncomfortable and wish he would stop. Not so much the singing, because I myself like to sing along with every song, and I would say I am almost an idiot savant of song lyrics, but I could do without the re-enactment of *Breakin' 2, The Electric Boogaloo* the entire meal.

Then the winking starts. Just a PSA to any men (or women) who may be reading this: If you must, a strategically placed wink in a conversation is acceptable. Several winks during said conversation is awkward and borders on socially unacceptable. Craig tells me after our dessert and the next location, we will go dancing. I am trying to formulate excuses to extract myself from the situation.

We get to our next destination. A very hot spot right now where it is nearly impossible to get a table. Craig knows the "bouncer" or "host" or whatever they call the man in charge. Maitre'D maybe? Who he gives a big bear hug to. He quickly shows Craig our table. As he walks through the restaurant all of the staff, waiters, hostesses, and bus boys are slapping his hand. It is a scene from Goodfellas, Craig's hair gel included. Craig tells me he brings people there for work all the time. Craig works with celebrities. That explains it.

We sit and Craig orders us dessert. He continues to wink at me incessantly, it is not a tick, he just thinks he is being sexy, and I ask him to take off his coat. He tells me it is part of his outfit and again mentions John Varvatos, but this time mentions that he spent 4k there earlier that day. I cringe.

The funny thing is, anger problem, hair gel and winking aside, Craig is a nice guy. Certainly a good-looking one. I felt like I was being hard on Craig. Craig tells me he has a confession to make. At this point nothing can shock me. He tells me he has a roommate. I am too tired to find it off-putting. He explains that when he moved back to the city post divorce he had his best friend live with him.

"But I have the Master Bedroom, and Master Bathroom."

I silently wonder why he would ever think that made a difference. Craig was a few years younger than me. Maybe this is what young single people do these days, I thought. I begin to yawn and tell Craig I should start heading home. Craig tells me he would never want me to take a cab this late at night and insists on driving me home. I think that is sweet and certainly makes him a gentleman. His apartment is literally on the corner and we can go pick up his car after dessert.

Craig asks me if I want to see his apartment which he is very proud of (obviously forgetting he is a grown man with a roommate). Out of morbid curiosity I oblige.

"Only for a second" I say.

When we walked in, it was exactly how I expected it to look. It looked as though Huffman Koos threw up in his living room. Black leather couches, faux modern art in shades of brown and taupe, also probably bought at Huffman Koo's or won on The Price is Right.

"Very Nice," I said through my teeth, "We should leave before the roommate returns."

Craig drove me home, lip syncing and break dancing the whole way home. Craig keeps trying to book another date. I have yet to accept.

7

JDON'T 101

May 2, 2010

This entry I do not have to write myself. These are actual lines from JDate profiles.

"I am an investment banker, but not a douchebag."

"Manhattan girls only, no Murray Hill please."

"I like my job so much I want to hump it."

8

THE BAIT AND SWITCH

May 2, 2010

I ALWAYS BELIEVE people have pure intentions. Some would call this nice. Many would call it naive. I like to think of it as positive.

This year I made a career change. I will not say what industry I am in for fear of outing myself but what I can tell you, is when I got my new job I updated my Facebook work information and some people took notice. One person in particular was a very old friend, or should I say an acquaintance, whom I met on a family vacation when I was a sophomore in college. At the time he was older and in law school. My mother thought he was cute. I did not. She told me I was just not ready for a nice guy. She still tells me this.

So, my old friend/acquaintance, Marc, contacts me and informs me that he is a lawyer in the very same field and he thinks he can make some client referrals for me. I am very happy to receive this email. It turns out Marc's office is only 10 blocks from my own and suggests we have lunch and talk about it.

"Lunch it is," I say, and with that, Marc is my first lunch meeting at my new job. What a nice guy that Marc is, I think as I start to fantasize a lifelong partnership. Me and Marc referring business to each other. Two nice people who just want to help each other out. In business. I always thought Marc was a little dorky, but that doesn't mean he isn't nice right?

As the days pass I can be overheard saying to people "Oh, I can't do Wednesday at noon, I have a lunch. For work."

I sent an email, "Sure, let's see if I can fit you in, I have lunch Wednesday, but maybe after?"

Wednesday arrives. I get dressed for my lunch. Professional, yet fashionable.

The day of my lunch, I can be overheard in the office, "Oh what Susan? Sure I can do that for you, I just have a business lunch and then I will be back."

"Shoot, I can't make the meeting Tom, I have another meeting. 21 Club. Yes, work."

I told everyone I passed on the way out of my office building. The mailroom guys, the doormen, someone from another company entirely on the 5th floor. At some point, I am pretty sure my colleagues fell into a figure 8 behind me, doing some type of choreographed dance routine as I walked out of the building to the song *"Who's That Lady"*. By the way I was describing this lunch, it might as well have been with the President. In fact, I may have taken a car with bullet proof windows to get there, but that part is blurry now.

Marc suggests I first meet him in his office and we will walk to the restaurant together. His office is one block from the restaurant. I arrive and tell the receptionist I am there to see Marc. I am expecting to meet some of his partners. Maybe some other people in the office. Why else would he have me come there if we were about to have lunch.

"Hi Marc, Darcy is here to see you. OK." She looks at me, "Marc will be right out."

I wait.

"Hey Darcy!" Marc says as he grabs his coat from a closet behind her desk."

That's it? I think. We are leaving? No introductions? No referrals around the office?

Till this day, I will never understand why Marc had me come up to the office.

We head to the elevator. I am distracted by my persistent wondering why I came upstairs to get him. I can't really think of anything else at that point.

"You look great Darcy. You haven't changed at all since I saw you last!" That was maybe 14 years ago. I would say he was being kind, but he hasn't changed that much either.

We head down in the elevator and we make nervous small talk trying to fill the awkward silences. We didn't have that much to talk about, since we were never good friends.

We walked towards the restaurant. Marc regales me with tales of his wife and two children. He didn't get married until he was 32, he and his wife had dated once earlier, lost touch and reconnected. He is in love with his two girls. It sounded like the Cleaver family, I thought to myself. I am glad Marc is so happy.

I can't wait to get to the restaurant. I want to get down to business and be out of there ASAP.

We get to the 21 Club and Marc gives his name. "Right this way Sir!"

The host basically takes us over a bridge and through a tunnel to the most desolate table in the restaurant in a dark back corner. *Did he plan this?* I think to myself, but quickly suppress the thought.

When we arrive at the table, the host asks Marc if he wants to sit on my side of the table,

"I would if I were with such a beautiful woman," the host says.

I am grossed out. Marc doesn't immediately say no. He lets the idea hang in the air a little longer than he should have and stands next to me. I vomited a little in my mouth.

"NO! We're good. I will sit on this side and he will sit on that side,"

I say quickly. I give my most phony smile. I am confused why I had to answer the question at all.

I look over the menu. I love the 21 Club. I am planning my meal. A lettuce wedge to start? Maybe tuna tartare? I am interrupted by Marc suddenly telling me most of the men he knows cheat on their wives. Huh? I am scared to look up from my menu.

"But not me," he says.

I am glad we cleared that up?

He continues, "But I haven't been married for seven years yet. Talk to me after this summer when it's seven years." I am not sure what prompted this as we were not talking about anything near this topic. *Note to self, don't contact Marc at all after the summer for any reason.*

I am suddenly incredibly uncomfortable and want to go home, or at least back to my office. I suddenly would rather stuff envelopes. PLEASE Susan, may I collate your papers? I silently pray the gross host returns to kidnap me.

Let's get down to business and get off this creepy train, I think.

"So, you are a lawyer in my industry?" I ask casually.

"No, not really anymore."

I heard the sound of a record screeching to a halt.

I want to scream *ARE YOU KIDDING ME??? WHAT THE FUCK??? WHY DO YOU THINK I AM HERE CREEPY MARC?* But I keep it inside. I want to say, *"But you said you were a lawyer in my industry and we could refer each other business and you had all these clients to refer to me."* But I was so floored I couldn't even formulate the sentence.

Crickets.

"Oh," was all I could say.

I lost my appetite. I didn't know where to go from there. Do I run from the table screaming? Do I call him out on it? What is the etiquette here? The waiter arrives.

"I'm just going to have a salad," I say, knowing it doesn't have to be cooked and I will be out of there in ten minutes.

Marc orders a seventeen course meal including a well done steak. I pray for a power outage in the kitchen.

I can't tell you what happened next, because I went numb. Marc talked and talked about his life and the law career in a field that was not my own. Of course he ordered dessert.

At the end of the meal I basically long jumped out of the restaurant and told him I had to get to my next meeting. I walked back to my office nauseated by Marc, but thankful I had the sense to not date him back in the day when my mother told me he was a nice guy and I just wasn't ready for a nice guy.

9

HELLO, OLD FRIEND

M AY 3, 2010

ONE OF MY early post divorce dating ventures involved a membership to a special online club for "the chosen people." JDate. If you want to make it fancy like tar-jay you can pronounce it jah–dah–tey, as in Je'nate but different. No matter how you choose to pronounce it, it's the same embarrassing mess. Or hot mess as they say.

It didn't take long to realize that when people posted "Tanzania" as their location, they weren't being funny as I had originally thought, they were just married or dating someone and didn't want to come up in any of the New York City searches. It also didn't take me long to write "please be the age and height you say you are" in my profile. I never could have imagined people would lie about such things, as you will eventually meet them in person and it doesn't take a rocket scientist to tell that you aren't really 6 feet but 5'9" and the pictures from this past summer were really from the past summer 11 years ago. But I was a newly single person and in this century, online dating was as normal as organic milk and google. Only painful, creepy and embarrassing.

For reasons unbeknownst to me I am quite popular in the under 30 bracket. I explain to them that while I am a mom, I am not Stiffler's mom, and then I turn into a mom and ask "aren't I too old for you?"

I remember one day getting an email on jah–dah–tey from a man named Nate. 39, Never married. Tall. Cute. A money manager of some kind. After a couple of emails Nate asks for my number. He calls me immediately. After Nate told me he lived in a very fancy co-op on CPW (he told me the name and then asked if I knew it and then explained to me that living at that address is like living in a private members only club that only few people can understand- to which I reached for the nearest lamp and tried to strangle myself with the electric chord) and a number of other nauseating details about his financial status which Nate wanted to portray as very good (at one point he may have asked for my fax number to fax me tax returns from years past). I was trying to politely excuse myself from the conversation when Nate exclaims,

"Oh my g-d, I am looking at your profile. I didn't realize you had a child."

"Yes. I do."

"Oh. That's not going to work. I'm sorry. I wouldn't be very good with a child. You see, I smoke a lot of pot and…"

"No problem. Thank you for being honest. It's good to know this right off the bat. Nate, I enjoyed speaking with you. Have a good night."

"I feel sorry for you," he says.

Huh?

"Dating is hard enough, but to have a child and have to date. That must be really hard for you."

I almost died after suddenly stabbing myself in the eye with a fork. I want to stab him, but I can't get to him through the phone. Instead I stab myself.

"Interesting that you feel that way." I say, "I have never found that to be the case. In fact, my child is my greatest joy and asset and I am so fortunate to have my child, so you see, I have already hit the jackpot."

I cannot believe I am still on the phone with this loser. "Nice speaking with you Nate."

Two weeks later I met someone fabulous. A divorced dad with a child and we dated for a year.

Fast forward two years since my first encounter with Nate. I hadn't tried JDate in about that long and decided to go crawling back and try to give it the old college try. Or in this case the old Yeshiva try.

After a slew of emails from people named "MotleyJew", "PSILove-Jew," "DontJewWantmeBaby," and so on and so forth, I see a blinking IM. Someone is trying to instant message me. The username is NateNYC41 (ah he is older now,) and I recognize him immediately. I ignore the IM. I figure he doesn't remember me from 2 years ago. The next day I logged in again. NateNYC41 is trying to IM me. That loser, I think to myself. He probably doesn't even remember that we spoke 2 years ago.

I decide to accept so I can remind him of our first encounter two years prior if he tries to pick me up. As g-d as my witness, and we are talking about JDate, which is religious so I would not lie, this is the conversation that ensues. Verbatim. I copied the entire thing:

NateNYC41: Hi Mom, how have you been?

(HOLY SHIT! He remembers!)

DarcyDates: Excellent, you?

NateNYC41: Awesome thankfully.

DarcyDates: Good to hear. *Always take the high road.*

NateNYC41: You know, you are so freakin' hot. Why didn't I try to meet you before? I can't remember, but I am an idiot.

DarcyDates: Because I had a child and you said you felt bad for me.

NateNYC41: Man, what an asshole.

DarcyDates: I know, it's my favorite JDate story ever. I tell it all the time. *This was a lie, it was really a tie with my other favorite JDate story ever when someone looked up my address through some type of court records and sent me tons of CD's because he thought I would like them. He was a stalker, and we will get into another time.*

NateNYC41: Oh man, I'm sorry, my statement was completely misinterpreted, whatever it was I said. You are way too hot to feel sorry for.

DarcyDates: Don't be sorry. I laughed (at you,) and then met someone two weeks later who I dated for a year.

NateNYC41: Are you kidding?

DarcyDates: What's up with you? Still no kids I see?

NateNYC41: Kids? I can barely take care of myself. *At least he is honest*

DarcyDates: Well, I have some names of some good babysitters.

NateNYC41: What is your number?

DarcyDates: No, sorry, we have been down that road before. We are old friends at this point.

NateNYC41: Okay, but your favorite JDate story needs a postscript.

DarcyDates: Thank you, but I can't. I don't want to ruin my favorite story with a lovely dinner.

NateNYC41: You are so meeting me it's not even funny.

DarcyDates: Cute, but no can do.

NateNYC41: Here is my number. Please call me. I must take you to dinner. *212-555-jdont*

DarcyDates: Goodnight Nate. Nice catching up.

Maybe Nate had matured with older age, who knows. In the two years Nate was trying to date every single girl under 35 without a child, I was raising my child. I had watched my child learn to read an entire book, and watched as my child learned to dive in the deep end. These things and all the smaller moments in between were a zillion times more rewarding than any guy I could possibly meet. Like I said, I had already hit the jackpot. I already had my Bashert. I, as far as I am concerned, am the luckiest lady alive.

Don't feel sorry for me. Feel sorry for Nate.

10

AS LONG AS YOU ARE HAPPY

MAY 4, 2010

THIS IS why I love my mother:

After a string of gross dates and deciding that I no longer had any interest in dating men, I sent my mother a text.

"I am becoming a lesbian."

"Haha. no you aren't," she writes.

And like any good Jewish mother, who wants to factor in the slight chance I was telling the truth and she would never want me, for one second to think I would not be the apple (dipped in honey) of her eye she writes a follow up text:

"If you do become a lesbian I will love you the same and you and your girlfriend are always welcome in my home."

It was very afterschool special of her to come around like that.

My mother has always lived by the "as long as you are happy" motto. But she really means it. I love you mom.

11

REAL TEXTS FROM REAL MEN

M AY 4, 2010

THESE ARE actual texts from real men.

Remember Andre? Andre, by the way, holds two advanced degrees. He plays in a basketball game on occasion with friends I introduced him to. My friend sent Andre a text inviting him to play in a Sunday night game. Andre responded:

"No can do, I am headed to Brooklyn tonight to see BJork. Chicks dig Bjork and I like to F**k chicks."

"Good luck with the sex," my friend replied, then called me immediately to ask what the hell was wrong with this guy.

Andre, apparently, also holds an advanced degree in being an idiot. Not that we didn't already know that (see: *Can You Be Friends After a Defriend*).

One CFO of a very very large company asked me out for Thursday night. I said I could not go as I had a fundraiser to attend.

This is his actual response. Not doctored in any way. Swear on my Blackberry:

"Can I please come to this fundraiser? I want to put my d**k in a puff pastry and lay in on a platter and then serve it to Muffy Jane Dusty C**t and see if she ups her donation. It's for the kids."

I am speechless, which is rare.

Who is this Muffy he speaks of? This is wooing? How does one even concoct such a text or idea for that matter? WTF??? This is how he asks me on a 3rd date?

I tell him I am horrified, which takes a lot.

"Does this mean I don't get a 3rd date?" He asks.

Crickets.

Note to self, stay away from the pigs in a blanket.

A very big lawyer sends me a text that he is out with an old friend playing "Buck Hunter" (a video game involving shooting and hunting down bucks- I explain because why would anyone ever know that). He invites me to come along:

"I just shot and killed three bucks. I called them all Darcy."

"Um...hmmm" I respond

"Are you scared?" He asks

"A little?" I say

"You should be. I'm a mighty buck hunter!" (See, *As Long As You Are Happy*, about how I am becoming a lesbian).

12

DO NOT TOUCH

May 4, 2010

On the subway today I saw an ad placed by the MTA in regards to sexual harassment being a crime in the subway:

"A crowded train is no excuse for an improper touch."

Neither is a date, I think to myself.

PSA to all my dates:

"A date with me is no excuse for an improper touch." I contemplated running this announcement in the NY Post.

13

HE WILL BOIL YOUR BUNNY

M AY 5, 2010

WHAT IS it with these needy men? Is this a new thing? Was it always this way? Isn't it supposed to be the women that are needy? But first let's discuss the book. There are a gazillion books on dating that state women should be elusive, bitchy even.

The one common theme is basically to never ever under any circumstances contact a man or show the slightest bit of interest. EVEN after you are married. DO NOT MAKE THE MISTAKE OF BEING AVAILABLE *EVEN* AFTER YOU ARE MARRIED, they claim.

"I'm sorry I can't be home Saturday night with you and the kids. I have plans. With who? Oh, that's not important." That would go over swell.

These books are insane and I am concerned people might actually listen. There are some different schools of thought in this book genre. Some will tell you to basically wait in silence in a closet somewhere until the man you are involved with comes looking for you...

when he feels like it. He may or may not have some sort of animal he just hunted hanging over his right shoulder. In the meantime you should be taking up hobbies like knitting in a group of local women, you should be taking up some type of meditation, maybe have a spa treatment. You should be volunteering with charities (the proverbial "they" are very into recommending charity work to single people).

I picture soup kitchens and clothing drives to be filled with single people walking around aimlessly. Does anyone else do charity work? Or does everyone go by their match or JDate moniker as they offer up another serving of potatoes?

"MustLoveDogs, can you hand me that stack of plates?"

"Sure JewCan'tTouchThis, right after I stir the gravy."

"ShabbatShiksa can you help me fold these sweaters that we just received?"

"Sure Hot2Trot, right after I fax this press release. By the way, I'm willing to convert."

But, I digress.

These books will tell you to let them go into their caves, men are like rubber bands, and so on and so forth until ultimately they are actually living on Mars and you on Venus and you never get to see each other because the commute is way too long. I like to call it locationally undesirable dating.

Then there are the aggressive books like "Why Men Love Bitches." They will tell you not to call a man back, leave your laundry at his door with a mere note telling him to do it and then tell you to set his house on fire, kick him in the face, and when he is left bleeding on the floor with no house and a bloody face and as he is calling for help, lean in close and give him the finger. It is only then that he will love you, and maybe even put a ring on it.

Let me tell you what I have learned in the modern dating world: If they are into you, they will *need* you. If they like you they will actually stalk you. The guy who wrote, *He's Just Not That Into You* has a point. If he ain't callin' he doesn't like you. Because if he does like you he WILL hunt you down (see: *Real Texts From Real Men* - specifically Buck Hunter text).

If you don't call them back they will send a follow up text, possibly a piece of certified mail requiring you to sign for it. They will call again. They will then send another follow up text confirming you received their voicemail, they will have their lawyer subpoena you for a mere response of whether or not you want to be in a relationship. Just when you think you have blown them off and they should be getting the point and you haven't spoken in two weeks you will receive an email:

"Are we going to go out again or are you moving on?"

WHAT IS GOING ON HERE??? I thought the women did this and it was completely against "The Rules." I thought it was horrifying and you are never, EVER, under any circumstances whatsoever, to show you actually LIKE them. I thought it was the women who wanted commitment. Guess what folks. It's the men. I have gotten bitched out by guys for my disinterest in something more than a casual date or two. Between the invites to meet the parents, to the "who are you texting?" to the "who did you have dinner with?" to the "why can't you see me more than once a week," sometimes I feel like I am actually hearing, "Now? Now? What about now? Do you want a relationship now? Now? How about now? Are we exclusive now? Now? Maybe now? Are you ready now? Can we go out again now? Now? Now can we? Now???" That's what I hear. And when I do, I shut down. Wait a second? Am I becoming a man?

To be completely honest, I like a man that is not afraid to tell you he likes you. I like a man who emails the next morning and says "That date was incredible and I can't wait to do it again ASAP," and then actually puts a date on the calendar. I like hearing that he is interested and not having to "wait it out and see." Life is too short for games, for waiting, for rules. Live life for today, as you never know what tomorrow brings. If you like someone, tell them. If they don't call you back, leave them alone.

14

CINCO DE MAYO

M AY 6, 2010

On Cinco De Mayo I had a date with a Mexican. A Mexican Jew.

Roberto was handsome in an intellectual kind of way, but more importantly, he was tall. We decided to meet for drinks, coincidentally on Cinco De Mayo.

"We will stay away from any Mexican places," he says.

What fun is dating a Mexican if you don't get tequila on Cinco De Mayo, I think to myself. He tells me Mexican restaurants will be too crazy tonight. I think we may not be a good match.

Roberto walks in a couple of minutes after I do. Is he carrying a murse? I panic.

Phew, it's a backpack.

He says hello. I like Roberto's accent. We walk to our table. Roberto is not typically my type, not that I have one, but if I did he would not be it. Roberto has a great smile, which I like.

"What are you having to drink?" He asks.

"I'm just going to have a glass of wine," I say.

"I'm going to have a fruity drink," he says.

Not sexy, I think to myself. I wish he would ditch the word fruity.

As I watch Roberto peruse the menu for his fruity beverage, I see it. Glaring at me. Roberto is wearing *man jewelry*. It is a necklace. With something hanging off of it that is more big than small. Like a car wreck I want to look away but can only stare.

The waiter approaches our table.

"I will have the Pinot Grigio," I say.

"And you sir?" the waiter asks Roberto.

"I want something fruity. I want a fruity drink."

I cringe. I wonder how many times Roberto can fit the word fruity into a sentence. Apparently a lot. I picture Roberto's drink to arrive with a ton of umbrellas. Possibly a cabana perched on the top of the glass.

"What is your best fruity drink?" he asks. Twenty seven…I silently count the word fruity.

The waiter suggests a drink with limoncello and 100 of the bar's other fruitiest ingredients that may or may not come with skittles and sprinkles on top.

"No, I don't like that," Roberto says. He doesn't smile. In fact he was rude. The waiter must have thought so too because he responded in a huff, "Well what do you like sir?"

Fight fight fight, I silently chant in my head.

Roberto tells the waiter he would like a fruity martini. Thirty eight…

While we are waiting for the drinks to arrive I notice Roberto is not talking. At all. He is just sitting back watching me. I squirm. I think Roberto must dislike our date. Maybe I am not fruity enough for him. I asked Roberto about his job. He answers in one sentence. I quickly look through my bag for a set of pliers, as I realize this entire conversation will be like pulling teeth. Damn it. I left them at home. *Sigh*.

An hour into the date I realize Roberto has probably said 120 words, 95 of them being "fruity."

I tell Roberto that I used to speak Spanish nearly fluently after studying it for years, but I don't speak it anymore so I have lost it. Roberto tells me I will re-learn it with him and we can speak it together. I wonder what date he is on. I also wonder if I would only learn the word fruity.

I tell Roberto a story about my uncle, to which he responds, "I hope you introduce me to him one day." Roberto is having fun?? He thinks there will be another date? I have already counted how many tiles were on the floor of the restaurant and played I spy with myself 4 times, all to prevent me from lighting myself on fire with the votive on the table.

Two hours, two drinks, and two appetizers later I tell Roberto I really need to get home to the sitter (thank g-d I had a curfew). We walk out of the restaurant, Roberto clutching his murse, I mean backpack.

When we get outside Roberto says, "Promise me I will see you again." I am confused but smile politely. Roberto seems like a nice guy even though I know next to nothing about him. I can't understand why he would want to see me again as he just stared at me the whole time and didn't interact with me whatsoever.

Roberto compliments my necklace. I do not return the compliment about his. In fact, I am wishing it away. I say goodnight and begin to walk away. I am not even down the block when Roberto calls me on my cell phone. I panic. I don't answer. What did he want to talk about? We had two hours to talk and he didn't say a word! He doesn't leave a message but sends a text:

"You looked so sexy walking away from me down the street. I hope I get to see you again."

I am surprised. Where was *this* Roberto in the restaurant? I wonder if Roberto is just shy and I am being hard on him. He seemed like a wonderful father. Maybe there was a language barrier? Whatever the case, he didn't watch reality TV (I have very low standards,) or make me laugh.

Mañana is another day I think to myself. Seis De Mayo here I come.

15

REAL TEXTS FROM REAL MEN

May 10, 2010

A man that has been asking me out on a third date made a donation to a charity I am involved with. After first sending me an email that he made a donation, he sent me the following text:

By the way, I had my brother make a donation too. I told him if he made a donation I might get in your pants. He said sure."

Cannot. Be. Real.

16

TOWNIE-RIFIC

May 16, 2010

One weekend, one spring, I went to visit my friend who lives in "the country." She is a dear friend who I love spending time with. Our friendship developed when my ex-husband and I owned a house in this "country" town. We have remained friends ever since. I love to visit her and our children have remained friends throughout the years. It's always a nice time for us to catch up and for our children to run wildly through the fields.

On this particular visit she informed me we were going to a party.

We arrive at the aforementioned party and the house is beautiful. It's even more beautiful at night with lights strategically illuminating the house and the pond just so. There is a bonfire in the backyard, ducks on the pond, candles and tiki torches lining the walkway. The host and hostess are the best looking couple I have ever seen. After a good hour chit chatting around the fire I tell Lizzie I need to get back home. I wanted to make sure my son was okay with the babysitter and I had had all the charcuterie one girl could eat.

I grabbed my jacket and was getting ready to leave when the host came running up to me.

"You're leaving??" She asks, and actually seems genuinely disappointed and a bit frantic.

"Yea, I have to be getting home, I have to wake up early and..."

"Don't go! Stay! Please!" She cuts me off. Is she pleading? Really? Suddenly I felt very important.

"Oh, you are so sweet. I really enjoyed meeting you too!"

She squints at me for a second with a guilty smile.

"OK! Here is the thing. I texted a guy. A single friend! I told him you were here and I thought he'd really like you."

I am shocked. I glanced around and suddenly realized everyone was in on it. It's like I had a Scarlet letter, except it was not an A, it was an S for single, which in the country is a rarity. I was like a unicorn. I was flattered and felt awkward all at the same time. This must be what it feels like to be a single Jewish lawyer visiting your grandmother in a Boca old age village, I thought to myself.

"Oh. Okay. Thank you?" I was not sure what the correct response was in this awkward situation. I re-loaded a plate of charcuterie (what non-Jews feed party guests), and I sat back down with a flock of antique dealers and landscapers (country jobs, in case you were wondering).

"He will be here in 10 minutes."

"Great!" I say. Not really sure how I feel.

I am sitting on my Adirondack chair gnawing on some type of salami/pepperoni/date/parmesan chunk, when I decide to gather up the facts.

"So Michelle, tell me about your friend. Does he live in the city?"

You see, this particular area is mostly city folk with weekend houses, so chances are he was only here for the weekend.

"No, actually he lives in Pleasantville." Pleasantville is not really the name of the town, it's changed for privacy reasons, and there is nothing pleasant about it. It's one town over from the town I was visiting (which by the way is amazing and my own private heaven). Pleasantville is a place where no one really lives. Well they do, but not people I date, per se. It's hard to describe Pleasantville and maintain diplomacy, so I will skip this part for now.

"Oh, what does he do?" I ask. Hoping for the best, but predicting the worst.

"He is a model!"

Crickets.

"A model?"

Now keep in mind we aren't in NYC or LA or even Miami. We are in the country. I didn't even know people modeled in the country.

"I don't know if he is your type but I figure it's someone to kiss at least."

Where is my Binaca when I need it? Did she just really just offer up someone for me to *kiss*? I actually think it's kind of cute and funny. I love her immediately. I wonder if she met her husband when she was 16 and hasn't dated since then.

"Oh! Here he comes." she gets very excited.

With that I see some type of pick-up truck/Mustang/Saturn extravaganza pull up to the house. I die a little inside. I know this is going to be bad. I am sitting in a dark field waiting for my model to show up. My model who lives between an A&P and a Stewarts.

I see him walking towards me.

"He is also a bodybuilder," she adds quickly. I wonder if she thinks that's a good thing.

Was it too late to get trampled by a deer? It's too late. He is getting closer fast and sees me. He is wearing a members only jacket and dress pants. By dress pants, I mean pleated parachute pants for some type of desk job in 1984. He has a ton of hair, but for reasons I still can't explain, his hair is shaved an inch above each ear. We are basically in the woods so there is no oncoming traffic to throw myself in front of. DAMN YOU COUNTRY LIVING. If I'm lucky, maybe a falling tree will land directly on my head. Is that a helicopter I hear hovering over my head waiting to airlift me to another location? Nope. Dead silence. We are in the country.

"Hi!" I say politely.

"Darcy, this is Skylar," Michelle says. Of course it is. I picture him to have a sister named Kayla and a brother named Braden.

Skylar smiles at me (kind of) and immediately looks at the ground. Michelle disappears into the night and I am pissed. I have no idea what to say to this man.

"So! You're a model?" I realize how ridiculous this sounds, but it's all I could muster up.

"Yea, I am. I am also a bodybuilder. And an actor."

Skylar doesn't look up at all. He continues to look at the ground. He suddenly rattles off a string of some type of automotive certifications he has. Something about coolant and Roto-Rooters. I wonder if Skyler is autistic.

I look down at what I am wearing. A cream cable knit sweater and a Barbour coat. I wonder why Michelle thinks we would be a good match. Maybe it's because I am alive. That could be all they require in the country.

"So! You live in Pleasantville?" I am wondering why no one, particularly Lizzie, is rescuing me from this situation.

"Yea. I live with my parents."

"That's sensible," I say

TAXI!!!! I want to scream. I keep it all inside. I am in the forest and there isn't another car for miles.

Skylar tells me he is acting in a movie. About Zombies and bodybuilders. He tells me about all the famous people in the movie, and by famous, he means the understudy for Mr. T in *DC Cab*. Before I know it Skylar, who still has yet to make eye contact with me pulls out an iPhone and is showing me his modeling pictures, shots of his abs, and a power point presentation of the proteins vs. carbs he eats in a day. WHERE THE FK IS LIZZIE?

I tell Skylar I really need to run. It was so nice chatting and the five minutes seemed like an eternity. Well, I left that part out.

"You on Facebook?" He says.

"Yes"

"Okay, well friend me and we can hook up in the city. I am there a lot for my movie."

"Will do."

Skylar starts to spell his last name for me so I can find him on Facebook. He kept spelling, and re-spelling. He changed the spelling several times.

"No, that's not it," and he would start again. Does he not even know how to spell his last name? I am confused. Can it be this bad? My next thought is that I can kick Skylar's ass in Scrabble.

I feel my way through the dark to find Lizzie. I see her face illuminated by the bonfire.

"You ready?" I ask.

We say our brief goodbyes, and on the way to the car I ask Lizzie if she could believe what just transpired.

"I didn't even see him. It was so dark. What did he look like?"

I couldn't believe I had no one to share this experience with.

When I got home I googled Skylar. After all he was a model/actor, he had to be somewhere on the Internet so I could show his pictures to Lizzie. Sure enough, there he was. Actually he was everywhere. Although Skylar wasn't famous for his movie, Skylar was famous for being some type of beef cake model popular with the gays. He was a gay icon of sorts. There were blogs written about Skylar and his hot body with dozens of men commenting on Skylar's good looks. Skylar was kind. He would respond to all of their posts. I never friended Skylar, but I did friend the hostess who wanted to set me up.

17

YANKEES V. RED SOX

May 16, 2010

NOT ALL DATES are bad dates. While the bad dates make better stories, it is possible, given America's love for romantic comedy, that the good ones do too. For this reason, I will bring out Colby.

My first date with Colby was a blind date. He was from Boston, very tall, dark and handsome and had a hot Boston accent and for the first time in a while I was excited for the date.

Colby suggested we meet to go ice skating in the park. I was psyched for this. I love to skate and used to play ice hockey when I was little so I knew I could hold my own on the ice. When Colby asked where I wanted to go skating, I suggested Lasker Rink. I had taken Bear skating there a bunch of times and thought it would be a good spot, away from the crowds at Wollman. It is right by the Harlem Meer. A completely desolate (read dangerous) spot of the park.

Right before the date, Colby sent me a text.

"I will be wearing my favorite sequin Brian Boitano one piece."

Funny, check. I loved him already.

It was an oddly warm day in New York City for January. I didn't even need a jacket. I took a cab up to 107th street and entered the park. It was pitch black. As I walked deeper and deeper into the dark park I started to think of all the rules I was breaking:

Walking through the park at night, check. By myself and a girl, check, check. To meet a stranger, check, check, check. I suddenly got nervous, but ignored my instincts. Dumb, check.

In the distance I see a well-lit oasis in the scary dark rape rambles of the park. It was the skating rink. I walked as fast as I could, praying to arrive safely. Note to self: Buy mace. Addendum: Don't make plans in the park at night with strangers.

I walked down the stairs into the rink and there he was. Cute, super super tall, and a smile that could light up the entire park. He helped me put my skates on and pulled the laces extra tight for me. Colby was also strong. So far so good. Colby discloses that he played ice-hockey for his law school team. I secretly think I want to race him. We walked towards the rink and the second our feet hit the ice he took notice.

"A girl who skates on hockey skates, pretty impressive."

"Yea, I can whip your ass on this ice," I fire back.

We are immediately best friends.

I don't know what we talked about but Colby skated backward with the ease of an NHL player as I skated toward him and we spoke that way for a good solid hour. He confided in me that he was bummed I could skate so well and I didn't need him to hold my hands. Something about it didn't even sound cheesy or skeezy. Colby was normal and cute and I felt like I had known him forever.

We walked out of the park and Colby helped me put my jacket on. He was a total gentleman. We had so much to talk about. So much so in fact we sat on a random bench on fifth avenue and kept talking and talking until Colby suggested we grab some dinner. I jumped at the opportunity. Colby and I were now extending our date, and I actually wanted to.

We walked a little further and chose a restaurant that looked good and casual enough for Colby to wear his sequin skating unitard. Okay, he didn't really wear it, but thinking about Colby now I can laugh at the idea of that. Dinner flew by and we shared our stories, our love for reality TV, our love for our children, and what we had learned about co-parenting with our exes. Most importantly, we realized we had the exact same sense of humor. I rarely think someone is funnier than I, but it may have been a tie. I loved it. Finally, a worthy adversary, I think to myself.

After dinner Colby walked me home. This was the first date who walked me home since moving to my new apartment. My doormen thought I was celibate. What would my doorman think? Why was Colby walking me home? How could I stop him from making it to my actual building? There was a deli on my corner.

"I am just going to go in here to buy something to drink."

"Ok," he said, and followed me into the store.

This wasn't going as planned. I was trying to ditch Colby on the corner before the doormen could see him. I buy a Gatorade and start to say goodbye to Colby. Like a puppy who you just fed bacon, Colby is trailing along right next to me until we get to my building. I glance at my doorman and glance at Colby. *Sigh*.

"So, it was really nice meeting you," I say.

"Yes, you too Darcy."

We chit chat for a nervous minute or two, he offers me his nanny on Mondays, I wonder if this is what all dating divorcées do. I gave him a hug and as I walked away I realized it was strange that Colby didn't mention wanting to see me again. I thought our date had gone so well.

I got upstairs and suddenly realized I would be disappointed if Colby didn't ask me out again.

He waited for the standard one day and then called and asked me out for the next day. I said yes.

I think it was my sister who called it first.

"YOU LOVE HIM!" she said one day while watching me text with Colby.

Or maybe it was the old lady in Starbucks who said something similar watching me read an email from him, "Who is it that is making you smile like that?" I was walking around with an eternal stupid grin that only love can give you. But whoever called it first, from the day we met, Colby and I went out again and again and again until we fell in love. Which was not difficult to do. Over the next year Colby would teach me about love, loss, and the Red Sox. More on Colby later.

18

CAN YOU HEAR ME NOW?

MAY 18, 2010

IF YOU ARE WEARING a Bluetooth in your ear, please don't. If you are driving and it's a necessity, I may let it slide. But only if it's an emergency.

If I can only see you from the neck up and you have a Bluetooth in your ear, I can only assume it is coupled with a fanny pack and phone clip of some kind on your belt. If you are wearing one as you walk around, or better yet, when you aren't even on the phone and it is part of your outfit in some way, please don't. I can't take you seriously.

Will there be a sudden emergency as we are standing around talking that is SO monumental you can't actually take the phone out of your pocket and answer it? Are you factoring in the slightest chance that pirates may show up, tie your arms behind your back and you will have to smash your ear against a wall to answer the phone? I am reasonable. If you gave me an explanation I may understand. But I probably won't.

If you post pictures of yourself on a dating website wearing said Bluetooth it will be an immediate turn off. Please believe me.

19

JONATHAN, 47, REALLY HAD A GIRLFRIEND

MAY 18, 2010

IT'S springtime in New York City. The weather goes from hot to cold within an hour, manicures turn from Chinchilly to Lilacism, allergies are at their peak, and so are benefit galas. May is that time of year when every benefit for every charity you ever had any involvement in schedules their biggest gala. Just when you think you can't eat another mini-slider, or chicken skewer, you best find it in your heart to make room for one more, as it's the season for good deeds and passed hors d'oeuvres.

My best friend Alexis is like my Oprah. By "my Oprah" I mean, I am her Gayle. And by that I mean I am constantly the third wheel to her and her husband, who we will call Stedman. Me, Oprah and Stedman head to one of these fêtes together. By the time we arrive, all three of us are in a marital fight. It's him against us. We are close enough that Stedman fights with me as though I am his spouse. I love him, but I am always happy he is going home with Oprah at the end of each night.

So, remember Jonathan, 40, is really 47? (See, *Jonathan, 40, Is Really 47.*) He was there. I saw him from across the room and grabbed my Oprah.

"That's him! That's Jonathan! My gay boyfriend!" I squeal. I am ecstatic she can finally put a face with the name.

As she turns to get a good look, he sees me. We are quite far away from each other. Close enough that you must wave and acknowledge one another, far enough that you don't have to actually talk. We make eye contact, even though he appears to be...hiding? As I am about to lift my hand to wave, he has already waved and turned away. All done in under 2.5 seconds. It was an awkward gesture where he dismissively waved his glass at me. I don't even think it was coupled with a smile. In fact, it could have been the most non-wave wave I have ever received. Alexis and I turn to each other with our mouths agape.

"That's it??" she says, "Don't you think you two were further along than a simple toodaloo?"

"YES!" I said. Afterall, he had told me he wanted to have children with me and told my mother he hoped she'd be his mother-in-law someday. This seemed like an under-reaction from my almost spouse-to-be!

We laugh hysterically. She tells me he actually looked like he threw up in his mouth for a second when he saw me. That's why I love her. This is what best friends are for.

Well it didn't take long to figure out why his reaction was what it was. Before you know it, Roberta (remember the girlfriend he had that I didn't know he had,) comes strolling up behind him. My best friend comments that she is an older version of me. Twelve years older to be exact. Of course I had done my research.

Now, I am not *that* girl. I do not confront, I do not make scenes. I keep it all inside. I am not the girl to approach an ex and say to his girlfriend,

"*Hi! I'm Darcy. Have we met? I dated Jonathan in March. What? You were dating then? He didn't tell me he had a girlfriend. Ohhhhhhhhh! Wait!*

Yes! This is vaguely familiar. Hmmmmm. That's right. Yes! When he told me he was visiting his family in LA, he later came clean and said he was visiting you. That's funny. Not funny ha-ha of course, funny awkward. Okay. This is all coming together now." No. I wouldn't say any of that. I'd just think it.

The snub didn't upset me, as we determined in the previous entry about Jonathan I didn't much need a gay boyfriend anyway. What upset me more was I somehow got so caught up in conversation I missed my meal. They had cleared the table before I had a chance to eat my salmon. Damn it. I was starving. Luckily, one of the bus boys that had cleared our table must have also doubled as an hors d'oeuvres waiter, as he had left a full tray of passed hors d'oeuvres on our table. I sat alone at the table, eating the leftover dumplings off the tray. A vision of class really in my festive attire. They were cold by this point. Kind of like Jonathan. At least I had my Oprah who I'd prefer to road trip with cross country any day over Jonathan. That's what friends are for I think to myself. Well, *that* and to tell you your ex looked like he threw up a little in his mouth when he saw you.

20

GAYDATE

May 21, 2010

Here follows the story of my worst date ever. Out of all the worst dates I have had, this certainly took the cake. For now at least.

Once upon a time, I was logging on to JDate to take my profile down. After an attempt to re-try the world of on-line dating, I had decided to un-try it. I was de-friending JDate. As I am logging on to take my profile down I get an instant message from Philip. Philip was 36. Single. Tall. I accepted his instant message.

After a brief chat, and quick display of a massive red flag:

"I am actually divorced. I was married for 5 years." (Even though he is listed as being single and never married).

I agreed to go out with him. The red flag, by the way, is not that he was divorced, but that he was lying in his profile. Apparently telling the truth is a moral that didn't apply to him.

He suggested we meet for a drink at a spot right by his office. And by spot, I mean a gay bar. I walked past the gay pride flag on the door. *How very progressive of him*, I thought. I stood by the bar which was filled with gay couples. Gay men. There were piles of free gay magazines at the end of the bar and I was quite possibly the only woman in there. The bartender kept leaving his station at the bar.

"Can I get you anything? A drink? Some water?" *A mirror so you see you are a woman and don't belong here?*

"I'm fine. Thanks." I text my friend, "I am on a JDate in a gay bar. I am on a GayDate."

Just then my date shows up. He looks like his picture but I immediately knew he wasn't my type. He just seemed uptight and I was obsessed with the idea of how such an uptight guy picked such a gay bar. He suggests we go sit in the back room. The back room had blasting music and must have doubled as a gay disco. There was even some type of stage/catwalk.

We sat across from each other and had to practically scream over "Man-Eater" blasting over the speakers.

"This is so weird," he says. I thought he was going to say it was weird we were meeting in a gay bar. "I have never been out with someone my age before."

I am not his age. I am actually 3 years younger than he is.

"What do you mean?" I ask. Genuinely confused.

"I don't know. It's weird. You are like a peer. You will get all my references. You are my age!"

I nod.

"My ex-wife was 4 years younger than I was," he says. I am still nodding. "My ex-girlfriend was 22. I dated her for 3 years."

I continue nodding to myself, to the little voice in my head screaming *'isn't this guy an ass*?' I nod.

"You were married for 5 years? You never had children?" I ask.

"No. I didn't want to have them with my wife."

"Oh. You saw signs of trouble?"

"No. I just didn't want to have them with her. I don't know. I wasn't into it." He said this with about as much sensitivity as Steve Martin's character as the sadist dentist in *Little Shop of Horrors*.

"She is remarried now and has a baby." *Thank goodness she got out*, I think to myself.

"Are you two still friends?" I ask.

"No. She wants nothing to do with me." He admits. *I can't imagine why.*

"Do you come here often?" I ask. Code for "Are you gay?"

"No, I have been here only a few times."

"I thought it was a little funny you picked a gay bar."

"This isn't a gay bar!" He insists. I glance around only to see two gay couples making out next to us and our male waiter in some type of hot pant shorts.

"Look at the gay pride flag on the wall. And the Stack of *Next* magazines on that table. This is a gay bar."

"It is???" He is still not convinced. Philip could be the most oblivious man I have ever met. The scantily clad man dancing to *It's Raining Men* was not enough evidence. He takes a walk around the restaurant looking for clues. *A real Sherlock Holmes*, I think to myself.

"Oh my Gd! You're right. It is a gay bar!" He says. I think about how often I will be frequenting this place, as I have decided to go gay after this date.

Philip sits back down with me. "This is a lot of firsts for me. First time in a gay bar (*yeah right*), first time going out with a woman who I knew had a child, and the first time dating someone my age." I hate Philip. I want to beat him, but it might be seen as gay bashing, since we are in a gay bar and I really wasn't up for jail.

"You are like a cougar," Philip says.

"What do you mean?" I ask.

Suddenly jail didn't seem that bad of a place.

"A cougar. You are like a cougar," He says over and over again. I am confused as he is 3 years OLDER than me. I wonder if Philip has age dysmorphia.

"You are older than me! How does that make me a cougar?" I ask.

If by cougar he means a wild animal that is about to claw his eyes out, yes. I am a cougar. I am a friggin' cougar, you idiot. ROARRRRRRR.

"I don't know. You are a grown up. I guess you are just more responsible than me, with a child and everything."

And you are an imbecile, I think.

After I sit through a brief dissertation on Philips' rise through the investment banking ranks from Associate to Managing Director and I am done gagging, I decide to wrap this evening up like a tight little present.

"Well, I have a dinner and I really need to run." *Right this second.*

I don't even remember how we made it out of there, other than I was grateful to be heading home.

"I bet you have a hot date now." He said on our way out.

"Yea, I do." I want him to vanish.

"I bet you have a date with a young guy so you can really cougar it up."

I want to say '*Actually, I have a date with a straight man, so I can really heterosexual it up.*' But I keep it all inside. I am actually heading home so I can plan my coming out party. One for the books, I think. Or at least, it's one for Darcy Dates!

21

REAL TEXTS FROM REAL MEN

MAY 25, 2010

A GUY who I have never slept with asked me if I wanted to hang out. I told him I couldn't. He sent me a text with a picture of his actual penis.

Crickets.

"Why don't you send me one now?" he asked.

I don't have a penis, I think to myself. I then wonder if this is what people do these days.

Next time I ask my friend if she wants to go get a manicure with me, and she declines, I am just going to send her a picture of my tits. Maybe it will make her change her mind.

22

REAL TEXTS FROM REAL MEN

May 27, 2010

A PERSON TRYING to book a third date with me sent me the following text:

"Are you afraid that date three obliges you to sex? It doesn't. I am not a piece of meat either."

I feel much better that we have established that.

23

HOUSE ARREST

MAY 28, 2010

I WAS SET up with Matthew by a very dear friend. This friend has incredible judgement and wouldn't just set two single people up just because they were both single, as my mother would do.

"But mom, she is 57 and he is 28?"

"You don't think he would like her? She's nice."

UGH.

I knew that Max wouldn't steer me wrong so I agreed to be set up and was kind of excited by the prospect. Max used all the adjectives one wants to hear about a blind date to describe Matthew. Max was a tough crowd to please, so I trusted his judgement completely. According to Max, Matthew was a good-looking, successful guy who lived in Tribeca but was born and raised on the upper east side of Manhattan which meant he would have that semi-dysfunctional side which I find endearing. I was slightly concerned that he was 39 and never married, but I agreed to go out with the bachelor.

We set a date at a great restaurant downtown, one of my favorites. He asked me if I would meet him at his apartment for a drink before the date. It was one block away from the restaurant. Translation: my apartment is amazing and I'd like to impress you with it. I figured I'd let him have his moment of glory, and after all, he wasn't a complete stranger so I agreed to the pre-dinner impress you cocktail.

Matthew opened the door. He was handsome, by anyone's standards. *Yay Max.* I walked into Matthew's apartment which was certainly swank. A 5-star renovation. I sat down on the couch. *Make yourself at home Darcy*, I think to myself, and he offered me a drink. I glance down at Matthew's feet. He appeared to be wearing...motorcycle boots. *How very 1990 of him.* Luckily for him, he had the high heels, I mean motorcycle boots, paired with an old beat up t-shirt from a nondescript hotel only a very select bunch know about. It had that "I am too cool to talk about it, but I will wear this t-shirt so you know I know about it but don't really care" look. It worked for him.

Matthew opened a bottle of wine and placed two glasses on the table. The bottle is neatly placed in a wine bucket. I decide he is metro. It's all way too smooth.

As we are drinking our wine I notice a guitar in the corner of the room.

"Do you play?" I asked.

"I tried to learn, but it's very hard. Do you?"

"Yes."

"Cool, want to teach me something?"

"Okay."

This date was turning cheesy fast, but I couldn't resist a little jam session so picked up the guitar and showed him the easiest chord for him to play.

"This hurts my fingers," Matthew whined.

"You need to develop proper callouses," I say. I quickly realized he would be the soft one in this relationship.

After our music lesson, he brings me into the living room.

"What do you think of these fabrics?" He asks.

Matthew had a variety of fabrics laid out by his decorator for the chaise that was being upholstered.

"The pink is a little too Huffman Koos," I say. I pinch myself quickly. Darcy, wake up! Are you on a date with a man or a woman? Stay cool Darcy, it's a man. Phew. With womanly interests. Sigh.

A couple of glasses of wine and two hours later, I realize we haven't yet headed out to the restaurant. I am suddenly starving. My stomach must have roared a terrible roar.

"So Darcy. We need to feed you."

Phew, we are going to be leaving the love nest.

"Shall we order in or go out?" he asks.

"Oh, we can go out. What's near here?" I want to scream 'WEREN'T WE GOING TO THE RESTAURANT ON THE CORNER AND THAT'S WHY I MET YOU AT YOUR HOUSE????' But I scream it on the inside.

"Well, we were going to go to Nobu. Let's order sushi." He says.

I die inside. I am fully trapped for life. I picture, years later, to be sitting as an interviewee on Oprah telling my tale:

"*Well Oprah, when they finally discovered me chained to the acrylic Jonathan Adler chair, I smelled like Chai tea, and he only fed me things that were organic. I was forced to learn words like wheatgrass and Kashi. It was terrible.*"

Is this a joke? I glanced down at his ankle to make sure he wasn't wearing some type of house arrest bracelet. I glanced down at my ankle. Maybe I was wearing one. At least if I was I could run out of the front door and an alarm would sound and they would come to take me away, and by they, I mean anyone else at all.

Matthew steps out of the room for a second. Was my mind playing tricks on me or did the lights just go dim? IS THAT SADE PLAYING? HELP ME JOHN QUINONES!

When he comes back he smells like mouthwash and he leans in to kiss me. Um? WTF!? It was very quick and very awkward. I pretended it didn't happen. I changed the topic to something about Matthew, I don't even remember what because in my head I am secretly singing 'food waiter, waiter waiter food waiter, waiter,' and I am too distracted to really pay attention to the conversation. Damn you Darcy, why did you have to be so cool and teach him how to play the guitar. Note to self: be a little more lame next time.

Matthew tells me he dated a German woman for a long time who was very rigid and organized, something he really liked. I tell him I am the complete opposite. Almost like a walking tornado. My next thought is that it is creepy that he found a rigid German sexy.

The food comes. I thank Jesus and promise to donate canned goods to the next food drive I see.

"Lets eat in the kitchen Darcy. I just got a new rug here."

Yup. I am still the man of the house.

I picture how quickly Bear and I can destroy the rug.

"Okay" At least we were getting out of the Sade infested romance den. I follow Matthew through his home. It is like a museum of sorts. Beautifully decorated for a couple, creepy for a single man. It had a very *Sleeping With The Enemy* vibe. I was dying to peek inside his cabinets and see if all the cans were turned with the labels facing outwards. I was able to control myself, only because I wanted to get to the table and eat two hours ago.

While we were eating Matthew was trying to kiss me. I tried to take the chopsticks and build some type of wall between us, but there were not enough of them. As dinner is winding down I decide it's time.

"It's time for me to get going," I say. I had been in Matthews house for four hours too long. Our first date felt like our 100th date. Or at least our 100th hour of this date.

Matthew seemed surprised I was leaving. The thing about Matthew is he wasn't on a bad date. He had been a good date. An excellent date. That was just a lot of date in his house very quickly. I don't know that a love connection was made, but someone learned to play the guitar, and canned goods were going to be donated, so the world surely became a slightly better place that day.

24

REAL VOICE MAIL FROM REAL MEN

June 1, 2010

One guy who I went out with two times about a month ago called me up and left me a voicemail last night. I had to share it with you immediately. Please keep in mind that after our 2nd and last date, I have never accepted another date since then.

"Hey Darcy, I realize our month anniversary is coming up and I think it's time to take our relationship to the next level."

Obviously, I think this is odd, as we went out one and a half times one month ago but I should have expected this. Two weeks ago he left me a similar voicemail:

"Darcy, it's me. I want to make sure you are a team player and you are getting on board for kids and a dog. Let me know."

25

GHOST OF RISOTTO PAST

June 7, 2010

My mother, happily remarried for years now to a wonderful man, likes to tell a story about one of her early dating experiences after her divorce. It involved her dating a man who acted very interested in her, and one day out of the blue not only did he not call her anymore, but he never returned her calls.

"I was so confused by it, I actually thought he was dead. I went into a restaurant one day and he was there having dinner with his friend. It's as though I saw an actual ghost. I walked up directly to his table and said to him, 'I thought you were dead!!!'"

When my mother tells me this story I always giggle and or roll my eyes. My mother can be so naive I think. I also think there are parts of the story I am missing, or signs she didn't pick up on…until now. You see, I have met my first ghost, although I have not yet seen the ghost so I can't say for sure whether or not he is actually dead, but I now know the feeling of having someone fall off the map over night.

There is a general idea, a myth, a story passed down by each generation, that single people should be volunteering for charity events. It is at these said charity events that they will meet other single people. It is these events that people will be hard at work doing good for others and suddenly meet that special someone. The bond will be so pure, so beautiful, as it is rooted in the work of that comparable to Mother Theresa. Besides they come with automatic credibility; how can anyone be that bad when they are so pure of heart and intention.

Well one evening, one particular charity I am involved with had an event that I was working on. The night of the event there were tons of good-looking party goers for someone such as myself, read single and tipsy, to meet. The crowd was a sea of business suits and cocktail dresses when I suddenly saw *him*. He was dark and sweaty with sleeves of tattoos, oh yea, and he is one of the chefs for the event. We meet quickly and we make the type of eye contact that makes other people around you uncomfortable. I ask his age. He is 29. I tell him my age. He tells me he doesn't care about that. I figure I don't either. This seems to be my new demographic anyway. More on that later. At the end of the night Chef Hottie asks for my number and I give it over. We are both going to be in the Hamptons that weekend and we make a plan to meet up.

Over the next week we text each other sweet things, and we put emoticons on our texts, I learn he doesn't know how to spell but realize I don't really care. What did spelling ever do for anyone anyway, besides I think, it's 2010 and there is always spell check. He apparently doesn't know how to use it but it doesn't bother me one bit.

The night we meet up I bring my step-sister as my wing woman. She tells me she is so uncomfortable with our chemistry, which I admit is outstanding, that she felt funny standing next to us. We spoke for hours and drank champagne. He told me how cute I was. We held hands. It was all very sweet and incredibly sexy. I didn't even mind that he was touching me. We made a date for that week. He was going to cook for me. It all sounded very romantic. At the end of the evening he gave me a big kiss and I actually wanted him to. I was happy.

Over the next few days we are furiously texting and getting excited for our date. He is asking me what type of vegetables I like and I offer to bake the dessert. We are fast friends. I picture our dinner date to be a scene from *Like Water For Chocolate*.

"Oh no." Max says, "You are not going to date a chef?"

"Why not?" I ask.

"They keep terrible hours and their lives are filled with addictions."

I decide to never tell Max about Chef Hottie's pension for alcohol and lots of it, and I ignore the advice completely. There is really nothing that can stop me other than death at this point.

The night of my cooking date arrives. Chef Hottie shows up to make sea bass and asparagus risotto. We dance to country music on my iPod and polish off two bottles of wine. It is a scene out of a romantic movie starring Matthew McConaughey and Kate Hudson. Only neither of us are Blonde. Well I kind of I am, or some people say I am. But, I digress. We head up to my roof and talk for hours. He smokes cigarettes and tells me about his wants in life. He tells me I am the coolest date he ever had. I believe him. I eat the whole thing up, including the dinner he made me. I present him with the dessert I made. He tells me how great it is. I should have known at that moment what a good liar he was. I am a horrible cook.

Chef Hottie and I are talking until the wee hours of the morning when I finally invite him to stay over. Afterall he lives in a different area code which I joke makes him locationally undesirable. We fall asleep to the sound of my iPod and the heavy smell of wine and smoke. He is respectful and doesn't try anything too major. In the morning he asks to see me again ASAP. We made a date for Friday. We can hardly wait.

Friday comes along and we go for drinks and dance a bit. We are having a great time. We behave as we are the only people in the room. He continues to tell me he can't believe how much he likes me. He likes that there are no awkward silences or long pauses in the conversation. We sneak out of the bar for a midnight dinner at an excellent sushi place. We feed each other sushi until about 2:30 am, and Chef Hottie puts away a large bottle of Sake. Chef Hottie can drink more than most men I know. I tell him I probably won't have a chance to see him for at least a week as I have so many commitments coming up and then I am leaving for the weekend with Bear. He starts to mope and asks me if he can come with us.

"I am sorry, but no one I date meets Bear. I keep that very separate unless I was in a long-term committed relationship."

"Oh. That makes it hard. But I guess it's good for him right?"

"It is."

He pretends to understand but continues to mope at the table.

"What's wrong?" I ask.

"You don't seem upset that you aren't going to see me for a week."

I find it insanely cute and uncomfortable all at the same time. I guess he really liked me. But it was actually okay because I liked him. He was all wrong for me. Wrong state, wrong religion, wrong age, he liked veal, he drank too much, he had one too many tats. But even though he was wrong, he felt very right. I liked him.

We found our way home at 3 am and the next morning he had to leave to prepare for a wedding he was attending. Before he left he let it slip that he was 28.

"You told me you were 29. Twice." I said.

"I told you I was 28. I think I know how old I am."

My memory is never wrong. I should be registered as a federal memory weapon. I knew he was lying but I overlooked it.

That day was like any other. He texted me that he wanted to make sure we found the time to get together this week. I told him it was important so we would. We texted a little throughout the day and then he texted me from the wedding asking me how my lunch was. All very normal. He then texted me a picture of him at the wedding. Still normal. I asked if he was going to be in the city that night as he said he might be. He said he didn't think so but he would let me know. That was the last I heard from him. Literally.

The next evening I was so surprised I hadn't heard from him again. I sent him a text:

"You okay?"

What if his car had fallen into a ravine, or he was tied up by the bride's garter belt and unable to escape. Maybe there was a flash flood and he was clinging to a tree in the middle of a river, maybe his "side business" had gotten him into trouble and he was now living in Federal university. Whatever the case, I could not imagine that someone so crazy for me would never contact me again.

Days passed and I finally sent the text that you know you shouldn't send, but sometimes you do, because you are human, after all:

"I can't believe you used me and you couldn't even give me the dignity of a response. No one has ever made me feel so terrible."

He texted back.

"Hi. I have Chef Hottie's phone. He is not available right now, but he will be back. PS- He probly didn't use you. His friend, Bob."

What I wanted to write back:

"You and Chef Hottie spell probably the same way (probly)"- but I kept it to myself.

I never heard from him again, and I never found out why. I did care, and it did sting and everyone party to this blossoming sweet relationship was in utter shock and awe and couldn't imagine what had gone so terribly wrong. I guess this is what a diss is. A straight up diss. The kind you hear about and you think only happens to other people.

One day I too may see his ghost, and tell the story and people will roll their eyes. *She is so naive*, they will think, or they will wonder what part of the story is missing. The truth is nothing is missing. I am telling all of you how it really is. The good, the bad and the ugly. The upside to this tale is that I probably saved myself a great deal of money on tolls and the path train! There is always that...

I ended up finding out what the real story was after this was written. Stay tuned.

26

REAL PHONE CALLS FROM REAL MEN

June 14, 2010

Remember the guy who told me it was time to take our relationship to the next level, as it was our month anniversary of our 2nd and last date? Well, he has been in touch. Often. I get periodic texts from him that say things like:

"I am not giving up on you," and "We are meant to be. I know it inside." By inside I imagine him to mean he has multiple personalities that are discussing this amongst themselves. I would think he was crazy, but being a doctor gives him a credibility that I can't quite explain. *Trust me, I'm a Doctor.*

Last week my phone rang. It was him. I answered as I felt he needed a concrete explanation of why it wouldn't work with us. I had given him other real explanations the other 22 times he asked, but maybe I wasn't clear. Even though we have only had one and a half dates, I explain to him in detail, spending 25 minutes too long, on why it won't work, and why we aren't a good fit, and how I think he is a nice person, but not the right fit for me. I think he understands. He then texts me about 20 times that night asking more questions about our breakup. Which I think is nuts because I haven't seen him in two months and we only went out one and a half times! What is there to talk about?

This morning my phone rang again. It's him. I am not sure why he is calling exactly, but I was distracted and answered.

"Hello?"

"Darcy?"

"Yes?"

"Why did you answer?"

"Huh?"

"Why did you answer?"

"You called?"

"Yeah, but you don't answer anymore. Are you keeping me on a leash?"

"Excuse me?"

"A leash. Are you keeping me on a leash?"

"What does that mean?"

"Well, you stopped answering or returning my calls, and now you answer. Mixed signals Darcy!"

Huh? Is this a joke? Ahhhhh. I now see why they say no good deed goes unpunished.

"Can I see you this week Darcy?"

"I really can't. And I thought we went over this."

"Just for a minute."

I think what a good salesperson he might have been had he not gone to med school. He is persistent. Persistently creepy.

"I need to go. Really."

I hang up before he has a chance to argue. He calls BACK. 30 minutes later.

"Darcy, I really need to see you."

I imagine him shoving me in some type of oven or black garbage bag. I picture waking up in the trunk of his car and dialing my mom.

"Mom, Help! I have been kidnapped. He is driving me around in the trunk of his car."

"WHAT," she would scream, "Does that mean you don't have a seatbelt on??"

Sigh. I decided to not answer anymore. I have done the good deed of explaining it 27 times. I think that is about 26 times too many.

27

SINGLE MAN DROUGHT

June 18, 2010

"Standards, I used to have some standards.

But man by man every standard meandered from me.

Lesbian, I should be a lesbian.

If I was born to love women, how wondrously sane I would be."

These are some of the greatest lyrics ever from the show *I Love You, You're Perfect, Now Change- Single Man Drought*. Sometimes, when I close my eyes, I can actually hear this soundtrack playing in my head.

28

SCENES FROM A NIGHT OUT

June 20, 2010

I was out with Max as his date for an event he had to attend. I love being a gay man's date, well, not when they are masquerading as a straight man. But this was different. This was Max. Gay, out, and bringing me as his date. Since I have sworn off men and dating for the time being a gay boyfriend is just what the doctor ordered. And by Doctor, I mean Phil, as he is the only Doctor I listen to.

Guy approaches: "This is love at first sight. I don't even need to speak to you. I already know I love you." He says.

This line is so pathetic. Tell me more, I think.

I pick up on an accent of some kind.

"Where are you from?" I can't believe I am engaging Mr. Love at first sight, with his cheesy pick-up line, but Max was in the bathroom and I had nothing to do at the moment. Oh, and he was cute.

"Brazil."

"Falo Portuguese?" I say, shamelessly flirting in his native tongue.

"Si! Fala?"
"Como Vai Voce?"
"Oi Tudo Bem! I am impressed."
I grew up with a Brazilian Nanny.
He looks very young.
"How old are you?" I ask.
"I am 27."
"27?"
"Okay, 26."
"I am too old for you."
"NO! No such thing. You are beautiful."
"That's sweet, but I have to run, we have to go to our next location now."
I see Max approaching.
"Awwww. Can I come with you?"
I am trying to be polite and extract myself from the conversation with this adorable newborn, when I glance down at his hand. Staring at me is a shiny gold WEDDING BAND???
"IS THAT A WEDDING BAND?"
"Yes."
"You're married???"
"Yes." He says this with zero embarrassment, shame or remorse.
"That's terrible. You are gross."
It's really all I could muster up. I know men do this, but really? With an actual wedding band on?? I turn on my very high patent heel and walk away.

I start to wonder to myself: When I decide to become a lesbian will I watch things like *The L Word*? Will I think Suzie Orman is hot?

We walk out of the event and jump into a taxi. We head to a gay bar. A gay bar filled with straight people.

Somehow Max and I befriend a motley crew of bar patrons. This all takes place after 12 am. You know what they say, and by they, I mean the NYPD: "Nothing good happens after 12 midnight." They become our entourage of sorts. One of them is adorable. He is 29 and Puerto Rican. Let's call him Danny. Danny takes a liking to me, and I am not going to lie, Danny is cute, but not for me. I ask him where he lives.

"With my grandma. But if I ever need privacy there is another apartment in the building I can use. It's my uncle's and he is in Florida, but I have the keys."

"That is quite the hook up," I say.

Let's just say I don't plan on meeting Danny's grandma anytime soon.

29

THE ROBBIE REPORT

June 23, 2010

Remember Robbie? (See: *Real Phone Calls From Real Men, Real Voice Mail From Real Men, Real Texts From Real Men*). I have decided to name him Robbie for the sake of Darcy Dates.

Robbie and I have decided to no longer speak. And by *we* have decided, I mean, *I* have decided to no longer speak to him. My politeness has gotten me nowhere. We have had the conversation way too many times already, but it doesn't seem to stick. I have stopped taking Robbie's calls. Well, that's not entirely true, I answer on each 30th call.

Yesterday Robbie called. I am so bewildered that he still manages to call 2-3 times a day I decide to pick up. Exactly what Gavin De Becker would advise against in *The Gift of Fear*, since I am basically now teaching Robbie that for every 30 phone calls I will pick up.

"Yes Robbie?"

"Darcy? You picked up!" (*Gavin would kill me*) "You stopped picking up."

"Well, it's a catch-22 with you. If I don't pick up you leave messages that I am mean for screening your calls, and if I do pick up, you complain I am keeping you on a leash."

I am not sure how this happened. He is like a pen pal at this point. Only with telephone calls and craziness.

"That's okay baby, I'd rather be on your leash than not in your life at all."

"You realize your nuts right Robbie?"

"I'm nuts about you is what I am."

For reasons I can't explain, I imagine if Robbie had a theme song while he walked it would be *Black Betty*.

"So Darcy, I am hanging out with a great girl now. I like her a lot."

"Awesome Robbie. So why are you still calling me?"

"Cause I like you Darce. I want you in my life."

"Awesome. I hope you get married and invite me to the wedding. I love a wedding band and pigs in a blanket. I'd stay in your life for that."

"I'm serious. You are a cool girl Darce."

"Thanks. I hope it works out with this girl. It sounds like you really like her."

"Yeah, she's cool. She's a nice girl. She's not as thin as I like. She is more voluptuous."

"Cool."

"What's the story with voluptuous? Why isn't it fat? What's the difference?"

Is he asking me this really? I'm confused.

"She hasn't slept with me yet, which I like."

"Nice."

"I mean, if she slept with me on our first date or whatever I wouldn't like her. I mean, I would, it would just change things. It probably wouldn't go anywhere."

"Well, if that's the case, then don't try to sleep with her until you know it will go somewhere." Am I giving relationship advice to Robbie? How does this kind of thing happen to me?

"No. I'll always try."

At least he's honest.

"Ok. Well, I gotta run. Work."

"BYE!" Robbie hangs up in a huff.

I go back to work for an hour or so and completely forget Robbie exists.

Ring Ring.

"Hello?"

"Why didn't you call me back?"

"ROBBIE. I AM WORKING."

"When can I see you? I want to go out with you again."

"Robbie, you are dating someone. We just had an entire conversation about your sex life with her, or lack thereof. Please, focus on the new girl and leave me be."

"Now you are playing games with me Darcy."

"WHAT?"

"You are blaming it on the girl, but that's not why you won't go out with me."

"No Robbie, you are right, that's not why. However, I still think you should focus on her."

"Can we go out as friends?"

"We aren't friends Robbie."

"Let me take you out as a friend."

Robbie and I are in an abusive relationship of sorts. I am not sure how or why. I put my foot down and somehow I still speak to him several times a day. In a few weeks Robbie and I may be living together. In fact, there is a good chance Robbie is sleeping under my bed at this very moment or lingering in one of my closets. I should stop writing right now and go look at some online wedding registries to make sure he hasn't registered us anywhere. More on Robbie Later I am sure, as he is the gift that keeps giving.

30

STEP AWAY FROM THE BLACKBERRY

June 24, 2010

If we go on a first date that is surprisingly not *terrible* and you text me 3 times and send me 3 emails post date that very same evening with no response (because I am sleeping), and I wake up to another text sent at 6:30 am, an email from google maps showing the distance from my house to yours, and a voicemail saying you just wanted to hear my voice, I will no longer think the date was good. Just saying.

31

NO GIFTS PLEASE

JUNE 28, 2010

I NEVER UNDERSTOOD why people write "No Gifts" on an invitation. Let's be honest, gifts are fun to give and to get. I am *pro* gift. But there have been cases when gifts can take a turn for the creepy. Not possible you say? Well, let me prove you wrong.

If we are dating, seeing each other, in love, married, divorced, friends, if you are a host, I am thanking you, it's your birthday, engagement, wedding, anniversary, you just had your first or fourth baby, maybe you won a Nobel prize, you are retiring, it's a get well gift of some kind....I find a gift, even a token, appropriate. Even if it's just "thinking of you and I thought you would love this gift," I support it 100%. However, even a "thinking of you" gift can go terribly wrong.

The following is not appropriate: If it has been 24 hours since our first date, and I am only responding to 1 out of your 20 texts, please do not send me an iTunes gift certificate to a Natalie Cole song that made you think of me. It will be weird and creepy and I will never be able to like and or listen to the song in the same way.

Also not appropriate: If I meet you, and I find you interesting, but I know we can never date because I live in New York City and you live in Philly and you are newly separated and have two kids that will keep you in Philly, and I tell you such on our first phone conversation, I will not like if you look up my address which is not published and send me a gift. I assure you, I will see your return address and wonder how you got my address without me giving it to you, especially because it is not published. I will open the corner of the package to peek inside. When I discover it contains approximately 20 CD's of my favorite artist I will NOT find it sweet. I will find it creepy. I will hand it to the mailman and ask him to return it to sender and to stamp it with something that contains the words "wrong address," or "recipient does not live here," or even "Are you kidding me???" I will never acknowledge receipt and we will never speak again. Every time I leave my building for the next two months I will look both ways to make sure you don't jump out from behind the car I believe you to be hiding behind.

32

FULL DISCLOSURE

July 1, 2010

On my second date with my ex-husband I told him a story and he told me I was too forgiving. I told him I was terrible at holding a grudge.

"Don't worry," he said, "I am an excellent grudge holder. I will always hold all your grudges for you."

Over time I learned he wasn't being funny. He was being serious. He was telling me who he really was. I love him dearly and he is one of my best friends till this day, BUT the man can hold a grudge like nobody's business.

My favorite quote ever is one that Oprah says all the time (I am very well-read like that). It is something she learned from Maya Angelou.

"When people show you who they really are, believe them the first time." It's simple but so true. People don't usually fake being bad people, but they certainly fake being 'good people'.

I have learned that this is a good rule of thumb to live by. Particularly in the world of dating. When people say things such as:

"My nickname used to be the prince of darkness."

"I would make an excellent con-man."

"I am always scheming for one thing or another."

"Men are much smarter than women."

"I have a side-business of selling drugs."

"I'm a good liar."

If they show you a text from their old boss that says "What's wrong, you have already fucked everyone in your office so you need a new job?" and so forth and so on...believe them. They are not "pretending" to be bad. They are bad. Pack it up, and run the other way. Do not wait to see it unfold, do not wait to see if you are different, do not, do not, do not, and do not. It's real. If they are showing you a flawed moral compass, it's broken and does not come with a one year warranty. You can't swap out their moral compass for a new one.

I am not saying I have mastered this advice, but I am getting a little better. And by a little I mean not much. (See: *Jonathan 40, Is Really 47*). I want to get better. But bear with me while I try.

33

CHANNELING DEMI

July 6, 2010

Robbie called me again today. I told you he would, as he is the gift that keeps on giving.

"Darcy?"

"Robbie."

"Remember when you told me it seemed like I was paranoid. Like I always spoke like the whole world was against me?"

"Yes."

"Was that a turn-off?"

No Robbie, it was a turn ON. Nothing is sexier than someone that suffers paranoid delusions. It's like Spanish Fly, only different. Because it's crazy. I silently think this. I don't say it. I just ask,

"why?"

"Because the girl I am dating said that to me yesterday."

I cannot believe I have become Robbie's dating coach of sorts.

Something went terribly wrong here. Note to self: See a shrink. Ask how this happened.

Many of you, at this point, are probably wondering what my only two dates with Robbie were like, so I am going to provide you with a walk down memory lane, if you will.

As I have discussed before, there is something about me and the under 30 crowd. One of my dates who is not representative of the human race in any way, recently 30, explained the reason he likes older women is because they are comfortable with their bodies. He was looking for one thing, and it didn't involve things like talking. Well, talking dirty maybe, but that is for another entry. I decided to give the younger generation one more chance. My good friend Victoria, also divorced with two kids, was seeing a gorgeous 26 year old. She just turned 38 last week. I figured I would use her as my role model and go for it.

My date with Robbie started off like any other date, only he was 40 minutes late. In all fairness to him he gave me ample notice that he was behind schedule, and by ample, I mean I was walking into the restaurant to meet him when I received his text. One of his patients was about to die and he had to save him which put him totally behind schedule. Fair enough I thought.

Robbie was cute. Super tall, 6′ 2″, but only 29. Okay FINE 28. Not a day younger! I figured why not? If Demi can do it, so can I. I have long hair too. We sit down and order our drinks. I order a glass of wine, Robbie orders a Jack and Coke. Hard living. I like it. Robbie is a doctor, or a resident at least, is that the same thing? I have no idea. All I know is if I choke on an ice-cube, he can probably save me and for now it seemed good enough for me.

I ask my usual younger date question.

"Aren't I too old for you?"

"No, who cares, age is just a number. I have dated people my age, older, younger, it doesn't matter as long as we jive."

I actually believed him. I ask if he has ever dated a mom.

"No. But I like children."

I wondered if saying he liked children meant he liked them like one likes spaghetti or Twinkies. I don't know that he realized kids are a full-time job. But he started to cite examples of all the time he has spent with children.

"Do you want more children?" he asks.

"Yes."

"Good. I like that you want more."

He is calm and collected. It doesn't seem fake or phony.

"I'd like to be engaged within the year. I am serious and don't want to waste my time. I am not looking to serial date," he says.

WHOA! If a woman said that to a man on a first date it would be game over. I suddenly felt an oppressive pressure that dating Robbie would mean ASAP commitment. I would never even utter the M word until the 18th date, and only then would I use it casually. And by casually, I mean asking if he ever watched *Married With Children*. I am good at assessing these things and nothing read fake. He didn't seem like he was trying to get me into bed. He was just talking. Like a regular person.

"Cool." I said.

I am not sure what led to the next disclosure but it seemed I should pay close attention.

"I don't like when people take advantage of me."

Fair enough.

"I REALLY don't like it. It really makes me crazy. For example, Direct TV."

I nod, unsure of what was coming next.

"When I signed up, they implied they were tight with Time Warner..."

I didn't hear the actual story, as I had tuned out, but I did hear what came next.

"So I called them and began to fight with them regularly. I insulted the education of the phone operators, I threatened them. I wished I was a lawyer so I could read up on contract law and sue them. I had fantasies of calling them up and citing laws and cases."

I stared silently. Is he really telling me this? He wasn't done with his angry confessional. I know it's wrong but I am egging him on with 'I understand!' and 'what else makes you angry?'

"I also feel this way about Dell. When I call and they transfer me to India I flip out. I am much smarter than people in India. I am a doctor."

WHAT? He was dead serious, which concerned me a great deal.

We weren't done with the stories.

He told me about his fight with the broker who rented him his apartment, and then topped it off with the fight with the paint store owners.

"They mixed the paint wrong. It was more pink and not red. I flipped out on them. They told me I was an asshole."

I am nodding still. I really wanted to ask why he was showing all of his crazy colors right out of the gate, but I just kept nodding.

"I kept screaming, 'I don't want this color red. This color red is gay. This is a gay color!' There were two gay guys in the store. I think I offended them."

I can only wonder why he didn't think he was offending me.

Then my favorite story: The one where he confesses he drove to a random law office in New Jersey to fight a hospital collection bill for $26 that he didn't even know he had. He showed up unannounced to fight with them. At this point I think he actually jumped the shark from crazy to cool.

He told me he loved fighting with people. He *LOVES* it.

I envision a life with Robbie. Me, holding his hand, him in a UFC fighting leotard trolling the streets looking for a brawl. At one point, I believe he slipped me an invitation to Fight Club under the table. *"I know,"* I whisper, *"never talk about Fight Club."*

I know it sounds terrible, but Robbie actually wasn't bad. A bit of an anger problem, but he was able to laugh at himself about it which is incredibly important. After my glass of wine I told him I needed to be getting home. He offered to walk me.

"If you don't feel comfortable I will only walk you until we get a block away. Don't worry, I won't try to come upstairs."

Huh. For such an angry guy, he certainly was a gentleman. Breaking news: Chivalry is NOT dead.

As we walked towards my apartment he turned to me.

"I can't believe you were going to walk by yourself."

"What? I was born and raised in this neighborhood. If someone tried to mess with me I'd kick their ass." I say. Only half kidding.

"I LOVE that! I think that's hot!" Robbie exclaimed. I forgot the fighting. Robbie loved fighting. My next thought is that if I had whipped out a box cutter and challenged him to a street fight he would have dropped to one knee and proposed.

Oddly enough, I liked walking next to Robbie. He was the perfect height and super cute. He smelled so good. When we were two blocks from my apartment I told him he could leave me there. He said goodnight and leaned in and kissed me softly on the lips.

"Is that okay?" He asked.

Robbie was like some Seinfeld-esque type character. Angry from one angle, super soft and gentle from the other. He reminded me of a hot Larry David. As I walked away I glanced back over my shoulder. I could swear I saw him shadow boxing on the corner.

The next day Robbie sent me a text, "I had such a great night. Are you up for doing it again?"

I ask if we can do it the following Friday (I needed some time to think about it).

"Absolutely."

For a young guy he was very grown up. He had cleared the reputation of the other younger men out there, and by other younger men, I mean one who was particularly yucky.

As Friday approached I thought long and hard about whether or not I was able to date Robbie. For as sweet, cute and angry as he was, I didn't think I could date someone that much younger. I always believe honesty is the best policy. I receive a text from Robbie:

"Are we still on for Friday?"

"About Friday…I have been thinking about it and while you are adorable, I am not comfortable with the age difference. I am so sorry. If I was younger I would be all over it, but I just can't."

"What is 5 years? In the long run, 5 years is nothing. When I am 50, you will be 55. When I'm 63, you will be 68. Will that really matter then?" I thought that it was sweet that he was thinking about the long run. My next thought was that Robbie didn't know how to add. I was more than 5 years older than Robbie.

"That is very sweet Robbie. I just can't."

"That's too bad Darcy. I thought you were very special."

I am touched by this. Robbie seemed to be more grown up than many men I had met. Later that evening I am on the phone with Nicole when I see Robbie calling me.

"Robbie is calling! Do you think he wants to discuss our relationship?" we laugh. Robbie and I had been out one time, and it was for a quick drink. "Let me call you back."

"Hello?"

"Darcy? Hi. Is it really just the age difference?"

"Yes." *And the anger issue.*

"Well who cares about age? Do you really care if you are 5 years older than your husband?

My husband? I didn't realize we were engaged. I'm glad he filled me in so I could buy a dress. It would suck if I didn't have a dress for my own wedding.

"Robbie, it's more than 5 years. And I am really not comfortable with it."

"Darcy, I had a patient today who was 98. Her husband was 88. She told me that before she came into the ER, she said to her husband, 'thank you for the most wonderful 60 years.' And Darcy, she was 10 years older than he was."

As I listened to Robbie talk it was so...cute. Why not, I thought to myself. Is age that important? I mean, look at Anna Nicole Smith and J. Howard Marshall. That was true love right?

"Okay! Ok. You win. Let's go."

Our next date was fun. But I knew we were in different places. I told him.

"Darcy, that's ridiculous. We are getting married. I know it."

I text Nicole, "I think I am engaged."

"Congrats," she texts back.

Little did I know that I would have a never ending relationship with Robbie. Not in the happily ever after sense, but in the ever after sense nonetheless.

I had found a prince of sorts to live in a land far far away with, unfortunately the land was bizarro land. Welcome to my twilight zone.

34

WHEN YOU LEAST EXPECT IT

July 8, 2010

"Darcy! Are you awake?"

"Yes, just walked in from dinner."

"Okay, we are picking you up in 10 minutes and taking you to a party in South Hampton."

"It's 11:30 at night! That is 20 minutes away from here. Won't the party be ending?"

"Darcy?! What are you? 80?"

"I can't."

"Why not?"

I sit and think for a second. Bear is with his dad for the weekend, and the truth is I really don't have anything better to do than have my nightly call with Alexis. *Accept every invitation*, I hear in my head. This is advice my psychic (for another entry obviously) gave me once.

"Okay."

I hung up. My phone rings. It's Alexis.

"Hey," she says.

"Hey, I am going to South Hampton for a party. Want to come?"

"Are you nuts?"

"A little. Get busy living or get busy dying." I say this. It's my new thing. I picked it up from someone's Facebook status update. I kind of like it.

"Where is this party?"

"At Bryan Mark's House."

Bryan Mark is a very well-known author who has published a number of best-selling books. Apparently none are on the art of getting a good night's sleep.

"You are driving all the way there?"

"No, Sam and Stacy are picking me up."

I hang up with her when I hear a faint honking outside. I grab a shawl as the party will be on the beach and head out the door. *You are too old for this*, I think. I then realize that Sam and Stacy are 3 years older than me so I guess it's fine.

Right before we pull onto Bryan's street I ask how they know him.

"We don't. But anyone can go. It's a house party."

WHAT??? I want to jump out of the moving car. Did they just tell me it's a house party and they weren't invited? Do they think we are 14? People still do this? Were we riding in a DeLorean and we had gone back to 1989?

"You don't know him??? I thought you guys were friends with him. UGH."

I knew I should have taken my car so I could make a U-turn.

How did this happen? I wonder how I will get home. My phone battery is almost dead with very little reception. Switch your thinking Darcy! Think "*The Secret.*" I try to visualize the best night ever. Instead I am visualizing getting arrested for trespassing. The truth is, the best things happen when you least expect it, so I suddenly just let go and decided that if I wrapped my Pashmina around my face they may not realize I wasn't an invited guest.

We walked down to the beach, and the party looked...fun. It looked like the parties I had attended as a teenager in the Hamptons.

On the beach, bonfires, s'mores, and a reggae band. Huh. Not bad. Not bad at all. A nice change from the regular run of the mill stuffy parties I usually attend. I had been there less than 3 minutes, when I ran into an old friend from college.

We catch up on her life, on mine, and I tell her all about Bear.

"I am divorced," I confide, "Know anyone?" I say. Kind of kidding.

"YES! I do!" She says. Sometimes people say this, but she really meant it.

"There is this guy. He works with my husband. I hear about him all the time and what a great guy he is and I just met him for the first time. He is really cute. And he's here!" she says.

I panic a little bit. This could end terribly with me jumping into the ocean and swimming to Cuba, or New Jersey, or whatever is across the ocean from the Hamptons. Her husband approaches. After saying hello and quickly reuniting she tells him her plans immediately.

"I was thinking we set Darcy up with Kyle."

He looks at me and his face lights up, "That's an EXCELLENT idea. Really. I likkkkeeee it." He is nodding with an approving smile as though she is really onto something.

Before you know it he disappears into the crowd and I am trying to plan a polite escape in my head for when I *don't* like Kyle. I have been through this before 'He is so cute,' 'He is great,' 'You will love him.' Only to meet him and silently pray for an earthquake so I can get lost in the rubble, dig myself out and end up on the other side of the earth where they can never find me. And by they, I mean the people who have set me up, and of course, the date to be.

"That's him," she says.

Silencio.

In a good way.

He is tall, dark and so damn cute. Wow. When you least expect it is right. At a party you are crashing at 12 midnight. He was actually so unexpectedly cute I lost my entire game. I, Darcy, was speechless. I gave a brief wave, a quick hello and walked away? GET BACK THERE DARCY. I couldn't. I walked aimlessly through the crowd towards the bonfire, looking to roast a marshmallow, or my arm, or anything that would make me look busy.

After a good 20 minutes of re-grouping I found my way back to Kyle.

"Hi."

"Hey."

We started talking. It was slightly uncomfortable as the crowd was filled with the ghosts of boyfriends past, but I managed to block it all out. At that moment Kyle's friend came over and brought him a beer.

"This is Darcy," Kyle said to his friend.

"Hi," I shook his hand.

"Those hands are freezing!" his friend said.

"I know, I am holding a cup of ice."

The second this comes out of my mouth I feel like Baby in *Dirty Dancing* when she says, "I carried a watermelon."

"I'll fix that for you," Kyle said.

Just like that, he took the cup out of my hands,

"I will hold it for you," he said, "here, let me warm up your hands."

He put my hand in his and started to rub it gently. He then put my hand under his arm to warm it up. Finally he held my hand and blew some hot air on it. I was watching him alternate his heating methods. It was...adorable. Here's the thing: When you actually like someone and are attracted to them, you think touching that you would normally think was creepy is cute.

"You have tiny hands," he said, as he held my hands in his.

"You're good," I said. "You always got this much game?"

He smiled.

I asked where he was from originally.

"I think my cousin is from there. How old are you?" I asked.

"Old."

"How old???"

"38."

"What? That's not old! I am (insert mid 30's age here. I would tell you all, but you aren't supposed to know that much about me)."

"WHAT? NO! I thought you were 26!" He looked like he meant it.

"Come on. I LOVE you." Awkward that I just told him I loved him. I wanted to vacuum that sentence back into my mouth, yet he was still standing there.

Leave now Darcy. On a high note.

"Well, it was really nice meeting you Kyle."

"You too Darcy. Hey, any chance I can grab your number and we can get together sometime? I have a really funny story that will take an hour and a half to tell you, but I can condense it into 45 minutes." Funny. I liked him.

I gave him my number and said goodbye.

He waited the standard 3 days, and called me. More on Kyle later.

35

THE PIOUS LIFE

July 12, 2010

"Come to my house on Saturday for a BBQ Darcy! Hot work guy will be there!"

"He lives with his girlfriend, remember? But I would love to see you." A laid-back night with friends is what I needed right now, so I threw on something short and some kick ass wedges and headed over to the shindig.

I know you are probably wondering who hot work guy is. It's quite simple. Jill works for a guy who I find very attractive. I met him 6 months ago at her office when I stopped by to grab lunch. It was crush at first sight. We only talked a minute, but he was cute by anyone's standards. He was a mix of JFK Jr. and Christian Bale with a hint of Superman thrown in for good measure. My friend later informed me that hot work guy was divorced with child. I had also learned over time that hot work guy had a serious girlfriend. They lived together. Great for hot work guy. Boring for me.

It was the perfect Hamptons dinner party. Small and intimate, no more than 10 people. It was set up beautifully in the backyard with tiki torches and citronella candles. Wine was flowing and Janet Jackson was playing. The perfect storm for bad lip syncing and faux dance routines performed by tipsy dinner guests.

I enjoyed getting to know Jill's friends, and even got to learn a little about hot work guy who was there sans live-in girlfriend. I had learned that he was married, met his wife at a young age, they became more friends than anything else. He started to have an affair with his now live-in girlfriend, which is when his then "live-in" wife became his "live-out wife." He announces this to me, a virtual stranger, as though he is catching me up on the latest episode of Entourage. He spoke from a place of complete detachment, as if it were a script he learned from a shrink, or his mother, or a judge. Hot work guy was a little odd. Maybe it was a kind of divorced parent camaraderie that made him feel like he could tell me his deepest darkest secrets, or maybe it was poor judgement. After I got to know him a bit, I was happy he wasn't mine, but he was easy on the eyes and just looking at him was entertaining.

After dinner I sat down to relax on an outdoor sofa of some kind wrapped in a pashmina, hair looking like a rat's nest from the salt air and sea breeze. I was enjoying this perfect summer night. Suddenly, through the crowd of people eating dessert and possibly dancing the electric slide, I see hot work guy emerge from the crowd and make a bee-line towards me on the sofa.

The sofa is big. Very big. An outdoor sectional of sorts. He sits directly next to me on the corner of the sofa. Did he just put his arm around me? I am pretty sure he now has his arm tightly fixed around my body. I smile awkwardly. I want to say hot work guy is drunk and mistakes us for being new best friends, but the sudden caressing of my thigh would lead me to think otherwise. He tells me he is glad we had a chance to hang out and I should come to Jill's dinners more often. He tells me what a great place he is in since his divorce was finalized. He tells me he loves hanging out with Jill and this particular group of friends since no one is trying to have sex and none of his single friends are pushing him to get laid, and none of his married friends who are 'miserable in their marriages' are living vicariously through him. I start to wonder if hot work guy is a sex addict. I get the sense that he is selling me on his new-found wholesomeness, and nothing about it feels convincing. He has mentioned several times how he was so fixated on sleeping with women during his marriage, and that he was very unfaithful. A self-proclaimed womanizer, but completely reformed. This, apparently, has all changed now that he is with his live-in girlfriend.

Huh. That's funny hot work guy. I could swear you are rubbing my thigh.

I learned they (hot work guy and his live-in girlfriend) had hit a rough patch during his divorce, but they worked through it and are now in a better place because of it. Is he playing with my hair? If this is a great place, I would hate to see a not great place. I am narrowing my eyes and contorting my face as though I am asking someone sitting across from me, "WHAT THE FK?" but no one was there except my imaginary friend, Sanity, who agreed this guy might be insane.

"Me and my girlfriend plan on having a baby next year together." He announces, as he tightens his grip on my body. I am frozen in confusion. I now know what it must feel like to be a deer in headlights. You want to run but can only stare. He tells me he isn't sure he wants more children, but he must have one with her to be fair to her as she has no children of her own.

"Maybe I should be dating someone who already has kids."

I pray he isn't talking about me. *Not it!* I scream in my head. I don't know that he heard me, but I am hoping he got the telepathic message.

Somehow I extract myself from hot work guys death grip and chit-chat with Jill a bit more. As the night is ending I announce I must be getting home. I say goodbye to hot work guy who may or may not start humping my leg by this point. The whole thing is so uncomfortable I am not really looking. I am more squinting, like I am watching a scary movie and I was afraid to see what came next. Hot work guy calls over to Jill,

"This one is amazing!"

AWKWARD. Jill knows that he lives with his girlfriend and Jill *knows* his girlfriend.

He then turns to me.

"You are very lucky I live a pious life now Darcy or you would be in big trouble."

I wonder how pious a guy's life can be when he is living with a woman and says this to a girl he just met. I smile quizzically. I am not up to speed on the pious life handbook, but I am pretty sure it would advise against such a thing. I tell him he is safe as I don't date married men. At all.

"I am not married, Darcy."

But you just spent the entire evening telling me you are having a baby next year with your girlfriend. I die a little inside.

I go to give him the token nice to meet you handshake, air kiss extravaganza when he grabs my face and kisses me. On the lips. Hard. He uses his tongue!!! I actually started laughing. In his face. I can't even kiss him back because I am in a full belly laugh at this point, yet the narcissistic side of me is screaming, "DARCY, HE IS GOING TO THINK YOU CAN'T KISS!" (Yes, I can be *that* vain.)

I tell him that this is a horrible idea. Not only am I not interested in kissing or being kissed by someone with a girlfriend, but I don't want to feel like I have to avoid Jill and Jill's fabulous *So You Think You Can Dance* dinner parties. I tell him I need to get out of here before there is any more trouble.

"Oh Darcy, there is plenty of time for trouble," he says, "the summer has just begun."

I actually feel dirty. It was so confusing. He looked so scrubbed and innocent like some type of all american football star, but at any moment he could have ripped off his face and revealed he was actually Ron Jeremy. I glance around to see if there is a sprinkler I can run through on my way to my car. Is that a slip-and-slide I see sprawled across Jill's lawn? Maybe I can take a running leap onto it and rinse off. YUCK. CLEAN ME.

Anyway, just like that, hot work guy turned into hot jerk guy. Another crush bites the dust.

36

REAL TEXTS FROM REAL MEN

JULY 14, 2010

ROBBIE IS BACK. He has been calling daily and I have stopped answering. Last week he sent a text:
"We could have gone to the stars."
I didn't answer it.
This morning I woke up to a text that said:
"My heart longs for you," sent at 4 a.m. For those of you just joining us, Robbie is someone I went on one and a half dates with about 2 months ago.
I actually laughed when I read it. I wrote back.
"You are nuts."
"You bring feeling to my life, you're the inspiration."
"That's a Chicago song."
"No it's not. I wrote it myself."
"Robbie, really. I am laughing. You are crazy."

"Just got off the night shift. I wouldn't chase you if you weren't so great. So save a little face, avoid the mace, and give me first base."

Folks, when Robbie references the night shift, he is talking about his shift in the ER. As a doctor. These are the people taking care of you and me in times of emergency. Just saying.

37

BREAKING THE RULES

July 18, 2010

As mentioned in an earlier entry, there are a plethora of books written on the rules of dating (see: *He Will Boil Your Bunny*). These books give step by step advice on how to make a man fall for you. Don't call him, don't act interested, don't even smile, don't let him see you eat ever, unless it's a basil leaf, and don't ever let him know you like him.

If you have seen the movie *How To Lose A Guy In Ten Days*, then you can pretty much liken my behavior on my first date with Kyle to that of Kate Hudson's character. I realize many of my entries rip apart actions and choices made by my dates, but you see, I am not always that innocent either. On my first date with Kyle I was in rare form and made some of the worst first date mistakes to date.

It was about 98 degrees in New York City. You couldn't walk a half block without breaking out into a deep sweat. I was looking forward to my date with Kyle, as our first interaction was pretty promising,

(See: *When You Least Expect It,*) and he was cute. He didn't set off my creepy meter in any way. That day I was running around from meeting to meeting with very little time to spare, culminating in dropping Bear off at his dad's house for the night. After a quick shower and a mad dash to the meatpacking district (which from here on out I shall refer to only as "the first-dating district,") I arrived to meet Kyle at his restaurant of choice.

I had one concern about our date. Kyle didn't yet know I was divorced or that I had a child. It is always the first thing I tell people, but it all happened so fast I didn't get a chance to tell him. The fact that he initially thought I was 26 put extra pressure on me. Here is my feeling about dating people who have an issue with the fact that I have a child: You are not for me. My child is my everything and my most favorite part of my life. If it doesn't work for you, great, but then it certainly doesn't work for me. So we're cool.

I showed up and found Kyle sitting at the bar. I immediately felt at ease. We hadn't even been sitting for 4 minutes when I asked,

"So, what do you know about me?"

"Nothing." Kyle said.

"Well, did you know that I am divorced and I have a child?"

"No. I didn't, but that's awesome. Kids are great."

"I agree!" I said. I felt relieved that he knew. Not because it is some secret I had to get off my chest, but because if this wasn't okay with Kyle, I wasn't okay with Kyle.

Kyle talks about his divorce briefly and confides that he got the sense his ex-wife never wanted to have kids and kept putting it off. He tells me he really wanted kids and felt that was what life was about. Excellent.

It was immediately easy to talk to Kyle. He had a good sense of humor, he loved that I was a mom, and we quickly admitted that we were psyched when we met. Kyle was drinking beer, and for reasons I still can't explain I chose to go the vodka route.

"This is an unlevel playing field," I announced, as the tall glass of vodka and soda was delivered to the table. Famous last words.

"No, I will drink much more beer than you will vodka."

Between the excessive heat and my PMS, the drink hit and it hit hard. I was all warmed up and ready for the confessionathon you should never really have on a first date. After I ate the majority of the food we ordered (it was sushi, so we ordered for the table), the waiter asked if we wanted to see a dessert menu.

"No, we're good."

"WHAT? We need dessert. That's so boring Kyle!"

This will not be the first time my behavior on this date will make you cringe. Just a warning.

"I'm not really a dessert person." He said.

"That could be a deal breaker," I said and I wildly summoned the waiter and asked for the dessert menu. *The Rules* girls would have officially died by this point.

I am more of a dessert person than an actual food person so I was bummed. Given that I had gone pound for pound with Kyle I was now well into my third drink. I should have stopped at two, but I didn't. It was hot, the drink was refreshing, and he was cute. The trifecta if you will, one quite similar to the Bermuda triangle where judgement gets lost instead of people.

At the end of my second drink I asked the waiter if I should go on a second date with Kyle.

"Don't you think we should get finished with our first date first?" Kyle asks.

Awkwaaaarrrrdddd, I hear, as a high pitched sing song voice in my head.

I invite Kyle to move to my side of the table. Why wouldn't I? I was bombed at this point. Kyle accepts and moves next to me. He tells me I am completely adorable. Then he kissed me, and I was okay with it. Maybe it was the vodka, or that he was cute, or that I was averting my eyes away from his short sleeve button down. But it was all good. I was having a grand ol' time.

"Did anyone ever tell you you look just like Denise richards?"

"No, because I don't." I mean, maybe I did, if by look like her you mean we are both blondish, and are moms and you have no eyes. Kyle must have been drunk too.

I am not sure how it happened but before you know it, I believe *I* asked Kyle out on another date mid-date. Gone was the *"let him chase you"* rule. We make a plan for the following week. I know my behavior is terrible and I want to make it stop, only I can't. DARCY STOP. Nope, I keep going. We wrap up the dinner and Kyle is about to call it a night.

"Hey, we are young! Let's go out!" I say. I may have even performed the perfect cheer.

"Where should we go?"

"I don't know, for a drink somewhere." If I had to guess what was going through Kyle's mind at that point it may have gone something like this: *'Lush party of 1, Lush party of 1, your table is ready.'*

We are heading to the next location and I see Alexis calling.

"OHHHH! It's my best friend Alexis! You need to talk to her! She is the best. She talks to all my first dates. ANSWER IT!"

I may or may not have been yelling this at him. They speak for a while. I don't really know what they talk about exactly, but the next day she told me that he said he needed to hang up because, "Darcy was shaking her ass at a homeless man."

When we got to our next destination I sat down at the bar. I believe I kind of fell off the chair. In all fairness, the chair was a stool, and the seat was an actual basketball. Even on my best day I may not have been coordinated enough for a surprise like that.

"Were you ever a fire-fighter?"

"No."

"Awww. Too bad. I can't marry you."

"Marry me? This is our first date."

"I know. Just saying. My psychic told me I was going to marry a firefighter." Gone was the *"don't talk about the future"* rule, or the *"don't be a crazy freak who talks about your psychic or shrink"* or *"you live in your parents basement"* rule. DARCY SHUT THE FK UP. What's worse? The fact that you brought up the M word or that you said you had a psychic? You are *that* girl Darcy. Why don't you go buy 9 cats while you are at it and call it a day.

Kyle is yawning and asks if I am ready to go. It's 12 midnight.

"Go? Now? Come on Kyle! We are having so much fun!" And by we, I meant I, as I was too drunk to know if we were having fun or not so I had just assumed we were.

"Where do you want to go?"

"I want french fries! Let's go somewhere for french fries!"

"Okay."

I had officially held my date hostage after he already said he was ready to call it a night. Gone was the *"leave him wanting more"* rule. We walked into a dive bar around the corner and I ordered up french fries and a Diet Coke (at least I had the sense to cut myself off, though it was probably too late).

"What are you having?" I asked.

"Nothing." Kyle said. He may have been sitting silently, or sleeping. I am unsure. When the fries arrived I offered him some.

"No. I'm okay."

About 15 minutes into my fry binge, Kyle asked, "You ready?"

I had fries hanging out of my mouth, but realized he must have really wanted to go. Hours ago.

"Okay," I said, as I stuffed as many as I could into my mouth.

I realize I have completely blown up the night. Kyle put me in a taxi (I think), and on the taxi ride home I texted him thank you. He responded that he had a lot of fun.

The next night I received a text from Kyle, telling me he hoped I was having fun and he looks forward to seeing me soon. Kyle must like crazy chicks. Thank you lord! From what I remember, Kyle was nice. And funny.

On our next date, yes, there was a next date, I apologized for my drunken behavior. Kyle asked what I was talking about and said he had so much fun. He was the perfect gentleman and let me tell all the same stories I told on the first date and acted like he was hearing them for the first time (my memory of that first date is a bit foggy so I wasn't quite sure what I had and had not told him the first time around). Kyle discloses that he too was drunk. I told Kyle he was a sport for letting me hold him hostage while I ate french fries in a dive bar, and I teased him for wanting to leave before I could even finish.

"Oh, I wanted to leave a long time before that!" We laughed. He was teasing, but it was actually true. I only drank one beer that night. He even asked if I wanted dessert. I tried to send him home but he wanted to walk around a little after the date.

"Why are you trying to send me home?" He asked.

"It's the least I could do after keeping you as my prisoner last time."

We walked through Soho holding hands and stopped periodically to dance in the street. He even dipped me.

38

REAL TEXTS FROM MY MOM

JULY 21, 2010

Even though I am a mother, I still have to answer to my Mother. My mother, who has always been a somewhat nervous, anxious woman when it comes to her children, became even more "worried" about me when I got divorced. I get periodic texts from her that say things like:

"You okay?"
"Where are you?"
"Are you okay?"
How do you feel?"
"How is Bear?"
"It's raining very hard. Are you okay?"
"The news is reporting tornado warnings. Are you okay?"
Really mom? In New York City? For that one I had to text back,
"No! I got sucked into a funnel cloud and I am clutching onto a cow. Help!"

On my date with Kyle I received a text from my mother:

"Are you okay?"

So being the nice, loving daughter that I am, I text back:

"No! Help me! My date has kidnapped me and stuffed me in his trunk. SOS. Send Help."

She actually wrote this response, true story:

"Great. Have fun."

Thanks?

39

NEEDING SPACE

JULY 23, 2010

I DON'T WANT to share my closet. Is that selfish? I had never really thought about it when I first moved in with my ex-husband. I was so taken by the idea of "moving in" with someone, that I gladly interspersed my sweaters with his, used every other drawer, and put my t-shirts on one of his bookshelves. I used my shoes as bookends and crammed my toothbrush into his toothbrush holder. I was all set. I was so excited to get my first drawer that I could care less if it had enough room. You have never seen a drawer packed so tight as was my first drawer at his house.

When we were married, we were lucky enough to have his and hers closets. I had enough room to get dressed in mine. On rainy days I would go in there and play dress up if I wanted to. I would try on dresses I had bought but never really had the chance to wear. Sometimes I would sit in there and look over old camp pictures I had stored in a shoe box.

Then came my divorce. I downsized apartments, and this time the master only had one closet. It was a nice size, I'll give you that. But there was only one. For me. Over time I would stare at it and wonder how on earth a couple could share this *one* closet. In addition to my closet I have not one, but two dressers, in my bedroom, and I could still use more space.

One day I was sitting with my (then) boyfriend in my living room. He would stay over periodically when Bear was at his dad's house. He offered up the idea that he could possibly have a little piece of his own real estate in my apartment.

"Maybe a drawer? So when I stay here I don't have to go home first?"

I think my heart stopped for a second. Not in a good way.

I realize this is when the "drawer" celebration was supposed to begin. Possibly a telephone chain.

"Hi Kate? He wants a drawer!"

"A drawer? That's great! Congratulations Darcy!"

"Hi, Sue, it's Kate! Did you hear about Darcy? Yes! He wants a drawer!"

"A drawer? Really? Wow! So exciting."

There may or may not be a parade that was supposed to ensue. Possibly a conga line of some kind, picking up neighbors and family members as we danced through the halls. I am pretty sure I was supposed to set my facebook status to "He asked for a drawer!" 20 people would comment with a mix of congratulations and witticisms and at least 7 people would "like" it.

But I wanted none of that.

Like a selfish, cold-hearted bitch, it flew right out of my mouth,

"I don't really have a drawer to give you."

"Darcy, you have two dressers and a walk-in closet"

"Yes...but...it's taken?"

I watched his face fall, looking for reassurance of some kind. But I had none to give.

That is when I realized; I am pretty damn comfortable not having a roommate. I realize a love interest is not a roommate. I do. But it is yet another person in the house. The idea of "giving a drawer" to a significant other, which may have at one point sent my heart a flutter just seemed...well...downright annoying. I realize this sounds callous, and maybe it is.

"Um...let's see...hmmmm...maybe there is a shelf in the linen closet...or....I know...maybe...no, that won't work...(faux sigh)"

I sized up my apartment trying to find an extra closet or drawer, maybe there was some room in the freezer? Maybe he could fit into my stuff and didn't need stuff of his own? No. That couldn't possibly work. I didn't want him to stretch it.

I didn't know what to do about his "stuff," but what I did know is that I didn't want him to move-in in any way, shape or form. Had I become a bachelor? Was it him or was it just that I had become so entirely self-sufficient and comfortable with my life as being just me and Bear. Bear and I had our own special space and our time was ours. Our space was ours. Something to think about. For now, my closet is all mine. Let's just say I am more than okay with that.

40

DARCY PLUS PARTY

July 26, 2010

R*EMEMBER* *the tale of Chef Hottie (See, Ghost of Risotto Past). This was one of our good dates, so I thought I should share. 3 months earlier...*

Memorial Day Weekend in the Hamptons means the first day of summer for New Yorkers. I realize that sounds a bit New York Centric, but bear with me.

One Memorial Day weekend, I was invited by a handsome young gentleman to attend a party in the Hamptons that he had some involvement in, he was the chef.

"I will put you on the list, just tell me how many people you want to bring."

Hmmm. "The list." "The list," is something I left behind years ago. In another lifetime actually. The only real lists I am on these days are ones that involve some type of sign-up for volunteer work at the book fair or bake sale at Bear's school.

Several days, several texts and one or two phone conversations later I reluctantly agreed to attend this party. I called Alexis and Max on conference.

"He invited me to attend a party. He put me on the list." I announce this with as much excitement as one announces things like dental appointments or jury duty. It's not that I wasn't excited to see him, but I could do without the velvet rope gauntlet in order to have that opportunity.

"Wait a second. You are Darcy plus party?" Max says in his most facetious tone.

Alexis and I immediately break into laughter.

"I know. I know. I am embarrassed to even tell you both."

They mock me relentlessly.

"Darcy, you can't go there. That is the worst thing I have ever heard," Max says. He proceeded to rattle off a list of D-list celebs he guesses will be in attendance. I cringe knowing he is right.

The day of the event, Max and Alexis texted me and called me periodically to mock me some more.

"Darcy plus party? What did you do today?"

"Plus party, are you dusting off your cork wedges for the occasion?"

My ultimate favorite was Max calling me, or should I say PRANK calling me:

"Hi Darcy plus party, this is Troy calling from the Pink Elephant. I just wanted to confirm your table tonight with bottle service, you and your friends will all be comped, if you have any problem please ask for me at the door. You are on *Troy*'s list."

I can only laugh. The whole thing is completely ridiculous, and I realize I am way too old for this. That morning I drafted my step-sister as my wing woman.

"I am in." She says. I love her positive attitude.

I decide I want to be fashionably late, and by fashionably late, I mean, arrive as it's ending. I would like to duck in and duck out with a mere hello and nothing more. The party is called from 7-10pm. I have a leisurely dinner with my family and at 9:00 pm I head out. My step-sister and I load into the car, cork wedges and all, and drive through the pitch black back roads of the Hamptons. A few wrong turns later we are more late than fashionable. I stroll up to the hostess at 9:40 pm.

"Hi, I'm on the list." (*Vomit*).

"Hi, the party is closed. We are at maximum capacity and even though you may be on the list we can't let another person in. We are closed for the night," she says this with a voice as though she is feigning sympathy of some kind.

WHAT? I just got shut down at the door for a B&T party I am on the list for?

"Well, I am not really here for the party (*I'm too good for it*); I am here for Chef Hottie. Can you please tell him Darcy is here."

This is what I want to say: "I don't want to come in, in fact, that's why I am here as it's ending. I think this whole thing is beyond cheesy and I would actually rather get run over by one of the 40 Range Rovers in this parking lot, than set foot through that front door," but I don't say it.

"What's your name?" The hostess says as she rolls her eyes.

"Darcy." *Darcy plus party,* I mock myself silently in my head.

Another hostess overhears me give my name and comes running to the aid of the first hostess. She says that Chef Hottie had recently asked if I had arrived and that he was waiting for me.

"Well Darcy, while we can't let you in, someone will go find him."

Is this real?

I text Max. "You won't believe this, but I can't even get in!"

"Go find Dina Lohan immediately., he shoots back. I laugh.

Chef Hottie walks out of the front door and immediately I don't care that I am waiting in a sea of cheesy losers with a door person that won't let me in. He is THAT cute.

"What's going on? Come here," he waves me over.

The hostess sisters explain to him that they are at capacity and cannot let another person in.

"Why did you get here 3 hours late? I was waiting for you," Chef Hottie says. He seemed genuinely disappointed.

"Sorry, I was eating with my family and I thought you'd be busy."

"No babe. I was waiting for you. Can you hang out here for 10 minutes and everyone will be leaving and then we can do something together?"

Stand around and wait for you? No.

"Okay." I say.

"Max. You would die from this scene." I text.

"I don't understand. I thought they weren't letting you in. What are you doing in the parking lot? Are you a parking lot dweller? DARCY GET THE FK OUT OF THERE. WHAT ARE YOU DOING." He texts back.

I am laughing so hard now I can barely stand in my cork wedges.

"My step sister is asking for the party favor at the front door. She is saying she should get one since she is on the list."

"Explain that she is your STEP." Max says.

I am howling.

A few minutes later I realized I wanted no part of standing in a parking lot. I grab my step-sister and we decide to hit the road. Not only did I drag her to a party that wouldn't let her in, she didn't get her goodie bag either.

As I am pulling away in the car Chef Hottie calls.

"Where are you? I came to get you."

"Sorry Chef Hottie, I couldn't wait in a parking lot any longer."

"I am so sorry that happened. Come back. It's over and we will have dinner."

With that, my step sister turned the car around and I walked right in through the ropes. *Very VIP*. Granted the party was over, and the bouncers were gone, but I still walked right in! We all had a nice dinner, my sister got her goodie bag and in the end a good time was had by all.

Max still calls me "Plus party," and I love it.

41

REAL TEXTS FROM REAL MEN

JULY 29, 2010

As I opened my eyes this morning, I wondered what I would write about today. I suddenly noticed, the red light on my phone was blinking. It was a text. From Robbie. It said,

"You let me know when you want me to rock your world for a night."

And just like that, this entry wrote itself.

42

HE SHOOTS, HE SCORES

AUGUST 2, 2010

THE OTHER DAY I met some old friends for a drink. They are truly some of my funniest friends so I was prepared for a non-stop laugh fest of sorts which I could really use in this 400 degree heat wave that we are calling summer. One announced her new boyfriend would be joining us. I looked forward to meeting him. He walked in with a friend who was not bad looking. The friend had appeared to be drinking for a long while, which was odd, as it was only 8 o'clock.

I was joking around with one of my friends regarding something work related when the aforementioned cute drunk friend interjects,

"No way. You are too hot. You are a *really* pretty girl and I know that's not the case with you. I mean, those kinds of girls, you can tell by looking at them. It's obvious. But not you. No WAY!"

I mean, I love where he is going with this, but it makes absolutely zero sense in the context of our conversation.

"What do you think we are talking about exactly?" I ask.

"That you're easy to get? I know you aren't. You aren't that type. I can tell by looking at you. You don't need to be. You are beautiful."

Insert his drunk creepy stare here.

I am flattered, but we are talking about work. Obviously drunk Tom is having a conversation with his inner voice. Out loud. Awkward.

He sees my phone and asks what the picture is of.

"That is my son. Bear."

"Wow! I've dated women with kids. I don't mind it one bit. I am 36 so most of the women I date have kids by this point. I'd like to have kids."

Huh. I didn't realize we were going to be dating. I might have even said this out loud.

"I mean, I was never really dying for kids, but I guess if my wife wanted them, I'd have them. If I really liked her. Loved her. You know."

"Well, I would hope you liked your wife. Or loved her. Both, equally. Let's just hope someone doesn't deliver a baby in a basket to your door anytime soon!"

"Well, one slipped by the goalie once but that's it."

Insert sound of record screeching to a halt here.

"Oh my. That is *a lot* of information about you Tom."

"Yea, I mean, it only happened once."

"But of course! And what became of that?"

"Oh, yea, you know...it's...yea...no." This was coupled with hand movements and dramatic facial expressions of some kind.

And scene!

43

THE THIRD DATE

AUGUST 4, 2010

My parents always told me one of their favorite stories from when they were first married. They were driving somewhere and my father asked my mother if she wanted to stop and grab a bite to eat at Howard Johnson.

"I'm not eating there. They have plastic food," she said.

After a little finessing they pulled into Howard Johnson and grabbed a table. My mother got up to use the restroom, which is when my father called the waitress over.

"Excuse me. When my wife returns to the table, please ask her if she would like the real rolls, or the plastic rolls."

She did just that, and my mom fell for it.

On my first date with Kyle (See: *When You Least Expect it & Breaking the Rules,*) over cocktails and raw fish, the topic of sex came up. Naturally. We were discussing when sex should take place for the first time. On what date, were we guessing, would the magic happen, as they say on MTV cribs, which probably isn't even on anymore. I have just dated myself.

"Third date!" he announced, as though it were written in concrete somewhere, in some man cave in a faraway land. He may or may not have grunted a beastly grunt as he said it.

"That is so cliché!" I said. "Seventh!"

"Seventh?! No way. That's crazy"

"Fine, you just upped it to eleven."

"Eleventh??!"

We laughed. It became an inside joke with us. We would negotiate how many dates until we sealed the deal. Or the deal of the moment at least.

On our second date we discussed possibly moving it from the eleventh to the eighth. It was going well and I wasn't falling off furniture or holding him hostage.

We met at a restaurant downtown and I brought a condom with me. Nooo, not for sex, but to play a pretty good prank on Kyle, Mr. Sex on the third date. Inspired by my parents' Howard Johnson story, I excused myself from the table while we were eating to use the restroom.

While there, I flagged down an innocent unsuspecting waiter. I wrapped the condom in a cloth napkin and asked the waiter to deliver this package to us at the table on a plate. Plated, if you will. He was to announce, as he delivered the plate,

"In the event that this is your third date, this is compliments of the restaurant."

The funny thing was, the restaurant had offered us so many random things that night, that a visit from a waiter offering us complementary goods of any kind was not completely off base. So far they had offered us hot towels, cold towels, mint towels, a shoe shine and possibly a happy ending, but don't quote me on that.

I sat down back down with Kyle and we continued to eat when I saw the waiter approaching out of the corner of my eye. He presents us with the plate and says exactly what it is that we had rehearsed,

"In the event that this is your third date, this is compliments of the restaurant."

"Did he just say 'if this is your third date?'" Kyle said, shocked.

"I think so!" *Faux gasp.* "What do you think it is?!"

"No idea." Kyle said, skeptical of the folded napkin.

I opened the napkin delicately and out came the condom (wrapped). Kyle had a million dollar look of confusion on his face. Kyle fell for it. Poor Kyle. I told him it was me. Kyle said it was the greatest story, which unfortunately he could not share with his friends, as it didn't result in sex of any kind. We laughed. Kyle didn't get to use the condom that night, as it was only our third date. But he said he would save it for the eleventh. Or the 8th. Whatever I wanted it to be.

44

HE'S BAAACK

A UGUST 6, 2010

ROBBIE CALLED ME YESTERDAY. He was frantic.

"Darcy! I just thought about it. Since you're taking so long to figure out if you will date me or not, do you think you can freeze your eggs? I really want you to bear my children, and this is taking a long fucking time."

"First of all, what the fuck? Second of all, I am not 'figuring out' if I want to date you, I don't want to date you and I tell you that daily. Thirdly, isn't there some other girl you can find out there to torture?"

"I have no problem getting chicks. They love me. No. I like you. I love you. You're my girl. You're my action. You're where it's at. You are going to be my wife. Give in now."

45

MY GPS CAN SUCK IT

AUGUST 9, 2010

A FEW RANDOM thoughts about my GPS and terrible sense of direction:

WHAT THE FK? I mean, I could possibly be the only person who has driven to and from the Hamptons 10,000 times and still gets lost. This past weekend, on my drive back, I was comfortably driving along on the Long Island Expressway back to New York City when for absolutely no reason at all, I pressed the button to begin navigation back to my house, where I could pretty much drive to with my eyes closed. The friendly english voice starts to call to me,

"In a tenth of a mile, make a left turn."

That can't be right, I think. That would take me off the main highway home. Why would I make a left off the nearest exit?

Ignore it Darcy. Ignore it.

The GPS starts to make a dinging noise indicating the turn is coming up and I am about to miss it.

Ignore Darcy. Don't fall for this. Again. Yes, it's happened before. I am terrible with directions and if I had to guess my GPS is apparently set to "*You are an idiot if you listen to me,*" if that's an option.

Now she isn't polite anymore. She is curt.

"LEFT TURN."

IGNORE

And then again!

"LEFT TURN"

Is she yelling at me? That bitch. I will kick her English ass. Before you know it, I caved to the peer pressure and made a left turn, off a major highway which goes straight to my apartment practically. (Don't worry mom, I am not giving my address, there are about 11 entrances into New York City. It's fine).

Now she is back to being polite.,

"Continue on the current road for approximately 3 miles."

Three miles on this road? But it's going in a direction totally opposite of the city. I mean, she's from England. Does she really know her way around here? But her voice. It's so... calming. It gives her some type of direction authority. Maybe she knows something I don't. Maybe she is protecting me from an insane traffic jam ahead. Maybe there is one of those overturned tractor trailers you hear about on the news. She's so nice, that GPS lady. I love that she has my back. I listen to her. She is like the David Karesh of my car. I drove 3 miles in the wrong direction, because she told me to.

After 3 miles of driving on a stretch of road in a direction I don't need to be going, she has me get on a highway I never even heard of. As I am driving I am thinking, this feels wrong. Very wrong. And totally out of my way. Then she has me get off at a random exit in a town I didn't even know existed. Was this a bad neighborhood? On Long Island? Huh! Who knew? Now I am making turns, U-turns, she had me stop and mow a stranger's lawn. I played a quick game of hopscotch with some girls in the street.

"Mommy? What are you doing?"

"Sorry honey, the GPS told me to." I shrug my shoulders as I jump along.

I hop back in the car where the GPS lady tells me to basically "Make a left, then a left, then a left into a U-turn, kick ball change, pivot turn, jazz hands, and do the entire tour of this bad neighborhood all over again." But, she said it differently. She didn't use those exact words.

"Look kids, Big Ben!"

"What's Big Ben Mommy?"

"It's a big clock in london. It's a joke from a movie. Sorry honey. Mommy is frustrated. And lost."

"I'm scared."

Me too honey. I am scared I am going to strangle the GPS lady.

"Don't be scared. I'm not lost."

"But you said you were."

"Don't worry, I'm not."

I am lost. I'm fucking lost. Are we in Maine? Does this look a little like Texas all of a sudden? Cause it could be. At one point I think we stopped for pancakes in Vermont. But that's blurry now, because all I can think about are the crawfish we just had an hour ago in Louisiana. WHERE ARE WE????

Four and a half hours into a would be 2 hour trip, I called a friend for help.

"Hey, my GPS lady is an ASS, can you please get me back on the Long Island Expressway?"

I give my location. I glance down at my GPS to give it the finger. The "route" looks a little like a green silly straw with WAY too many loops and circles to ever get out of there.

"Oh. Really?" my friend said, "You are really far from there."

Of course I am. I have actually gotten 3 passport stamps out of the trip and I am possibly holding a work Visa in another country.

They gave me some directions of how to get back to another main highway and I was on the road home. Finally on a familiar road. Better watch out GPS lady. I got your number. I pressed the button that said "Cancel Guidance." Buh-bye GPS lady. Who's in charge now bitch! (Don't worry, I'll use you again soon...obviously).

46

ADVICE FROM MY EX-HUSBAND

AUGUST 11, 2010

"Darce, he must not like you *that* much because if he did he would try to bang you that night."
"But he-"
"No."
"You don't understand he was-"
"Nope."
"He was with all of his friends. It was boys night. He didn't even have to invite me to boys night, but he did!"
"Penis before friends."
"But he-"
"No, Move on. Next."
"Fine."
Why am I listening?

47

INTERPRET THIS

AUGUST 12, 2010

I SHOULD HAVE KNOWN my first date with Devon would be, well, interesting? Devon was super hot, tall, and wore Vans. He was from California and had a little bit of a hippy dippy doo quality I wasn't quite used to. On our first phone conversation he asked if I wanted to go watch interpretive dance.

"You up for that?"

Dead Silence. I actually heard my hair growing from the root.

Here is the thing, the fact that you wanted to take me to see interpretive dance on our first date makes you *not* my type. I just can't. I love dancing. LOVE. I'd go as far as saying I found MTV's "Dance Life" to be a real tear jerker of sorts. That being said, if you took me to see *interpretive* dance, I would be hysterically laughing the entire time, possibly even getting myself kicked out. If you were into it, I know this is wrong, but I'd think you were weird, which I am *sure* makes me a terrible person. I may in fact do my own interpretive dance and run away from you.

We met for our date and it was 112 degrees. Well almost. I saw Devon approaching and he was tall. Yes! We chose a table outside.

"Wow. It is super hot out!" I said, feeling for Devon who was wearing jeans which made me extra hot.

"I am a positive person. I am staying positive about the weather."

"Ah, I am a jaded new yorker. We love to complain about the weather."

Devon must have told me about 20 times in the first four minutes about his super positive attitude. It's as though I was on a date with Tony Robbins. I was expecting him to whip out hot coals at any moment and have me run over them with him.

"*You can do it Darcy!*" He would scream as I scolded my feet on the burning embers, "*You can do anything you put your mind to!*"

"*But they are burning me!*" I would screech.

"*Mind over matter Darcy!!!!!*" he would say as he dragged me along.

"I smile and laugh all the time," he said, with a creeptastic smile.

I wonder who says that actual sentence, unless you are one of the Wiggles, and even the Wiggles are a bit creepy no? I waited for him to bust out singing *"fruit salad, yummy yummy"* (if you don't have children, you can skip that reference. It is made for people who had to sit through countless hours of those creepy men dancing and singing a song about fruit salad).

You are also on mood elevators. Lots of them. I think this to myself. There is absolutely nothing wrong with mood elevators by the way. I support you 100% if you need them. My concern for Devon however is that he was on *too many* of them.

Devon then offered up my favorite quote of the evening. It is so good it should be framed on people's bathroom walls, similar to *Footprints*.

"Sometimes I am jealous of the gay man's lifestyle. With all the drugs and the sex."

I stared at him like a donkey's head just popped out of his chest. *I'm sorry? What the FUCK? WHO SAYS THAT?*

I wondered why Devon couldn't keep this to himself. Just a tip guys: if you think that, don't say it. At least to me. On our first date. I will think you are a gay drug addict. Just saying.

I look at Devon and see something peeking out from his neckline. Ah, of course. Devon is wearing my dear old favorite...man-jewelry. This particular man-jewelry was very large and cumbersome. A heavy chain of sorts. I wondered how this doesn't hurt Devon's back having to roam around with that all day. My next thought is there was a gas station somewhere missing their keychain. It was *that* big. There was absolutely no way Devon could make it through airport security with that thing. It definitely doubled as a nun-chuck.

After a quick drink I wrapped up the date as quickly as possible. Devon asked me out for the following Tuesday and I said...yes? UGH. It was so awkward I had to. DAMMIT DARCY. Now I would have to spend countless hours trying to figure out how to get out of that. WHY DARCY? I find dating to be entirely about getting out of things. It's just more commitments to break.

Devon insisted on walking me home.

"You can just walk me up an avenue and I will hop in a cab."

Devon spent the walk trying to cop a feel of my body.

"You have a really tight little body," he said, as he smiled his creepy mood elevator smile.

"Thank you."

Awkward.

The next day Devon texted me that I should "have a great weekend and to keep smiling, laughing and frolicking"

FROLICKING? I almost died on the spot. As I read the text I glanced around hoping, for the sake of watching Bear grow up, someone nearby had a defibrillator so they could revive me back to life. I am not much of a frolicker, not that I even know what that means, but I'd prefer a man who doesn't know what frolic means either. Devon and I were certainly no match made in heaven, but I didn't think this would bother him one bit as he was loaded to the hilt on happy pills.

After our date Devon would text me things like :

"How are youuuuuuuuuuuuuuu?"

"Enjoooooooyyyyyyyyyyyyyyyyyyy your day."

"Seeeeeeeeee you soon."

Really? Really? Who writes like that? Deeevvvvvvvvvvvooooooon does.

A week after our first date, and countless dodges and cancellations on my part I receive a serious text from Devon.

"Can I tell you something very honest?"

"Yes?" I responded. UGH. What can this be? I run through the scenarios in my head. "I am bi," or "I am an ecstasy addict" (which would explain the constant smiling, laughing and frolicking). I waited for the response with bated breath.

"Before I left California I started dating this girl. She is coming to stay with me for a week and I feel funny about it because I am really diggin 'on you (yea, he used that exact term), and I don't want it to mess things up because I like you alllllooooooottttt."

Seriously??? I quickly wondered if Verizon, the company in itself, was pranking me with text messages.

"Oh Devon! Don't be silly. We only went out once (and I was plotting my escape the entire time). Please. Enjoy the visit. Have the best time!"

"I knew you would say that. You are the coolest chick I have ever met. It makes me like you more. You and I are a perfect match."

Yippee. Now I am somehow in a relationship with a guy I never wanted to see again, who has a girlfriend.

48

ROBBIE REUNION

August 16, 2010

Out of pure boredom I agreed to meet Robbie for a quick drink. He basically beat me down and there is a good chance I also bought a water filter, life supply of Tupperware and a food dehydrator from him while I was at it.

We seemed to become friends, in a Stockholm Syndrome kind of way, and I figured why not.

Robbie was sitting in his chair, uncomfortably squirming, fidgeting with his shirt.

"Do you like when I wear shirts like this or belly shirts?" he asked.

"I'm sorry?"

"Do you like these shirts or belly shirts?"

"You wear belly shirts?"

"Yea. You know. Shorter shirts."

"Robbie, you shouldn't even say the word belly shirt."

"My friend Mike calls me Bobby Belly Shirts."

"Why?"

"Cause when I lift my arms up sometimes my shirts are short and my stomach sticks out."

Just when I thought Robbie couldn't be more strange, I come to find out he has a stash of belly shirts, which as far as I am concerned haven't been worn since 1984...on girls...but what do I know anymore. Clearly nothing, as I am here after all.

"Why won't you be with me Darcy?"

"The thing is Robbie, when you ask me to do things like freeze my eggs...I realize why I don't want to date someone SEVEN years younger."

"Darcy, I was kidding about the freezing of the eggs. I have super sperm. I would have no problem getting you pregnant."

"Robbie, there will be no sex."

"What are you doing for sexual activity?"

"What?"

"Sex, what are you doing for sex. What is your level of sexual activity."

The weird thing is, because he is a doctor, it sounded okay coming from him. WTF, Snap out of it Darcy, he is a doctor, but not YOUR doctor. He is your STALKER.

"Robbie, my sex life is none of your business. Not that I have one."

"Let me help you with that Darcy."

"No. I'm fine."

"What can I do to make you my wife?"

"Um, you don't know me. At all. We went on two dates, 3 months ago."

"I know all I need to know. I am not giving up ever. You are my dream girl."

"If by dream girl, you mean, we only have a relationship in your dreams, then sure, I guess I am."

"Give me your address."

"NO WAY. Why?"

"I want to start sending you things, like orchids."

"And ransom notes?"

"Darcy, you don't take me seriously."

"HOW CAN I? YOU CALL ME EVERY DAY AND OUR LAST DATE WAS THREE MONTHS AGO!"

"I call you more than once a day. At least *three* times a day." He says. Thinking that makes it better?

Why am I judging him? I am the one who came to meet him.

MR. WRONG RIGHT NOW

AUGUST 18, 2010

MY DEAR OLD FRIEND JOHN, who is also a life coach, unfortunately not my life coach, but gives me great advice from time to time asked me once:

"Darcy, as I read your blog one question comes to mind. I wonder if you are looking for Mr. Right or Mr. Right *Now*?"

Huh. I never really thought about it that way. While I would think I was looking for Mr. Right, he did have a point. My choices weren't always well...*that* great. It made me wonder; Did I want a long-term partner, or was I looking for someone to have some fun with? I had been married for 7 1/2 years and much of my adult life, if not all of it thus far, was essentially spent as being someone's wife. Maybe I liked the freedom to make choices and make mistakes, which I am nearly an expert on, by the way. I kind of like my life right now. I hit the jackpot of having the best child on earth and everything else is a bonus as far as I am concerned. But I did start to examine my life, by looking at it from John's perspective, and I came to a stunning revelation.

This is how I know I am not yet ready for "Mr. Right" and I am really just ready for "Mr. Right Now" :

Driving down the highway last week I was behind a motorcycle. It was a racing bike of some kind. I couldn't really see the guy on it, other than he had on shorts and a t-shirt and a helmet. Suddenly, out of no-where, on a major highway he popped a full on wheelie and rode for about a quarter-mile like that. It went on for so long, I didn't know that type of stunt was actually possible. He kept casually glancing over his shoulder, no big deal, just going about 80, popping a wheelie on the highway. Holding it for longer than I knew it was ever possible to even hold a wheelie.

My initial thought: *He's CRAZY. That is SO dangerous. What an IDIOT. He can die in a second. What normal person does that?*

My next thought: *He's so crazy he is hot and I want to drive behind him for hours and possibly follow him off at his next exit.*

Therein lies the rub of my romantic life. I want the nice guy who will be doting and kind and loyal, but I want him to be a wild man doing a wheelie down a highway like a complete dangerous nut job. I gotta work on this. Note to self: Get your head checked. See what can be done about this.

50

DEAR DATE FROM LAST NIGHT

AUGUST 20, 2010

Dear Date From Last Night:

If it is our first date, and the entire time all through dinner, you are begging to see my underwear at the table, and I say no, and you continue to beg, I won't want to go out with you again.

If I tell you that you are making me incredibly uncomfortable and you tell me what you are doing is completely normal, I will think you have a criminal record.

If you call me a prude for not showing you my underwear at said table, on our first date, I will understand why you are 42 and never been married.

If, when we get up to leave, you are walking behind me, and lift up my dress all the way to my waist, unbeknownst to me, exposing my entire ass to the restaurant so you can look at my underwear, you should understand why I punched you. Just be thankful you still have your teeth.

Love,
Darcy

51

BRIDAL SKELETONS IN MY CLOSET

AUGUST 23, 2010

LIKE ANY HEALTHY woman in her mid thirties, I have quite a few skeletons in my closet. Okay. I admit. It's a friggin' graveyard. There is one skeleton I would like to talk about in particular. It hangs in my closet with quite lovely bones covered in a black garment bag with the beautiful words *J. Mendel* written across the front. What is it you ask, buried beneath one too many Chanel bags and vintage tees? A wedding dress. Oh no, not the wedding dress I wore to my actual wedding. Noooo. That one is in storage somewhere collecting dust so I can pull it out one day for Bear's future wife and say, "Want to wear this honey?" and she will cringe. No. Not that one. This is a wedding dress that was sent to me as a gift from an ex-fiance. Yes, there was one. I haven't yet discussed him on my blog as I would not even know where to begin with him, but his name was Nick Hogan.

Nick Hogan had proposed to me after a year of dating at a rather complicated time in my life. When he proposed, it didn't feel, well, authentic. It felt forced and just…wrong. He placed the ring on my finger and we both looked at each other in awkward silence.

"Really?" I asked.

"Yea," he said.

I called my mother.

"I'm engaged?"

"You don't sound excited about it. Are you?"

"I gotta go." I hung up, frozen in fear.

I sat up in bed all night, not so much out of excitement but out of deep-seated confusion. It wasn't right. I knew it. That is when operation "Give Back The Enormous Ring" began.

I only wore the ring on occasion, and the rest of the time it was hidden in my closet.

"Why don't you ever wear your ring Darcy?" friends would ask.

"Oh, you know. I am not a big ring kind of girl."

Let's be honest, girls, who isn't?

Alexis would tell people I got engaged.

"I didn't know Darcy had a boyfriend?"

I would tell people, "I am engaged."

"To who?" they would ask.

Exactly.

I tried to get on board with the idea, but I just couldn't. I knew it was wrong, Nick Hogan knew it was wrong. It was like watching a train wreck in slow motion, only I was the train and really, who wants to be a part of that. Nick Hogan was always very good to me, and I was crazy about him, but he was a complicated guy, in ways I can't even begin to describe at this time.

"Darcy, I am taking you to look at wedding dresses," Alexis called one day, sounding very cheery and bridesmaid-like. Very unlike her. I think she sensed I was in some type of engagement like depression.

"Alexis, I am not getting a wedding dress."

"Darcy, yes you are!"

"Alexis!"

"Come! We are going to Bergdorfs."

That is an offer I can rarely refuse.

"Fine."

I picked her up in a taxi and as we headed down to the store I felt a minor panic attack setting in. We entered the bridal area and it felt...well...wrong. Like I was cheating on my first wedding. However, anyone who has ever been married can tell you they have fantasies of their next wedding gown, even in the most happy of marriages. *It would be short. It would be funky. A bit more casual.* I had this opportunity. For a moment I put my panic aside and started to comb through dresses...when I spotted it. It wasn't a wedding dress per se, but it was a white *J. Mendel* gown. The Rachel Zoe in me was screaming "*Oh. My. Gd. It's. Bananas.*" It was perfect. Subtle. Pretty. Just very Darcy. I looked at the price tag. Yowza. I didn't need a dress this expensive. I didn't really need a dress.

"I am going to think about it." I said to the lady. Not so much the dress, as the actual wedding.

I walked out. That was certainly the dress. I don't know what it was the dress for, but if there was something, that was definitely it. It was made for me.

Alexis tried to do what any best friend would and arranged for an amazing surprise. She had Nick Hogan send me the dress, as a gift. It was a beautiful, outstanding, overly generous gift, as most of Nick Hogan's gifts were. I wore it around my house. I loved the dress. I couldn't so much see myself walking down an aisle in it, but definitely through my living room. Man, I looked great in my living room. I pictured my neighbors in the building across the street who look directly into my apartment to say to each other,

"Who is that crazy wackadoo who is always in a wedding dress in that apartment across the street?"

"I don't know honey. It's sad. Don't look." The wife would say, as she would close their blinds.

In the end, I called off my engagement, but the dress remains in the archives of my closet waiting to be worn. If I do marry again, this is the dress I would like to wear, which might be kind of creepy. If any of these men I went out with knew I had a wedding dress hanging in my closet, they might go running for the hills. Maybe I should just wear it on all my first dates. See if it feels right. If they are a match with the dress they might be a match for me? Kind of like Cinderella's shoe, only different. Cause this was just weird and dysfunctional.

One day I may tell my future husband,

"Hey, you know that dress I wore to our wedding, well this is a funny story, not funny ha-ha of course, but funny crazy…"

52

SNOOKI SAID IT

AUGUST 25, 2010

"Guys are douchebags and I hate them all. They don't know how to deal with women and I feel that is why the lesbian rate is going up in this country."

-Snooki, *Jersey Shore*

This just in: Great minds really *do* think alike. I already said this! Well, differently of course.

While I love men, I have had just about enough of dating. I told my friend Gary I was going to change the name of Darcy Dates to Darcy Eats, about a girl who eats herself into oblivion until it becomes a full on airlift situation.

"Darcy Eats is brought to you by Ben & Jerry's and Purina Fancy Feast," he said.

Ugh. The cats. I forgot about the cats. I am going to need to get some cats. But I am beyond allergic. Sigh.

53

THE LIST

AUGUST 27, 2010

SOME OF YOU may remember the famous *Friends* episode where Ross and Rachel form a "list." "The List" contained five people, famous people, they were allowed to hook up with if the opportunity arose. It would be a day pass, so to speak, in their relationship. After this episode, couples everywhere began to compile their fantasy lists. Over the years my list would change. A new movie would come out, and a newer crush would replace older ones. The one thing I can say about my list is it was always quite unique. I never chose the pretty boys, the Brad Pitts or the George Clooneys. I am just not cut from that cloth. I always had some odd ones on there, which should not come as a shock to any of my readers by this point. I was always a stone throw away from adding Steve Buschemi.

At one point in my marriage Kid Rock was on my list. One night I had court side tickets to the Knicks game and he sat right next to me.

I remember calling my ex-husband from the Game.

"Bad news honey. I am sitting next to Kid Rock!" I say this, as though I had a chance.

"Out of all the people in America that dirt bag is on your list and now you're sitting next to him! Why can't you have a normal list like regular people?" I believe at the time he had Gwyneth Paltrow.

Kid, as I like to refer to him, was with Sheryl Crow, his girlfriend at the time. Not that it would have mattered as I didn't have implants or lucite heels, which seemed to be a requirement for him.

In case you were wondering, Kid is no longer on my list.

I was telling my friend Gary about my list and who was on it. I disclosed that both Christian Bale and Christopher Moltisanti were on my list.

"Interesting," he said, "so you have two mass murderers, both with names that derive from the word Christ."

Huh. What an unbelievably astute observation.

Who is on your list?

54

THE PRANKSTER

SEPTEMBER 2, 2010

IF I HAVEN'T SPOKEN to you in months, other than your bi-monthly texts saying hello, which I ignore, do not prank call me.

As an aside, if I actually tell you we aren't a good match and I do not want to go out with you again, I won't forget. Checking in bi-monthly will not trick me into a relationship of some kind, I promise. I will remember each time that I am not interested.

Do not call me from a blocked number and when I ask who it is, do not say:

"Darcy, you know who this is."

First of all, I don't, and I think that is a creepy game. Second of all, if I have a glimmer of an idea and I think it is you, and I already know, from previous encounters on the telephone that your number is *not* private, so you specifically blocked your number to fake me out so I would answer the phone, I will like you *less* than I already do. Also, if you are blocking your number, you obviously don't want me to have a heads up as to who you are, so no. I don't "know who it is." In fact I haven't heard your voice in months and we had only gone out once. As far as I am concerned, you are a total stranger.

When I ask you *again* who this is, and say I do not recognize the voice (as that is a chance I am not willing to take) do not tell me this is a fun game, and I should sit back and enjoy it and have some fun with it. I don't "enjoy" playing with prank callers anymore than I enjoy playing in traffic. That is on par with stripping in front of my window for a peeping tom or calling out to a mugger right after they steal my wallet: "Hey, you forgot to ask! My bank card pin is 7625! Write it down! Don't forget!"

Do not tell me this is a fun distraction from my busy day and when I announce I am hanging up the phone because I don't speak with people when I don't know who they are, do not tell me this is a conversation I will regret missing. I won't regret missing this, just like I didn't regret not getting swine flu or a spiral perm in the 80's.

Click.

Update: Right after I wrote this up last night, the pranker called again. One week later to the hour.

"Darcy?"

"Who is this?"

"You know."

"No. I don't know. I am with a client. Tell me or hang up."

Click.

Shortly after, and I mean within 5 minutes I got a text from the guy I thought it was.

"Darcy, I am not letting you get away so easily."

"Did you just call me?"

"No. I would not be so presumptuous."

"Huh. I just got a phone call from someone who sounded like you. It's the second one."

"Surprised you remembered my voice. It's been months."

THEN WHY THE FK ARE YOU CONTACTING ME???

"What did they say?" he continues.

"Doesn't matter. It was creepy."

Crickets. No word since. I'll never hear back. He is busted and he knows it. Although If there is one thing I have learned, it's to never say never.

55

THANK YOU? I THINK?

SEPTEMBER 8, 2010

I WAS SITTING with my friend Chet last weekend and he looked at me very seriously and said,

"Darcy, you are the only girl who has a kid, who can get away with having a kid."

Thank you? I think?

Footnote from the author: I know Chet was trying to pay me a compliment. No doubt about it. But it must be said for the record I don't think having a child is something you have to "get away with" similar to white after labor day or mini skirts on older ladies. I feel like the luckiest woman in the world to have a child like Bear. He is my greatest asset. If I could have him cloned 30 times over I would. Octomom would have nothing on me. Oh and Chet, I know you meant it very nicely, but I think I am much luckier than you. Just saying.

56

MY DATE WITH ROBBIE

SEPTEMBER 10, 2010

OH READERS, you will love this. Are you sitting? I had...(*insert sound of throat clearing here*)...a date. With Robbie.

Well, not so much a date as basic plans gone awry, but a meeting of sorts with only the two of us, involving the dark. Okay, it was a movie. Not shared popcorn, he insisted we each had our own. But, we did share sour patch kids.

"You don't share popcorn?" I asked

"No. Is that something I should do on dates?"

"This isn't a date. But yes. I'd share popcorn with strangers if they would let me."

How did this happen you ask? Let's see.

After a calling binge of epic proportions over the weekend, I think he may have been up to six calls a day, I received a call one Monday night from Robbie.

Apparently he had some trouble at work that day that culminated in him getting written up by his supervisor in the hospital.

"It's cause she wants to fuck me. The whole hospital does. That's my problem."

These tirades don't register much with me anymore. It's like white noise at this point. I sit, silently shaking my head, keeping one eye on the Real Housewives of NJ confrontation between the matriarchs.

"Where is Bear?" he asks.

"He is sleeping."

He asks me, as he always does, if he can come over, which you know I have never allowed.

"What do you think the answer is?"

"Listen Darcy, I have had all I can take. I want to be with a woman who wants to be with me. It's over."

"I'm sorry to hear that," I say as I turn up the volume on my TV. I am missing one of those awkward dialogues when Danielle gives her daughter an inappropriate lecture offering up way too much information about her personal life. The mother in me is screaming, 'Those poor girls!' but the reality show addict in me wants her to tell them even more!

Alexis calls.

"Robbie, I am going to conference you with Alexis. You can tell her why you have just broken up with me."

Alexis and Robbie have never met, but she loves him, as much as you all do. He is excellent entertainment.

I tell Alexis, Robbie has ended it with me. She feigns disappointment, and coaches him through it. We both tell him we will miss him and he hangs up in a huff, leaving us to discuss the minutiae of this show, down to Teresa's husband calling Chanel, "Chanels."

The next day, I didn't hear from Robbie until late in the evening. He popped up and sent me an instant message on my computer.

"I miss you. This is killing me."

"I know. I am sorry it has to be like this."

He disappeared.

I am proud of Robbie. He is really following through with this breakup. This breakup for crazy people.

The next day Robbie calls me.

"Darcy, I tried. But I can't live without you. It's killing me. Let me come over."

"No."

"Want to see a movie?" he asks. His last desperate attempt.

Beat.

"Okay."

Okay? I think to myself.

"Okay?" he asks.

Well, at least we were all on the same page about that.

"Yeah. Bear is with his dad for the night and I have nothing to do and there is a movie I would like to see."

"Great. I will buy us tickets. You just show up baby."

He hangs up on me. I have noticed Robbie never says goodbye. He just hangs up.

I hopped in a taxi and headed towards the theater. I am waiting outside for Robbie when he shows up. He is so cute and tall and just too young as always.

"I love you baby," he said as he approached.

I laugh. It's not even worth getting into at this point. No sense in fighting it, since I am clearly trapped for life.

We sit down next to each other in the movie theater and I can't even believe I am actually there. I glance around wondering if people think Robbie is out with his mother or his babysitter. I slump in my seat a bit as the movie starts.

"Is this a chick flick? UGHHHHHHH" Robbie says. Loudly.

As the movie starts he holds my hand. I let him. I know, this is so awkward to type and I am sure it's even more awkward to read.

Midway through the movie Robbie screams out loud, "THAT IS SOME FUNNY SHIT RIGHT THERE."

I die.

"You are that guy. You realize. The guy that screams at the screen. I am with *that* guy," I whisper to him.

I suddenly realized something sick. I didn't mind. I enjoy Robbie's company. A LOT.

After the movie we grabbed a quick bite to eat. We shared an entree and dessert. After the meal Robbie grills me on whether or not he ate most of it as he squeezes his love handles.

"I'm getting fat," he says.

"Want to come over?" I ask.

"What?"

"I don't know. Want to? Before I change my mind."

Folks, avert your eyes. This is ridiculous. I know.

"Seriously? You are letting me come to your house? To your *real* house?"

No. To my *doll* house.

"Totally platonic okay? We can hang out. And talk."

I don't know what came over me, but I wanted to spend *more* time with Robbie. I wanted to chit and chat and eat potato chips and make crumbs. I wanted to just hang out. Was I becoming one of those girls that would marry someone in prison?

Robbie came over and we talked. Well, mainly he just looked in the mirror and I rolled my eyes. And laughed at him. And we had fun. And it was okay. And we've been out a couple of times after that. He is crazy, but in a crazy way he is mine, similar to headaches or issues. And I like him. Who knew? Don't get ahead of yourself. There won't be a relationship. I am still incredibly uncomfortable with his craziness and of course, the age difference, but Demi has paved the way for us old chicks. Philip, aka *Gaydate* guy, would be happy to know I am officially cougaring it up. And Robbie is much hotter than *GayDate* guy anyway. *GayDate* guy, suck it. This old bitch is having a grand old time. ROAARRRRRRR.

Okay, let's get serious for a second. We are more just friends than anything else, but sometimes that is just what the doctor ordered. And by Doctor, I mean Robbie.

57

IT'S NOT ME, IT'S YOU

September 14, 2010

"It's not me, it's you."

I know this is not acceptable to say, but sometimes I wish it were. It's kind of like how *He's Just Not That Into You* revolutionized the way women thought about men and the fact that they were being blown off, or not pursued. It seemed people everywhere were breathing a sigh of relief that it was as simple as realizing he just wasn't that into them.

There are tons of dates I have been on, and tons of guys I have met where I have thought, he is super awesome, a great guy, incredibly smart, cute and dynamic...for someone else. Something about him just wasn't the right fit *for me*. Nothing you can put into words really, just that certain je ne sais quoi. But there have been other times, when it *wasn't* about me. I didn't want to say, "it's not you, it's me" because it *wasn't* me. It's *you* dammit. You are creepy, aggressive, angry, crazy, I might suspect you aren't into women, and if you were it was strictly so you could wear their shoes. Whatever the case it's not me, it's you. If only we could say that. Send that one sentence in a text, maybe we would breathe a sigh of relief. This isn't only in the dating world. It may work with friends as well.

"Hey Darcy, haven't seen you in a while. You must be really busy with Bear and work?"

Instead of having to write you are busy, life is getting in the way, you don't have a babysitter, you aren't feeling well, you're a flake, you are going through something, you are organizing your Lladro figurines, you can write back:

"No. Actually I haven't. I have been free as a bird. It's not me, it's you."

Insert shoulder shrug here.

Just typing it makes me breathe a sigh of relief. Ah, simple pleasures. It's like porn for the over-committed.

58

ONLINE D(EGR)ATING

SEPTEMBER 16, 2010

AT A LOSS of what to write about today, I suddenly remembered one of my experiences with online dating that had all the makings for a pretty good entry.

I had received an email from a seemingly normal, handsome guy. Divorced with two kids. Very vanilla. He worked in finance and started a charity for underprivileged children, which I liked. After a few quick email exchanges he asked for my number because he felt we should chat on the phone. I sat on the idea for a couple of days, unsure if I was interested, and finally sent it to him.

Here is the thing, *(insert dramatic sigh here)*, if I give you my number, I am hoping you will call me. I am hoping you won't use said number to *stalk* me. In other words, I shouldn't then receive a facebook friend request from you when I haven't yet provided you with my last name.

I do not accept said friend request on facebook, but do answer the phone when I see an unfamiliar number.

"Hello?"

"Hi Darcy. This is Freddie."

He sounded nice, but after a quick chat for 3 minutes which seemed like an eternity, I knew Freddie was not going to be Freddie my love. After speaking for a while he tells me he has googled me.

Yay

"You know, not to stalk you, but I wanted to just find out more about you. See if you look like your pictures. Which you do. You look great. You are very pretty. I also sent you a facebook friend request."

I know. I ignored it.

"Well, I am glad you think I look like my pictures. Do you look like yours?" I ask, thinking that he would of course say yes. It should be a given?

"No."

I laughed. He didn't. Bad sign.

"I have gained a ton of weight since those were taken."

"I'm sorry?"

I still think he is joking. Wouldn't you? Who admits this? Why put old pictures that look nothing like you??

"Well, they are a few years old. I don't really look like that anymore. I went through a hard time and put on a ton of weight. A lot of depressing things happened to me."

Crickets.

"Oh," I said. Not sure where to go from there really.

"Yea. Sorry."

"Huh."

"Yeah," he sighed.

Could. Not. Be. More. Awkward. Unless of course I showed up for the date and couldn't pick him out of a line-up.

"Are you still there?" he asked. I became unbelievably silent.

Oh me? Yes. But I am smothering myself with a pillow right now. That's why you can't hear me. My mouth is covered and I am just waiting to die.

"Well, anyway, you have my friend request. Take a look at my new pictures and if you are too shallow to go out with me because of what I really look like then that's okay."

Yep. I just died. The pillow did the trick. Or he did. Not sure which, but it was certainly over.

Sure Karl Rove. If you want to spin it on me that's fine. Because I won't accept your friend request and I won't be calling you back. Oh, and just a note to the online dating site in which I found you, I'd like a refund. Thanks.

59

DEAR CVS MANAGEMENT

SEPTEMBER 20, 2010

JUST WHEN I thought CVS could not be any more lazy, they have now swapped out their cashiers, with self check-out kiosks.

Note to the management: ARE YOU FRIGGIN KIDDING ME?

I have always wondered what the employees there did. One register is usually open, 11 employees hanging out behind the counter. People would waddle up to the counter holding heavy baskets overflowing with economy size Pantene and heavy cases of water. You could almost hear the cashiers scream in their head, "Not it!"

Now, there are 4 self check-out kiosks that don't work properly and those same employees stand around as tech support. They run over to press a button if the machine freezes or jams up as it often does and they use some sort of card that hangs around their neck to fix it. In fact, they usually end up doing it *for* you. So why can't they just ring you up? By the way, I would *love* to check myself out, if it *worked*, but it *doesn't*, so that is why I have a problem with it.

The lines have gone from 5 people long, to 25 people long, as no one can actually use these kiosks.

But here is my favorite part of the entire experience, and I think you will agree; There is ONE register left in the store. It is in the front next to the self check-out kiosks and it is used STRICTLY for those who either:

a) Want to have a passport picture taken.

b) Want to collect their photos that were being developed.

or

c) Anyone who wants to purchase a CVS gift card.

Now I ask you: Of the typical NYC drug store shoppers, what do you think the ratio is of people wanting their passport picture taken to those wanting to buy things like toothpaste, tampons, Advil or shampoo? Do you think the passport photo crowd outweighs the shopper category so much that it needs its own register? Just throwing it out there. Also, do people have photos developed anymore? No, Really? I am asking that seriously. I can't remember the last time I heard someone say, "I can't WAIT to get my pictures back." Plus, a CVS gift card? Really? Such a popular gift that, again, it needs an entire register designated for such? I mean, I would LOVE a CVS gift card. I can stay in there for hours, which I do, standIng in line. But is that a must have gift for the season? And it's not even gift season.

So when 25 angry New Yorkers, who, by the way, are in a rush, are waiting in line to check THEMSELVES out, it is my advice, CVS, that you don't have someone screaming (or mocking),

"Is anyone on the line buying a CVS gift card?"

As far as I am concerned they are screaming

"Has anyone seen Batman? Robin maybe?"

Here's an idea, how about I BUY a CVS gift card and use it to pay you to check me out at the register. Now there's a thought.

60

IT'S NOT ROCKET SCIENCE

SEPTEMBER 22, 2010

As I sat across the table from my date, an incredibly handsome Neurosurgeon, the thought crossed my mind; Every argument we ever had during our relationship would probably end in, "No, actually it *is* brain surgery."

61

PRETENSION IS A FOUR LETTER WORD

SEPTEMBER 27, 2010

IT WAS a cool September evening in New York City. The air had that perfect chill reminding you that fall was just around the corner. People were whipping out their cashmere wraps and warmest blazers. It was Fashion's Night Out. I am not sure what it's for, but it's a new thing they do during fashion week to raise money for starving models, or something to that effect. Stores leave their doors open past 10 pm and fill their spaces with DJ's, mini cupcakes, models and bridge and tunnel party goers who imagine themselves fashionistas for the night. The streets in the Meatpacking district looked like a night out in South Beach. Max and I headed into one of the stores where I immediately spotted a man in high heels. The store was owned by a friend of ours and the head of PR was Max's friend... So together we took part in supporting the evening's festivities.

After one too many hours on my feet I kissed Max goodbye and headed to meet some friends who were in from out-of-town at one of my favorite restaurants in the West Village. I was chatting with them at the bar when suddenly I locked eyes with a handsome stranger across the room. It was the kind of intense eye contact you can't really look away from, and you don't really want to. Suddenly the room begins to spin like a scene from *Matrix* where the people freeze but the scenery is spinning, and it feels like a good thing.

Suddenly he disappears. Yet another new york missed connection, I think to myself and continue on with my conversation. Not long after, a waitress approaches.

"Excuse me, you have a note."

"Me?" I say, knowing who it is from, but very shocked he sent it over. He was brave, I was impressed. I like brave. It felt like study hall, only better, because it was in a bar. And I was allowed to talk to my friends.

I opened up the note and written in very neat cursive handwriting it said:

"I am not sure who you are with, but I would love to invite you to come have dinner with me. I could stare at you at the bar all night, but then we would never eat," signed with his name and his number.

I was excited by the idea of this note. It's the type of thing you would like to happen when you make eye contact with strangers, but doesn't usually happen, if ever. I liked that he was very bold and stepped up to the plate and it certainly made for a good story.

I entered his number into my phone and sent him a text:

"I am sorry, tonight I am with my friends, but hopefully a rain check."

"Excellent, I would love that," he replied and we exchanged a few more texts. Suddenly he asked if I was feeling spontaneous enough to possibly have dinner with him the next night. It was perfect. The following week was busy and I couldn't imagine when I would get the chance again.

"I have a birthday party to attend but we can meet for a quick bite before if you'd like."

"That would be great," he said, "I look forward to tomorrow."

With that I turned off the ringer on my phone so I could get some sleep.

Please don't be gay. I thought to myself as I shut my eyes.

The next evening I headed downtown to one of my all time favorite restaurants to meet the handsome stranger for dinner. He was certainly as cute as I remember, but I had yet to hear his voice.

"Hi, I'm Darcy." I said, shaking his hand.

"Hi, I'm Adam. Nice to really meet you."

We are ushered to our table, where we are seated. Adam takes his chair and complains,

"He did it wrong."

"I'm sorry?"

"He was supposed to seat you on this side of the table. The lady should be the one to look out."

I'm sorry Countess deLesseps, I didn't realize we were being held to such high etiquette standards.

"Would you like to switch?" I asked, realizing that Adam was way more high maintenance than I was.

"No, it's fine. I'm just saying."

Why. Why are you saying that?

It didn't take long for me to realize Adam was much cuter from across the bar with no actual talking involved. He was...well... pretentious.

The waiter approached,

"Would you like something to drink? Maybe some wine to start?"

"What would you recommend to put with the Arrabiata sauce? Something to bring out the flavor," he asked with some type of faux Philip Seymour Hoffman-esque affected accent that only works on Philip Seymour Hoffman.

You could smell the pretension from across the table. I quickly wondered if I could somehow kill myself with a bread stick. There had to be some dangerous maneuver I could try. Possibly sticking it through my eyeball, jabbing myself through the heart.

Please, if you are out with me, please don't parade your foodieness around me. Also Adam, I'm pretty sure you don't know anything about wine, so please don't pretend. It's awkward and uncomfortable for everyone involved. Including the waiter, who by the way, was laughing when you asked that question.

His pretension didn't end there. He peppered the conversation with references to his handmade shoes, and custom-made blazer, his love of fashion and art.

"I mean, how have people NOT gone to Basel," he proclaimed.

I feel the same way about BBQ, I wanted to say, but kept it all inside.

I imagined myself in a cone of silence.

"Darcy? Are you listening?"

"*No, sorry Adam, I am officially in my cone of silence.*"

I was desperately trying to haul ass out of there and was looking forward to meeting my friends. Oh my friends. How I missed them. It was like being on an episode of Survivor, only it was a restaurant that was bold in Zagat's and I was wearing patent heels. We couldn't get the waiter's attention for the check.

"I think he is doing me a favor. He sees who I am here with. I think he is doing this on purpose so I get more time with you. I think he remembers me," he said.

I dry heaved in my brain. I know you are thinking it's not medically possible, but it is. Swear.

The end of dinner couldn't have come fast enough and when it did, he asked me out for another night. I laughed a nervous laugh and quickly hustled to grab a cab.

"So sorry! Gotta run to my friend's birthday party!"

I shook his hand goodbye and hopped in the cab the 3 blocks I didn't want him to walk me.

He texted me the next day.

"Hope you didn't have too much fun without me at your party."

He went on to name drop like a maniac, how many names can you drop in a text? He informs me he is headed to dinner with the former Chief of Staff to one of the presidents, and he was staying in a beach house lent to him by one of America's royal families.

I wanted to reply, "What type of wine goes well with douchebag?" but I held my fingers.

Adam was not a bad guy. He was a total gentleman and meant well. Just a little too showy for me.

Adam asked me out to dinner again immediately, which I liked. I am a sucker for a man with a plan. However, I did not accept his invitation. Sorry Adam. I did like your note! We will always have that, but sadly not much more.

62

THE DOCTOR WON'T SEE YOU NOW

SEPTEMBER 30, 2010

THIS IS what I love about the doctor's office: The never-ending wait.

You get there and have to first wait in a waiting room with bad magazines, things having to do with homemaking and crafts, gardening and baking. I am not sure why they subscribe to these magazines, or where they have even learned of such magazines. Why not the mainstream ones? Was there a study somewhere saying people will calm their nerves in a doctor waiting room by 20% if they are learning how to make a cupcake that looks like a spider for Halloween? Then you are sent into a cold exam room for 45 minutes before the doctor actually arrives. I am not sure why they call it an appointment, when it should in fact just be called a window. The cable company calls it a "window" from 10-2 or 4-6, which most people have a problem with. But the truth is, they are honest. Why don't doctor's offices start calling it a window?

"Hi Darcy? Please arrive on time at 10 am, your window for your appointment is 10 am- 2pm. No, no sorry, I can't tell you the *exact* time, or even a ballpark time, but you should be there for when the door opens."

Sometimes I think about bringing things to keep myself occupied as I will be there for hours. It's a good thing I switched to Verizon because T-Mobile used to never work inside doctor's offices. Sometimes I envision myself bringing gorp ,you know, that trail mix hikers bring on long camping trips to sustain themselves for days. That fruit and nut mix? Would it be odd to show up to my next doctor appointment with a flashlight, a canteen, a bag of gorp, a pillow/neck rest of some kind, possibly a Snuggie? Would they be offended if I had a pizza delivered as I was waiting naked in the exam room?

"What? It has been two hours. I got hungry. And I'm fresh out of gorp!"

In fact, I'd like to have visitors. I would like Bear's babysitter to bring him by so he can visit me at the doctor's office.

"Mommy, why are you staying here so long?"

"I'm sorry honey, it's my window. I will be home as soon as I can. Thanks for drawing me this picture. It's beautiful. I'm going to hang it up right here next to my exam table."

Maybe I can have friends deliver balloons and stuffed animals to my bedside. Maybe one of those stuffed animals could be wearing one of those little stuffed animal t-shirts saying, "Come home soon!" That would be nice.

Here is the question I have for all of you, because I am just wondering if we all think the same, or I am just a little weird. When left in a doctor's office, are you sometimes tempted to give yourself an exam using their equipment? Do you sometimes want to take that thing they use to look in your ears, and stick it in your ear really quickly? Maybe use a tongue depressor and give yourself a throat culture. When the nurse comes in, you can hand over the cotton swab and say, "Run this for strep will ya?"

The only reason I don't do that, is because I am sitting practically naked, freezing, wrapped in a makeshift gown of some kind sitting on *loud* crinkly paper. The paper, by the way, is pretty much there as an alarm system. They can hear that paper all the way in the waiting room. I imagine the receptionists (who are always lovely mind you, and by lovely I mean, not nice) to have a walkie-talkie system,

"I hear paper rustling in room 4, I think she is up and taking her blood pressure. Send someone in there to check it out. Yeah. Just say you are taking her weight."

On one occasion I waited so long, I was tempted to make a beard out of cotton balls so when the doctor walked in I would have a long white beard.

"Yea, I didn't have a beard when I came in 4 hours ago," as you shrug your shoulders.

The exam usually lasts 20 minutes and as you are getting dressed and leaving you see other people waiting in their rooms as you walk down the long hallway. You give a consoling glance, knowing they have a good three hours ahead of them as your doctor has only entered one of the 4 filled exam rooms.

So there you have it. Next time the cable company tells you to be home from 10-2, instead of getting annoyed, you can say thanks. Thanks for being honest and giving me a window.

63

FORGET PARIS

OCTOBER 6, 2010

I ARRIVED at a dark little bistro in Soho to meet my very cute, very French date.

I met Jack at a birthday party for a friend and he was very handsome, though I could not understand much of what he was saying with his thick French accent. I don't dig the accent thing because sometimes tiny things, little nuances get lost in translation. Humor is the number one most important thing to me. If you are making me laugh, we can fall in love. Well that, and some red-hot chemistry. My concern with a language barrier is something gets lost in translation and when you miss a flight, you lose your passport, you get a flat tire in a monsoon...having a sense of humor is SO important, and I actually don't know how you can do without it.

Jack showed up, looking hotter than the first time I met him in a suit. He was very well dressed. I liked him because he too was divorced with a child so he could relate to much of my life, even if I couldn't really understand what he was saying. He showed up for the date and immediately excused himself to smoke outside. How very French. I watched him inhale the Marlboro Red as though it were the last cigarette on earth and was just praying he wouldn't smell when he walked back into the restaurant.

In the first 20 minutes of our conversation I misunderstood almost everything he said.

"You work out with a trainer?"

"You *are* a trainer."

"OHHHHHH okay... you are a *trader*! Okay, okay. That makes more sense, given where you work."

This is how our conversation carried on for a good hour. I felt terrible. I smiled like a moron while he talked. *Such an American Darcy*, I cursed myself. He could have even told me he was fired that day, and I smiled politely and nodded. Uh-huh. Okay. Yes. Yes. Um Hmmm. *No idea*. Inside I was just hoping that his english would get better. Or I would miraculously learn French, which was improbable, given the fact that I had studied Spanish from the first grade till junior year of college and still do not speak it fluently, if at all. Sadly, I did sing him a song I learned in French in fourth grade, complete with hand gestures. He told me none of the words were actually French. I think I made the words up, as I didn't really remember the song. So yes, Jack wasn't being rude, it just probably was not French. It might have been Russian, Italian, Latin or German, as I was required to take all those languages too. Don't ask. I can say "Hello, how are you?"and "I can't complain" in all of those languages, but it really ends there. Apparently my school doubled as a training ground for CIA covert Ops, but I digress.

By our third bottle of wine Jack's English improved, or I was wearing ear goggles, which are essentially beer goggles, but for your ears. And made out of wine.

Jack knew everything about wine, but not in a pretentious way. It was in a natural French kind of way, and I liked it because it just seemed really authentic and second nature and he seemed quite passionate about it. Passion, check. Jack, who I felt was very conservative at first, started to loosen up quite a bit. He begins to tell me I am his American fantasy girl, the one he always hopes will sit next to him on the plane to France but never does. Before you know it got a little too heavy in the romance department. I felt like I was riding on the train with Ethan Hawke and Julie Delpy in *Before Sunrise*, yet I didn't want to be on that train. Here is something else about me. I don't love romance. Let me rephrase, I *do* love romance, I just have a twisted view of what I think is romantic.

For example, this would be romantic: You make me laugh so hard I hit my head on the table, which in turn makes you laugh because you in fact have a nervous laugh like I do. We are laughing so hard at my injury that the couple at the table next to us yells at us and asks us to be quiet. We then fight with the neighbors and gang up on them together which makes us fast best friends. The next day you send me an ice pack with a note from the table that says I give good head. THAT is romantic. Sick and twisted, yet romantic.

Holding my hand anywhere: romantic.

Showing me that you are into me: romantic.

Just checking in to say hello or asking how I am: romantic.

Giving me a piggy ride down a side street that is overrun with rats because they are my biggest fear: romantic.

Telling me you want to watch a sunset with me and sing me a song, just makes me nauseous and uncomfortable. I know that's probably terrible and Hallmark may send me some sort of cease and desist for writing this in a public forum, but it's how I feel. I don't like contrived romance. Or romantic romance. I like to be surprised. Surprise me. Buy me one of those pipes that are made of black licorice, because I am the only person in America who actually buys them. Yes, I do buy them. Really...

Jack tells me all the things he would like to do with me and all the places he would like to take me, which I find sweet and endearing. He seems like a very sweet gentle soul, a great dad and an overall good person. He tells me one day he would like to wake up with me in the morning to the smell of warm toast.

"You mean french toast?"

"No. Warm toast."

Warm toast? Is that a sexy smell? Kind of sounds gross in bed no? And itchy. I want to wake up to the smell of aftershave and soap. But warm toast?

He was being incredibly respectful and a full gentleman. Some of my dates could have learned a thing or two from Frenchie. Wait. I spoke too soon. Wait for it...wait for it...

"I probably shouldn't tell you this. But I have a very big dick."

Insert sound of record screeching to a halt.

Blink, blink, rapid blink.

WHAT? I wasn't sure if I was shocked by what he said or the fact that his English was suddenly perfect. Oh no! Wait...wait a second! Did he...did he think "dick" meant something else in English? What just happened here???

"People always tell me how huge it is. They are shocked."

Nope, he knows the definition.

"Oh. Wow. Well. That's...huh (furrowing my brow). Good to know... I guess?"

"I probably shouldn't tell you that, I guess. Just thought you should know."

"Oh. Well...thank you."

I guess I will just add that into my Filofax under "Jack's penis size," and if I need this data I will refer to it accordingly.

64

DATING DETOX

October 11, 2010

I, Darce E. Dates, have a big announcement. I am going on a diet. A dating diet. Maybe it's a dating detox? Well, actually, more like a fast. For 60 days I will not go on a date. I will not go to dinner, drinks, movies, concerts, sporting events, hiking, white water rafting (that would be hard to resist, to be honest, especially if it was within driving distance), staycation, vacation, one of the girls in your rotation, dancing, prancing, nary a *thing* with a guy that could potentially be a romantic interest.

Fine, in the spirit of full disclosure, just like anyone entering a rehab of some kind I have snuck one thing in my duffel bag. It's one last date that was planned before this announcement so I need to go on it.

I am burnt. I don't even want to become a lesbian, as that would involve dating. I want to become a monk of sorts. I want to wear an orange toga of some kind, a color that looks terrible on me. I want to only do things with Bear and my friends and watch 80 hours of *The Office* on DVR. I want to do nothing but the following:

1) Find out which of my neighbors is smoking pot 24/7 and making my bedroom smell like a frat house.

2) Wine and dine with old friends, new friends, friends that don't want to be naked with me in any way. I would like to go to 6th street and get Indian food with them. Possibly Chinatown for some dumplings, I want to eat tacos at that creepy place I love. I want to have some beers and wings and then go home and watch MORE of *The Office*.

3) I want to learn how to make a quilt. Or not. No. I don't want to make a quilt. It seems difficult if you really think about it.

4) I want to buy a new dresser. I'm bored with my old one.

5) I want to see a movie, in a theater, by myself and get bed bugs. Well, I don't actually want the bed bugs, but I can't talk about seeing movies in NYC these days without mentioning the bed bug epidemic.

6) I want to delete tons of email from my inbox so I don't keep getting "System Administrator Mailbox is Full!" Messages. It's incredibly annoying and prevents the sending of email from my Blackberry.

7) Speaking of Blackberry's, I would like to not carry mine when I am not working.

8) I would like to change my phone number and possibly take down my Facebook page. I would like to revert to making person to person calls.

9) I would like to subscribe to trashy magazines so they show up at my house without me having to be in an airport to read them. This, of course, would entail me checking my mailbox more often than I do, so maybe it's not such a good idea now that I talked it out.

10) I would like to go to the gym and not leave after 12 minutes, from what I understand that is not long enough for a sufficient workout.

11) I would like to enter and win a sweepstakes of some kind. I would like to win a big check. And I don't mean the sum, I mean the

size. One of those extra large checks they carry to your door when you win.

12) I want to visit Ellis Island, something I have never done even though I was born and raised in this city.

13) No. Actually. I don't want to go to Ellis Island. I will just believe other people who say it's cool.

14) I would like to work on my Poker face, which is horrendous.

15) I would like to ride the luggage carousel at the airport. I have always wanted to do that. Bear has too. We will do it together. I would *not* like to get arrested for it. I don't think you can watch The Office in jail. Do they have condiments in jail by the way? Just wondering.

16) I would like to buy my Halloween costume NOW so I don't have to wait on-line the day of Halloween and be a witch because it's the only thing left.

17) I would like to start drinking green tea, and understand what all the fuss is about. Actually, scratch that. I'm not a tea person. But, I would enjoy a milkshake. I wish they had *Friendly's* in the city. But I'll take one from *Shake Shack*, a place I have never been. Apparently, I am the only person in NYC to have never been to Shake Shack.

18) I would like to go to *Shake Shack*.

19) I would like vitamins to be something I take and not just something to decorate the shelves of my medicine cabinet.

20) I would like to join a nunnery. While I am Jewish, I am basically abstinent, so I may as well get some credit with g-d. As they say, "money in the bank."

So, you are wondering, what is it that I will write about? Well, I do have tons of stuff in the archives that have yet to be written or published regarding my previous dates, I will also let you know how I am doing as a social misfit, holed up in my apartment doing nothing but watching *The Office* and *not* quilting. Jim from *The Office* by the way, is now number one on my list. I am now in a relationship with Jim. He is tall, funny and cute. Only he doesn't know and he isn't real which is obviously an obstacle, and it probably isn't healthy. Let's be honest; it's possibly a tad creepy.

Bottom line: there is only one man in my life I would like to spend time with right now. He is a little man, and although he is only 6, he is the best one I know. Yesterday we went to a street fair, ate roasted corn and shish kabobs, and then we rode our bikes down West End avenue. If that is not a perfect day I don't know what is. He's my best guy and makes me super happy. Sorry, Jack and your big penis (See: *Forget Paris*), but this girl is on hiatus.

65

ANATOMICALLY CORRECT

OCTOBER 13, 2010

AT MY ANNUAL GYNO EXAM, my Doctor told me he wanted to set me up. At least I know I have a pretty vagina.

66

REAL TEXTS FROM ROBBIE

O CTOBER 15, 2010

I WOKE up this morning with a text from Robbie.

I opened up the attachment and it was a picture... of his penis.

Sigh.

This is really not something I would expect from Robbie. This was very out of character.

I text back:

"What the fk?"

And again.

"Seriously!? What the fk?"

"You don't like it?"

"Robbie. We are friends. Friends don't text friends pictures of their penis."

"Friends show each other their parts."

Parts?

"I have zero interest in your parts."

"FINE!"

I shake my head. Even for Robbie this was crazy. I receive another text:

"Why can't you tell me if you think it's nice or not?"

"Ask a girl you are sleeping with. Or a girl who cares."

"You're being immature."

Really? Because last I checked immature is texting a picture of your "parts" to girls who don't want to see them. But sure. I know the regular rules of society don't apply to the world I live in with Robbie so I just overlook it.

"Okay. You're right. I'm immature."

"Tell me what you think of it!"

Is he demanding I critique his penis via a picture he texted me?

"This is what I think: There are things I *love* about you, but overall you are a total douchebag."

"Darcy! You know that's not true."

This is when the calling begins. He continues to pass the phone around to his friends who are chiming in with "We miss you Darcy!", "When are we going to see you Darcy?". It's like I am on speakerphone in a kindergarten classroom.

He jumps back on the phone.

"I want to see you."

"No."

"Fine. I'll call you back."

I know, I think to myself, *I know*.

67

SPRAY AND WASH

O CTOBER 18, 2010

This entry is dedicated to Hogan Lipschitz.

After a seemingly good date with a guy I liked who never asked me out again…I asked him out. I told one of my good guy friends:

"So I am going out with him again tonight."

"Really? He asked you out again?"

"No. I asked him."

"What? *Why*? Why would you do that?"

"I don't know. Why not?"

"Well then I hope you plan on banging him."

"What?"

"You better bang him."

"Nice. You know me better than that. You know that's not going to happen."

"Well if a girl asked me out for drinks, I would basically go home and change my sheets and think it meant she was going to fuck me."

"Well, why change the sheets? Maybe I made it so easy he doesn't even need to go through the work of changing them. Maybe he just needs to *Febreze* them!"

The Darcy Dictionary:

Febreze:

noun-A spray product people use when they are too lazy to actually clean or wash something.

verb– What men do to their sheets when a girl makes it way too easy to get a date with her.

adjective– "She's not the kind of girl you need to change the sheets for. She's more of a *Febreze* kind of girl."

68

WHEN LIFE GIVES YOU CITRUS... DON'T MAKE A COLLAR

OCTOBER 20, 2010

LADIES, have you ever gone on a date and thought to yourself, "I have a real Mandarin collar situation on my hands"?

I have.

69

DRIVING WITH MY MOM

O CTOBER 22, 2010

MY MOTHER IS one of my best friends. However, sometimes her logic is a little off and she suffers from real Jewish mother anxiety. These are just a few of her gems, a compilation if you will, from some of our recent trips in the car:

She glanced over at me as I was texting furiously. I was sitting in the *passenger* seat.

"Darcy, it's very dangerous to text in the car."

"That's only if you are driving, which I am not."

"Still. It's still dangerous."

Okay.

She has also mastered the traffic tracker on her IPhone, which I admit to be helpful when initially planning our route, however, it doesn't end there. She often gives live traffic updates while I am driving.

"Darcy, traffic is moving. There is no traffic here," she says as she is staring down at her phone.

"Yes, I had derived that from looking directly out my window and actually *driving*."

It's not nice, but sometimes, while going 70 down an empty highway, no other car in sight I will ask, "Is there traffic now? How about now? Maybe now? Now is there traffic? Maybe there is traffic here? Can you check if there is traffic?"

"Darcy, you're teasing me." Then I see it. She can't resist! She actually sneaks a peek at her phone traffic tracker to see if there is traffic!

"No, there is no traffic," she says.

"Thanks mom. You're the best!"

She also has an intense fear of the HOV lane. Not because it's moving fast, but because she actually thinks you will get trapped in it and never be able to get out. When I am driving in the HOV lane, she literally sits forward, eyes peeled on the road, looking for an "exit" from the HOV lane. She will read the signs:

"Darcy, you can exit the HOV lane at exit 38."

"But we are going to exit 70."

"Are you sure? What if we can't get out of the HOV lane after exit 38 and before exit 70."

"I am going to really live on the edge and take the risk that I may have to stay in the HOV lane for the next 2 days. I may have to drive all the way to Canada. Or Cuba. Or whatever is all the way past the Hamptons because I can't exit the HOV lane. I'm a gambler like that."

"It's not funny Darcy."

"Yes. Yes, It actually is."

From my mom's perspective she basically thinks at some point there will be a news helicopter following us similar to that of the white bronco chase, only instead of fugitives on the run, the newscasters will be screaming, "Below you will see a family stuck in the HOV lane. They have been driving for hours. They can't get out. They missed the exit! We are trying to assist them, but we aren't quite sure how."

"Mom, you know it's just a white line, and we can drive over it at any time."

"That's illegal Darcy."

"Well, if there was an emergency, we can get out. That's all I am saying."

"Well, it's not legal."

Yup.

70

BREAKING THE FAST

OCTOBER 28, 2010

THIS IS DEDICATED to *my dear old friend "D," who asked if Darcy was in fact looking for love, and I just didn't know the answer...*

I have fallen off the wagon. Actually, I haven't fallen. I am jumping off with my very own two feet. I have never been one for diets or detox's (see: *Dating Detox*). I have never been one for anything that involved any type of *will* really. You know that saying, "Where there is a will, there is a way?" Yeah. I can't relate to that. In my case, I *will* not. I was never really good at fasting on Yom Kippur so why should this day be any different than any other day, as us Jews like to say.

Surprisingly, I got a lot of boycotts regarding my fast. Even my gyno didn't agree with it. I told him that it's probably because he wanted to make a little more money off of me, by me having another baby, or getting an STD of some kind. He laughed, but inside he knew I had a good point.

I have an old saying, I don't know where it came from. Probably a calendar or a mug, or a needlepoint pillow at a math tutors house in 8th grade: "Don't waste the pretty." It's the advice I usually give to my girlfriends who are spending way too much time on a guy who doesn't deserve it. I realized, by not accepting dates of any kind, I was in fact wasting the pretty. Not very green of me to be so wasteful. I needed to do it for the environment. Or at least my environment. It was much healthier than my aspirations of riding the luggage carousel or working on my relationship with fake Jim from the office, who by the way, I just found out is married.

The fast so far has given me a bit of clarity that I didn't have before. It's only been 18 days, but in ten more days, if it were February, it would be a month. It gave me a good chance to clear my head. However, the other night I caught a rerun of *Pretty Woman*. It's probably the twelve millionth time I have seen it but it made me realize, I *do* want to fall in love. Not with a hooker, but with a really great guy. This was a big breakthrough for me. With all the dating and the don't-ing I lost sight of what it was I was looking for. I want to find a soul mate, another great love of my life. There. I said it. Without even gagging. Very un-Darcy of me, but it's true. I have found one before and I will find one again. I want someone who can make me laugh and keep me on my toes. I want someone who I can't keep my hands off of. I want a worthy adversary and someone who will let me make the temperature 40 below when we are sleeping. I want someone who is great to me and great to Bear. I want someone to take the other side of my silly bets. I want someone who lights up when I walk in the room and someone who will fight to the death in the gauntlet for me. Is that extreme? I figure as long as I am making my list, why not. I know all of these things are possible because I was lucky enough to experience all of these things before. And some people don't even get that! And I believe I can find it again because I know there are multiple soul mates out there for everyone. Just look at the Polygamists! Those guys found lots of wives. And I am sure some of them can still find room in their hearts for a few more. Maybe I should move to Utah? Nah. I love New York. And I am not a great sharer. Well, I am. But not in a sister-wife kind of way.

My life is filled with love. I love my child, I love my family, I love my friends, I even love my ex-husband, but there is room for more. Maybe not in my closet (see: *Needing Space*), but in my life for sure. And I want that. And more kids. And more chaos. I have really enjoyed the time I have spent *not* quilting, and I have yet to make it to Shake Shack, but my me-time and my me and Bear time and my, me and my friends eating wings and drinking beer time (which doesn't often happen because they are more of a wine crew), does not have to be affected by my dates, not that it ever was.

By the way, do you know *love* is the most googled word on the internet?

71

REAL TEXTS FROM REAL MEN

November 1, 2010

I was asked out by a guy who I never really followed up with. I just didn't think he was for me. The following is how he chose to proceed...via text. Odd choice if you ask me, and or anyone else really...

"Darcy! What's up? I tried to make a plan with you and it never worked out and now another month has gone by and we still haven't gotten together! I thought for sure that by now we'd be coming over to each other's apartments for booty calls, right"

Crickets.

For those of you who were wondering if chivalry was dead, now you know. It is. It's more dead than the horse this guy keeps beating by continually asking me out with little response. Had this come only one day earlier I may have been able to stay on my fast for *at least* ten more days. Similar to the fit inspo picture people tape to their fridge to keep them on their diet, this could have been my reminder of why

I was fasting to begin with.

72

IT'S COMPLICATED

November 4, 2010

You know when you see someone's Facebook relationship status set to "It's Complicated," and you were never quite sure what that meant?
Yeah.
If you're Chef Hottie (remember that guy? See: *Ghost of Risotto Past & Darcy Plus Party*) *this* is what it means:
"Hey. Remember when I met you and I was pursuing you hardcore, and we started seeing each other and could barely keep our hands off each other? And then suddenly I vanished into thin air and I *hid* from you? Remember? I may or may not have faked my own death...or at least pretended to be my *friend* and never had the nerve to face you ever again once I disappeared and you never quite had the explanation you deserved? It's because I really had a *girlfriend*. The whole time. Actually, we've been together for *at least* a year. Oh yea, and we are *still* together. That would explain the "hiding." I was just

actually praying I would never get caught and I didn't really think our paths would ever cross, because I don't live in the city.

Oh! And before I forget, remember that long speech I gave you about how I don't understand cheating? How i'd never cheat on my girlfriend if I had one, because really what is the point, and why be with someone you weren't that into? Yeah. That was a fake speech, because I actually *was* cheating on my girlfriend when I gave that speech. It was pretty convincing wasn't it?"

Yep. I'd say that's pretty damn complicated.

I only know this because I found his Facebook account he said he never had.

MEET ROBBIE'S FAMILY

November 8, 2010

My faux relationship with Robbie is pretty much over, but other things keep coming up. Since we stopped speaking, his obsessive calling has resumed. Now he mainly calls and yells at me for never answering or saying I am too busy to speak, which is very often true.

He called the other night. I hadn't picked up in a few weeks... since the penis text incident. I decided to say a quick hello.

"Hi Robbie."

"Hi baby."

"How have you been?"

"Good. How are you?"

"Good."

"Are you dating anyone?" I love how he gets right to the point.

"Yes." This might keep him at bay. *Might.*

"Who is this guy? Is he hotter than me?"

"What else is new with you Robbie?"

"Things are good. What are you doing tonight?" He sounds rushed, frantic and semi-angry as always.

"I have plans."

"Is he taking you to McDonald's?"

I'm silent. I wonder why I do this to myself.

"Well, I am glad to hear you are doing well. I actually have to run though. Have to hop in the shower." I really did have to run.

"Oh. So you're playing hard ball with me now?"

"I'm sorry?"

"Saying you have to go and shower."

"Um, no. I actually have to take a shower. I just got back from the gym."

"Fine."

Finally an hour later he texted, "Can I see you tomorrow?"

I haven't seen Robbie in a couple of months, and it always makes for such good Darcy material, and Bear was going to his dads house for the weekend. I really had nothing going on.

"Okay. But it's *totally* platonic, and I would like to bring a friend or a group of friends." *Possibly a therapist for the both of us. For you, because you need one, and for me, because I obviously do too.*

"Okay."

The next day I check my phone and have 3 missed calls in the space of an hour, from Robbie. Coupled with a text that says "ANSWER!" I called him back.

"Why weren't you answering your phone?"

"I didn't even see it ringing. I was with Bear."

"Listen, I'm seeing you tonight right?"

"Yes."

"Can you come to my moms birthday dinner? It's at my brother's house." His brother who lives outside of New York City.

My eyes widened. I know this is terrible but my immediate thought: What excellent Darcy material! Meeting Robbie's family? That is a virtual goldmine. Come one readers, those of you who follow the Robbie drama, you know that to be true!

"Really? Okay." I say. I was actually ecstatic.

"Really? Cool! We will leave at 7."

"How are we getting there?" I ask, knowing the responsibility will probably fall on me.

"We can take a car or you can drive. Or I can drive your car."

"No. You aren't driving."

"Why not?"

"I'm pretty sure you have major road rage."

"I don't have road rage! Be ready at 7," he hangs up.

I texted him shortly after.

"Are you sure this isn't going to be awkward?"

"That's what I hate about you," he writes back.

He always had a way with words.

I call Alexis.

"Hi. Guess where I am going tonight? Robbie's. Mom's. Birthday. Dinner." I say this as though it's the Oscars, and I know she will feel the same.

"Shut up. That's amazing!"

"Yep."

"Where is it?"

"The brother's house. Do you think they are going to wonder why he is bringing an old lady with him?"

We laugh. Hysterically.

"Alright, I gotta run. I gotta go get ready for my Machatunim."

We laugh even harder. For those of you unfamiliar with Yiddish, Machatunim means in-laws. A word Alexis and I use constantly and it gets the same reaction every time. Never seems to get old.

"What are you wearing?" I text Robbie.

"Jeans."

"And what?"

"A shirt"

Alrighty then. I throw on Jeans and a pink button down. Robbie shows up wearing the exact same thing. There is nothing like making an awkward situation even more awkward.

"Don't mind the old lady in the matching outfit mom." I picture him to say as we arrive.

As we climbed into the car, I asked "You told your brother I was coming right?"

"Of course."

I start driving and he starts asking me about my love life. I tell him it is great and thriving. Which is obviously not the case, as I am driving out of Manhattan, over a bridge, with a guy who spends the greater majority of his free time torturing me. I already want to turn the car around but realize I am leaving his mother high and dry, and as a mother, I am sensitive to that, so instead I just wonder if I can do a slow drive by the house and he can roll out. For most of the ride, Robbie had the sun visor pulled down so he could look at himself in the mirror.

"I hope it works out with you and this guy Darcy," he says, as he stares at himself intently.

"That's very altruistic of you. Thank you."

We pull into the driveway and I slink up to the house. I want to jump in the bushes but Robbie has already kicked in the door. I walk down the hallway and silently wait for the disaster that I know is about to unfold.

Robbie's family says hello to him, they see me out of the corner of their eyes but say nothing.

"This is my friend Darcy!" He announces.

"I wish you would have told us you were bringing someone Robbie! So we could have set the table for her," his brother says.

His brother does not look at me.

This doesn't register with Robbie. He leaves me there to fend for myself.

"I am so sorry he didn't tell you. I thought he told you he was bringing me."

"No, it's okay," he says, still not looking at me.

"Get my guest a drink!" Robbie screams at his brother. He really knows how to turn a moment from bad to worse.

"Oh, that's okay-"

"How about a tour?" Robbie screams to me.

"Okay," I accept, desperate to get out of the kitchen.

I walk from room to room with Robbie. As soon as we are upstairs I ask,

"What the hell? You told me you told him I was coming!"

"Oh, It's fine."

As we walk back into the kitchen Robbie screams at his brother again,

"I told you! Get my guest a drink!"

I go to my safe place in my mind. There is cotton candy and possibly a unicorn there. There are also rainbows, and honey nut Cheerios.

"What would you like to drink Darcy?"

"I'll just have a glass of wine." I see it opened right next to him.

"No. I'm going to make you a mixed drink."

"Okay."

I see where Robbie gets it now. Apparently the whole family doesn't believe in listening to what other people say. It must be a genetic trait.

Now he introduces me to his mother. Robbie's mom was hot!

"Mom, this is Darcy!"

"Hi Darcy."

"Hi."

"How did you guys get here?"

"Darcy drove," Robbie said.

"Oh. You have a car in the city?" she asked.

"Yes."

"That's nice. What do you do?"

Really?

"Insert my job here."

I got the sense she wanted to see a copy of my tax return, but I didn't have that on me.

Now a new batch of relatives show up. Robbie introduces me to them.

"This is Darcy! Darcy, this is my uncle Mike, and my aunt Sara."

"Oh! Hi, we met," she said as she shook my hand.

"No. I don't...I don't think we did."

"Oh! I'm so embarrassed. So sorry!"

She whispers something to her husband. They look at me and then whisper to each other once again. This can't be real. No real people are like this. Wait. Yes they are. Robbie is like this. And these are his kin. Ah, it's all coming together now.

Robbie's mom returns to make small talk with me. I told her that I had some friends from her town. She knew the families well. I told her I was friends with their kids.

"So how old are you Darcy?"

Insert age here.

"You are?? You look 20! Seriously? You aren't (*said age*), there is NO WAY!"

I love her now. Maybe I can date her. She's divorced.

"Yes. I also have a 6-year-old son."

"No WAY. Really?"

She is really shocked. For a moment I like these people.

"Yes, I do."

With that she wanted to see pictures of Bear, and now the sister was warming up to me and she too wanted to see pictures. An activity I always like taking part in. I felt at ease. For a minute.

Robbie shuffles me to the couch and grills me on whether or not I think he looks hot.

"Can you not?" I say, "I can't take it anymore. Why don't you go make out with that mirror that's leaning on that wall in the corner over there."

Robbie's sister's boyfriend is watching our interaction. Robbie gets up to use the bathroom.

I wanted to feel out the family's stance on Robbie, "Does it scare you that Robbie is a doctor?"

"A little," he said.

Not good.

Robbie returns and sits back down next to me. His mother sits on the other side of him. He has his arm around me and she has his arm around him. Huh. I just never saw this moment for myself, that's all.

"What do you think of Darcy mom?"

I'm sitting right here.

"She's adorable Robbie."

"She is. I wanted her to bear my children, but she didn't want to be my girlfriend."

"Don't bear anyones children Robbie, particularly if they aren't your girlfriend."

Want to die.

"I had to break up with her because she was too possessive."

I look at him with my mouth agape.

"Don't talk about possessive Robbie. You can be possessive too. You know you had a problem with that," his mother said firmly.

Really? Um, Hello? This is fake. Has to be.

"Robbie? Your mom doesn't think you're kidding."

Robbie's mom turns to me.

"Robbie worked very hard to be a doctor. Very hard. He worked his ass off. He should be able to do whatever he wants to do."

Well, that's interesting wrong advice.

"Robbie, it's not funny. I want to strike that from the record."

He is laughing hysterically. I am wishing my car was like *Knight Rider* and would bust through the living room walls to rescue me. I press the unlock button on my car key with the hopes of hearing an engine rev. Nothing. Thanks for nothing, car.

"Why don't we tell your mom the real story."

I turn to her,

"The real story is that Robbie asked me to be his girlfriend. I said no and if you ask me, that's the complete opposite of possessive."

His mother doesn't want to hear it. She continues to defend Robbie. He is laughing and I decide I hate him. I narrow my eyes at him and he laughs even harder.

Saved by dinner time. I am seated next to Robbie and across from the mean aunt. The entire meal she is looking at me and whispering to her husband. He would then look at me and whisper back. Do people not realize this is rude? I want to go home. I need to get away from this dinner.

"*Can I help you in the kitchen? Can I caulk your tub? Need your bathroom tiles re-grouted?*" The brother ignores me as he always does.

I'm homesick. I miss Bear. I miss being able to use my phone, which Robbie by the way, was doing the entire meal. I miss my bed. I miss my mom. Mommy. Tell me if there is traffic!

By the end of dinner I have stopped even fake smiling at the mean aunt across the table. I hate her. I hate myself more for being there. Robbie saves me.

"Let's sit down on the couch."

Thank you Jesus. We are alone. Which is better than being with his crazy family, whispering about us right in front of our faces. Robbie is oblivious. He proceeds to try to cuddle with me the entire evening.

Robbie and I are on the couch and he has his arms wrapped around me. His brother sits with us and decides to talk to me.

"So you guys are just friends?"

"Yes," I say, quickly.

"We dated for a minute but then had a falling out," he said.

"Yes, we dated for a minute after he called me every day for 6 months, so finally I caved."

"I called you a *few* times a day Darcy. Not just once."

Okay. If you want to admit that to your brother, be my guest.

"So, I don't believe it. Coming to a mom's birthday dinner is a very girlfriend thing to do. If you weren't his girlfriend, why would you be here?"

"Actually, that is a question I have been struggling with all night."

"Can I ask you a question Darcy. You are obviously a very pretty girl, and seem to have a good head on your shoulders. Why did you pass thirty and never get married."

Oh, Okay. I thought the awkward portion of the evening was over, but it's not. Okay. Got it now.

Because he wasn't talking to me earlier in the evening, he missed that I was divorced and had a child.

"Actually, I did get married. I was married for 7 1/2 years. I also have a child."

"Oh. Wow. Okay."

This is the third time I have announced this evening. It's like being in DA, Divorced Anonymous.

"Hi, I'm Darcy, and I'm divorced."

Only no one says "Hi Darcy!" Because they are mean.

Robbie's mom starts to make a beeline towards us on the couch. Robbie has his arm tightly fixated around my body and I am falling asleep on his chest watching TV. I am exhausted from embarrassment. It takes a LOT out of you. She chose to sit directly on his lap.

AWK-WARD.

I am now in a three-way cuddle hug with him and his mom. She is basically giving him a lap dance and possibly nibbling on his ear. I guess I can't date his mom. She is apparently dating Robbie.

"Mom, I am going to marry Darcy. Would you mind if I married Darcy."

"Don't get married, you are my baby," she said as she hugged him tighter, possibly slipping him the tongue. He starts to pull me closer, and starts to kiss me on the head.

I could have sworn I heard one of them whisper, "It rubs the lotion on the skin or else it gets the hose again." But I wasn't quite sure which one of them said it, not that it mattered much.

"I'm going to marry Darcy. What do you think of that mom? I want her to bear my children."

"He isn't marrying me. He isn't even dating me." I say. *The only relationship he is in is with the mirror.*

She starts clinging to him, "Darcy is adorable. Don't get married, be a doctor. Stay with me!"

I finally break free of the most awkward family moment I have ever been a part of and I start looking for my car keys as an activity. I know they are in my pocket but I am so beyond creeped out I want to go home and cry, or laugh, or take a shower. I am not quite sure, I just know I want out.

Finally it's time to leave. Robbie stops and looks in every mirror on the way out. I have to peel myself out of the full body hug Robbie's mom is now giving me. *Friends close, enemies closer?*

When we get to the city Robbie asks, "Are you sure you don't want me to sleep over?"

"Yes"

"Have I ever slept over?"

"No."

I pull up to his building.

He has basically already jumped out of my moving car.

"I get it," he screams.

After meeting your family Robbie, so do I. So do I.

As I drove the rest of the way home I had Alexis and Max on conference. I re-capped my evening with them.

"You lost me at the part where you actually went to an intimate sit down dinner in another state for his mom's birthday," Max said.

We all laughed hysterically, and just like that I was home.

74

UNDER MY UMBRELLA

November 15, 2010

It was a rainy night in New York City and I headed out to one of my post-fast dates. I was rested and ready to go. Unable to get a taxi in the mini monsoon, I dashed into the subway. In my opinion, it's the easiest way to get around this city.

I got off at my stop to find it still raining. Given the fact that it was raining when I left my house, I actually had an umbrella with me, which is rare.

As I am about to open my umbrella and step out from the awning next to the subway stop a man calls out to me,

"Hey, can I buy that off of you?"

I look up. He was unbelievably handsome. He had an accent and was definitely a model of some kind, or at least used to be. He looked to be in his mid to late thirties.

"I'm sorry. It's my lucky umbrella," I said and flashed a quick smile at him. I stepped out from beneath the awning and walked into the rain.

Halfway down the block I feel someone nudging me.

"Excuse me, I am just going to walk with you a bit under here," the handsome stranger says.

He is about 6 2" if not taller and he was crouching to get down under my umbrella. I look over at him.

"Okay," I laugh a bit and raise my arm as high as I can.

Is this real? Obviously this story would have gone quite differently if he wasn't so cute. A double standard, I realize.

"I wanted to tell you your jeans look great on you. I import jeans from Australia. What brand are those?"

I smile coyly, "J Brand,' I say, unsure what to make of this.

"We are having a launch party for the new line at a new great place in the West Village. Would you like to come?"

"Oh..."

Who knew? In *all* that time, I could just find a date right under my umbrella!

"Let me give you my card. If you want to come, call me or email me."

With that he hands me a card. It has a tennis racket on it, "Oh, I'm also a tennis pro," he says.

Of course he is. Tennis players are always hot.

"I have to leave you here now. Sorry," I said to the handsome stranger.

We were about to cross the street and running into my date with another guy under my umbrella would be hard to explain.

"No problem. Call me! Don't forget."

I smiled. I didn't think I would be calling him. The story had all the makings of a romantic one, but something about him just wasn't for me. A little too good-looking and a little too smooth I suspected. Any guy with an Australian accent with model good looks and in the jeans business was also most likely in the jeans coming off quickly business. At least that's how I saw it.

I headed to the next block to meet my date, Leo. As soon as I saw him, I was psyched. He was so cute and much more my type, not that I have one, as I am not clear on what my type is, but he was closer to what I imagined it to be. We quickly bonded over our obsessive love of *The Office*.

"What's your favorite episode?" he asked.

"I'd say the sexual harassment episode."

"Mine too!"

We were talking about it in grueling detail and became fast friends.

The evening was going great and we basically closed out the restaurant.

"I have to use the bathroom quickly, but I have a surprise for you," he said, as he reached into his pocket.

"Please don't propose. It's only our first date."

We laughed.

Out of one jacket pocket he pulled out his IPhone, and headphones from the other. With a few swipes of his finger he had it set to my surprise and handed it to me.

"It's the sexual harassment episode of The Office. You can watch it while I'm gone."

"Really? Cool! I can't believe you have that on here!"

This is too good to be true.

I put the earphones in my ear and sat and watched. When he came out of the bathroom I handed him one of the headphone buds and we watched the rest of the scene together as they were basically cleaning the restaurant at this point.

It was fun, and he was normal, and it's very own way...it was romantic. And he invited me to come to an event with his friends three days later. I accepted.

75

DON'T ASK, DON'T TELL

NOVEMBER 18, 2010

When you live in an apartment building, you assume the doormen know way too much about your personal life. However, it's an unspoken rule, a don't ask, don't tell policy if you will, between tenants and their doormen, that they pretend to not realize when you are coming home at 4 am, and you pretend they didn't see.

This is what my doormen know about me: they know I use their desk as my own private *Staples*. I come to them for inappropriate use of their stapler, tape, possibly a paper clip here and there. Maybe even a band-aid if the need should arise. They also know that I am a mom and I am single. They see both sides of me. They see me taking Bear to school each morning and they see me going out on occasion when he is at his dad's, dressed in a very high Louboutin heel and the occasional sequins top. Sometimes, when I am headed out for a night on the town, Nick, my evening doorman will chant, "Party time! Party time!" It's like having a jewish mother in my lobby. Only one that doesn't offer advice. Actually, maybe it's more like a shrink than a mother. One who sits and stares and smiles and you aren't quite sure what they are thinking.

In all my years living here, I have had a gentleman visitor or two.

The doorman will ring me up.

"Colby is here?"

Are you asking me? Telling me? What do you think of Colby? What is that tone in your voice? Are you thinking he is a good match for me? Are you wondering why I am having a guy over? Obviously I am just thinking this. But I do wonder.

If I could find a rope ladder long enough from my window to the street, I would get one.

"Hi Colby, I know this is an odd request, but is there any chance you can bypass my lobby completely and climb up to my window? It's only 12 floors. Yea. It's easy. Oh yea, if you get blisters on your hand I'll just ask my doorman for a band-aid"

My doormen are essentially a gateway into my life. There is a system my building has in place, as many do these days. When you have a package at the front desk, UPS, FedEx, a package from a messenger or a creepy stalker, they send you an email that includes which doorman signed for it, what type of item it is, box, bag, envelope and then lists the sender's name and the time and date it arrived.

For example, recorded by Mike McCarthy 7/15 at 1:28 p.m., one box from Shopbop.com.

This is great and sometimes helpful. When I am out and about I get an email on my Blackberry that my package from Shopbop has arrived, it means I now have a top to wear to that party later that evening and I can relax and not think about it for another minute.

Sometimes it's exciting: recorded by Mike McCarthy 12/20 at 5:00 p.m., one box from Amazon.com. Yes! Bear's 800 piece Star Wars Lego space station has arrived. Oh...I mean...Santa came!

Sometimes it's scary: recorded by Mike McCarthy 5/03 at 1:28 p.m., One envelope from the IRS. Yikes, that's never good.

Sometimes it's awkward. Well, not often, but sometimes.

Like a few weeks ago: recorded by Mike McCarthy 10/23 at 3:07 pm, One USPS postcard from Dr. Gyno.

Sheer panic.

What? Why is my postcard from my gyno going to my doorman? Now he can not only see that I went to the gyno but find out my test results from my annual pap smear which are sent in a postcard form. They only send normal results by postcard, but *still*.

I am sitting at work mortified knowing that Mike the doorman knows I had a pap smear and it's normal. I guess that's better than it being abnormal and Mike thinking I had an STD, but...is nothing sacred?

The day I received the aforementioned "postcard" e-mail, I arrived home from work to find a substitute doorman, one I have never seen before. Awkward but better than having to face Mike, who I see every morning.

"Hi, I got an email. I have a postcard here." *A postcard that will make you think of my vagina.*

I'm sorry Ms. Dates, I don't see it. I will call you when I find it.

"No, noooo. don't worry about it. I'll just ask Mike when I see him."

Twenty minutes later my phone rings. It's the doorman I don't know,

"Ms. Dates. I found your important postcard."

Cringe.

"Thanks. I'll get it later."

For now you can just pin it up in the elevator. I don't want anyone to miss the good news.

I picture one man from the floor below who I always see walking his dog to give me a thumbs up in the elevator.

"Hey! Darcy! Nice results on your pap smear."

"Thanks." I would say. *Awkward.*

That evening on the way back from the supermarket I finally picked it up from George, the evening doorman, who tells me it's only at the front desk because a tenant found it in their mailbox. Awesome. That makes 4 more people more than I wanted to know about my healthy vagina. (Well, four people PLUS everyone reading this, which is a lot of people.) At this point it's basically a chain letter about my vagina. There might even be an entry dedicated to it on snopes.com. I have a brief moment where I think it might be a good idea to xerox the postcard, hand it out in my lobby or slip it under each person's door like a menu with a handwritten note on the back, "*Hey, just in case you didn't get a chance to see! It's normal!!*"

I wonder if this may be a topic at the next Board meeting.

"In other tenant news, Darcy had a pap smear and it's normal."

"So noted," the minute keeper would say. One or two people might clap.

Wow. How many times have I used the word vagina in this entry? Vagina, vagina, vagina, vagina, vagina, vagina...A lot!

76

MORE ON MY VAGINA…

November 23, 2010

I am not making this up. It seems like I am because the timing is uncanny, but I *swear* this happened yesterday. Just one week after my post about my pap smear.

My ex-husband called me last night.

"I just got a letter from our health insurance company informing me you had some type of pap smear. Do I, as your ex-husband, really need to follow your vagina that closely?"

"Yes. And I am forcing my readers to follow it that closely as well. Along with my doormen and the rest of my building."

See! I told you there was a chain letter re: my vagina!

77

DEAL BREAKERS

November 29, 2010

Think about the mate you would like. Now write down a list of all the deal breakers that you will not, under any circumstances, be able to look past. The person you end up wanting to go out with again, the one you end up liking, will have most of the things on that deal breaker list. Guaranteed. And you probably won't even care.

My best friend in the world, Nicole, grew up right here in Manhattan with me. Growing up she was the Bonnie to my Clyde. Or vice versa? I'd have to think about it. Whenever we found trouble, we found it together. We were born on the same day, in the same hospital, with the same delivery doctor and she grew up right around the corner from me. Literally. We went to the same schools, we went to camps in the same small Berkshires town, we ended up at the same college, we even married guys with the same name. I went first. She caught the bouquet at my wedding. Sounds creepier than it is. Or is it?

After our kids were born, we would meet up weekly and have a quick beer on a sunday at a secret old irish pub that was our special place. And by special, it meant we would never run into anyone we knew and we loved that. Early on in my divorce I would go to her apartment on the nights Bear was at his dads and she would cook me dinner. Her husband would yell at me for eating dessert before dinner and we would make faces behind his back. We would meet up in Central Park with our kids on the weekends and have them play in the Meadow just as we had years and years ago. Well, we played differently in the Meadow back then...but that's a story for another time. I had always assumed our kids would go to school together. The same one we went to. A couple of years ago she announced she was moving to Brooklyn. I didn't believe her. Until... she actually moved to Brooklyn. I was crushed. It's not that I have anything against Brooklyn. In fact, I love Brooklyn. My parents grew up there. I was raised on Nathan's hot dogs and the Cyclone when visiting my grandparents. But...it's just....well...not the city. Okay! Okay! It technically is. But I am very Manhattan-centric. Forgive me!

"How will I ever see you again?"

"I work in the city, Darcy. Right near your house."

"It's not the same."

And I was right. We didn't see each other as often as we used to. She is more like a pen pal in Sri Lanka now. A pen pal I write to on Blackberry Instant Messenger.

When I visit her in Brooklyn, I drive as though I am taking a road trip to the country.

"Bear, would you like a snack for the drive? Are you sure you used the bathroom?" I pack enough car activities for a road trip to Canada. I am always surprised when it takes me under ten minutes to get to her house with no traffic. There was no point in which I could stop at a look out, or even for gas for that matter. I can't even say for certain my car ever touched a highway.

When she takes a cab home from my apartment I am always in shock.

"You mean a cab to a train? A cab to a donkey caravan? A cab to a hot air balloon maybe?"

"No Darcy. A yellow taxi right to my door."

Just so you know her "door" is to a house. Which is pretty suburban if you ask me.

Every year on our shared birthday we would host get-togethers since we share many of the same friends. This year...she hosted her birthday in Brooklyn. Oh the betrayal! On the invite she wrote, *"Don't worry folks, the beer tastes the same in Brooklyn."*

But does it *really*?

When Leo (see: *Under My Umbrella*) told me he lived in Brooklyn I decided to go on the date anyway. I wanted to shake things up a bit and step outside my box. My box that doesn't involve a bridge or tunnel of any kind.

"This is going to be the guy I end up liking isn't it? The guy that lives all the way in *Brooklyn*," I said to Nicole, as I headed out to meet my date after work before *he* headed back over a bridge or tunnel to get back to his house.

On our first date I decided it actually didn't matter. I liked Leo even if he did live (*cringe*) in another borough. Apparently, not only does a tree grow in Brooklyn, but so does a really great guy. Leo lost his license so he is currently using his passport as an ID. I suspect it's because he actually needs a passport to get home. Maybe I was right this whole time. Maybe you *do* need to go through customs to get to and from Brooklyn.

78

HEY JEALOUSY...

DECEMBER 2, 2010

I HAD BEEN out for the evening with Leo and Robbie had called about 6 times in the space of an hour.

"Just answer it," Leo said with a furrowed brow as he watched the phone ring continuously on the edge of the table.

"No, definitely not." I said as I slipped the phone into my clutch.

At this point my life feels like that of Laura Linney's character in *Love Actually*, where her brother is constantly calling her from the mental institution. Although, unlike Laura, I wasn't letting this "brother" ruin my date like she did, and I certainly wasn't picking up that phone.

On my way home I took the phone out of my bag to see what other calls I may have missed. There were a few more calls from Robbie, coupled with his famous "ANSWER!" texts. I check my messages. He talks into my voicemail as if it's an answering machine from 1987.

"Hello? Hellllloooo. Darcy! I know you hear this. Pick up. Pick up now. Darcy? It's me damn it!" This can go on for several minutes. Could he possibly be the only person left to not understand that voicemail is not on a speaker that echoes through the living room?

Finally, when I am home, finished with my evening I text back.

"What?"

I didn't wait for the response. I turned off my phone, I laid down, shut my eyes and zonked out.

The next day at 10 am my phone rings. It's Robbie.

"Were you texting me for a booty call last night?" he sounds enraged.

"Huh?"

"You texted me pretty late."

"I was asking you what you wanted. You called me about 23 times last night."

"I know it was a booty call, and I have feelings too. You can't just booty text me. I gotta go, I'm in the hospital and this isn't an appropriate conversation."

He hangs up on me. I laugh. Every time he mentions "the hospital" I lose complete faith in medicine.

A couple of hours later I am walking to an appointment when my phone rings again. It's Robbie. I had a good 15 minutes to kill before my meeting so I figured I'd answer.

"So why were you calling me so many times the other night? What on earth could have been the emergency?" I asked.

"I was out with this girl, and I accidentally called her Darcy. She freaked out. I was trying to get you on the phone so you could explain to her that we are just friends."

"Damn. Sorry I missed that."

"What's up with this new guy you are seeing?"

"I like him. He's actually awesome."

"Did you have sex with him yet?"

"No."

"Are you going to?"

"Possibly, one day."

"WHAT? Over my dead body are you having sex with him! Did you see him naked??"

"Seriously Robbie…"

"I can't take this. I feel sick."

"*Whoa*. Can we dial back to the beginning of this conversation? The original purpose of this call, where you were calling me to confirm to a girl you were dating that you and I are just friends?"

"I can't talk to you. I can't hear about you and this other guy."

"You were calling me from a date!"

"It's different. You broke up with me!"

Really? We had a breakup?

"Robbie…"

"You are *naked* with this guy? *Naked*?"

"Robbie, this is really unhealthy."

"I just love you so much, but I screw it up because I have issues."

You think?

"I have abandonment issues. I have a fear of abandonment so I do things to push people away. I also want to fuck everyone I see. It's a problem."

"You realize those are two completely different issues."

"I know."

"Whoever finally settles down with you is going to be a really lucky girl."

I don't think he realized I was being facetious.

"So you are saying you don't want to settle down with me?"

"I need to go. I'm at my appointment."

I say goodbye. Another healthy conversation to write up for Darcy Dates.

TAKE MY EX-WIFE. PLEASE

D ECEMBER 6, 2010

JASON and I sat proudly watching Bear in his weekend sports league while sharing a mini buffet of food we bought from the vending machine. Suddenly, out of nowhere, Jason says something incredibly sweet and heartfelt. A compliment, which for Jason, is rare.

"I was watching *Client 9*, the Elliot Spitzer story. You should totally quit your job and do that. You'd be good at it."

"You're suggesting I become a prostitute?"

"Not a prostitute. An escort."

"That's the same thing."

"No it's not. They are looking for cute girls who you can talk to. You know, have conversations with. They'd like you."

"I see you've really thought this through."

I heart my baby daddy. He's always looking out for me. I wonder if he'd be my pimp. Kind of like a family business. But totally inappropriate and illegal.

80

HIGH STAKES

D ECEMBER 9, 2010

I RECEIVED A TEXT FROM ALEXIS' husband.

"I am setting you up with a really good friend of mine. I am giving him your number."

"What? Who?"

"Just trust me."

"Don't give anyone my number."

"Too late. I already did."

Here is the thing; You have to know Alexis' husband to understand how out of character this is. Not that he wanted to set me up. In fact, I would go as far as saying he has set me up with more people than anyone else I know. He is the Patti Stanger of my life, which if you knew him...is, well...hard to fathom. However...*Alexis* is the finder and the screener. She knows my taste, she knows what I will and won't like. I would allow her to pick out my wedding dress without me even being there. Oh wait, she practically did (see: *Bridal Skeletons In My Closet*.)

I call Alexis.

"Alexis? Who does Stedman want to set me up with?" As I mentioned in an earlier entry, Alexis is my Oprah, and I am her Gayle, which would make her husband, Stedman. Naturally.

"What?"

"I don't know. He said it's his good friend."

"He doesn't have any good friends."

We laugh.

"He won't tell me who it is and he gave him my number."

"UGH. Ignore him. It's probably one of the creepy freaks he plays cards with. Cowboy Johnny or Super Star Dave."

"UGH. Tell him not to give my number to anyone."

I text Stedman.

"Please don't give my number to Carney Dave or Movie Star Henry."

"It's not Carney Dave or Movie Star Henry. It's Cowboy Johnny and Super Star Dave."

Like that makes a difference.

Later that evening Alexis calls me on speaker. Stedman is in the background.

"Who did you give Darcy's number to?" She asked.

"Just trust me. She will love him. He is an actor."

"An actor? I don't date actors."

"This is going to be the best date of your life Darcy," Stedman says, with a determination I rarely see from him.

"You gave her number to Pete?" Alexis sounds repulsed.

"Yea."

"Ugh. Pete is not an actor. He's an out of work loser," she says.

"Wait a second, didn't Pete go to jail?" I asked. Something about his name sounded familiar.

Stedman laughs.

"Yea, didn't he go to jail??" Alexis chimes in.

All three of us laugh. Even though it's not actually funny. Because this is my life.

"Beggars can't be choosers Darcy," he says.

"BEGGARS??" It's terrible but I laugh even harder. So does Stedman. We have a good relationship and I know he is joking, which is the only reason I am laughing and not crying.

"She isn't even looking to date. She is dating Leo." Alexis takes my back like a best friend should.

"Yes. I am dating Leo."

"The Brooklyn guy? Come on Darcy, he is the best catch!"

Something about this suddenly rings as fishy. Why did Stedman, a man of few to no words, have such a desperate interest in me taking a date with his creepy loser friend.

"Holy shit. Did you bet me in a poker match? Oh. My. Gd. Is that what this is about?" I asked with genuine concern.

"No."

"Did you bet Darcy in a poker match?? Why are you pushing this so hard?" Alexis knows I may be on to something.

"Yeah. Something's not right here. Don't give anyone my number and I know you bet me! You gambled me away in your friggin' poker match. To an actor. An out of work actor. Who may or may not have gone to jail. Nice."

At the risk of sounding like a feminist, maybe I should have a say in these things? I don't know…maybe clear that with me first? Apparently single people are like cattle or handicrafts to married people. Fair trade goods of some kind.

The following day I receive I text from Stedman:

"Don't worry. He isn't calling you. I told him I found out you had herpes."

"What?? HERPES!? I don't have *herpes!!!!!!*??"

"I know, but I needed an excuse. It would have been rude for me to just tell him you aren't interested."

Is this really my life? How can I be sure? Is there an App I can download somewhere to check whether or not this is actually happening?

81

SONGS ABOUT DARCY

D ECEMBER 13, 2010

It was the summer of 1990. The summer that Bobby Banks was my boyfriend. Well, it was only for a couple of weeks between the end of school up until the day I left for camp. As I stood in front of my building saying goodbye for the summer, he handed me a lucite case. Inside was a cassette tape.

"I made you a mix," he said, as he handed me the tiny box.

He neatly wrote every song on each tiny line on the paper insert. In bold script across the top it said: *Miss You Mix*.

I popped the tape in my Walkman the second my camp bus pulled away from the curb and for the next few hours listened to it over and over again on my way to the Berkshires.

I will never ever forget Bobby Banks, I thought as I kept my finger on the rewind button, listening to each song 26 times. Until…I arrived at camp and reunited with Matt Lucas.

Next thing I knew, I was making a mix tape for Matt Lucas at the end of the summer, decorating his insert with hearts and stars and rainbows, and whatever else I could manage to draw, which wasn't much. It was the perfect balance of Richard Marx, Bryan Adams, Peter Cetera, and Depeche Mode, with a touch of Van Morrison. I dubbed a copy for myself and cried the entire way back to New York City, listening to it over and over again. I glanced down at the scratched plastic window on the Walkman which revealed the title on a sticker that was crookedly placed on the tape: *Summer Of 1990*.

I will never ever forget Matt Lucas, I swore to myself. I would listen to the tape every night before I went to sleep. Every night for *at least* three weeks.

Leo and I had been dating for one month, one week and three days. This weekend was our tenth date. If you count breakfast, it may have been our fourteenth. Not that I am counting.

On our last date Leo sat next to me and showed me his IPod.

"I have something for you. I made you a playlist."

"Really?"

"It only has 22 songs. But it's perfect. It's songs we listen to together and songs that just remind me of you. I'd like to make it 100 songs."

I think I stopped breathing for a second. In a good way. Leo had basically made me a mixtape. Which, as you know, you only do if you *really* like someone. I swooned.

He even named it, "Songs About Darcy," a play on the Maroon 5 album *Songs About Jane*, which he gave me as well in the good old-fashioned form of a CD.

"The girl on the album cover kind of looks like you," he said as I ripped it from the wrapping paper, "Ignore the amateur wrapping job. It's the best I could do."

It could have been wrapped in garbage for all I cared, all I knew was that every hair on my body was standing on end.

How awesome is Leo. I thought to myself.

My old friend Ricky said to me over lunch the other day, "Of all times Darcy, how can you get a boyfriend now? No one is going to want to read about a mom in a relationship."

"True," I said.

But they will want to read about the mix he made me. And I bet I am right.

82

MY MOM THE STALKER

December 20, 2010

The other day my mother made a startling confession.

"A while ago I tried to get you a date with this doctor I saw on TV."

"Huh?"

"I was watching that show I like in the morning, that medical show. There was this adorable doctor on there who was 41 and he was perfect for you, so I googled him and tried to find him so I could set you up."

"I'm sorry?"

She laughed, but only a little. She clearly thought this was a good idea.

"Are you nuts?"

"Why?"

"You have to ask?"

"Well I thought it was a good idea. At the time."

"Sure. If you are Robert John Bardo."

"Who is that?"

"Forget it. It's the stalker who stalked Rebecca Schaeffer from *My Sister Sam*. In addition to stalking, which by the way is illegal, you have become *that* mom. That Jewish mom who pushes her daughter on lawyers and doctors. What the hell!?"

"I know. I don't know what came over me."

"I know what came over you. Craziness."

"I googled him to see if he was married. I also found out where he lived."

"You found out his *address*?"

"Well, he lives in San Diego, California. I could have probably found out his address though if I wanted to."

"WHAT? Actually, don't tell me anymore. Make this story stop. Right now. I would like to know even less of this story than I already do. I feel like hearing this makes me an accomplice of some kind."

I'LL HAVE WHAT HE'S HAVING

December 23, 2010

My first fix up after my divorce was with a man named Drew. Drew was the best friend of my best friend's husband. Less complicated than it sounds. Drew was a big shot in the music industry and was used to dating women 10 years younger than me, which was odd since Drew was 20 years older than I was. This made me uncomfortable.

"He is young for 50," they would say. Whatever that means. In my very early 30's I felt 50 was 100.

I agreed to meet Drew, and he agreed to meet me, even though I was old.

I met Drew at his restaurant of choice. They were right. While he was 50, he had a boyish look with his Adidas sneakers and white t-shirt. We approached the hostess to get a table and they said they couldn't seat us.

"We are swamped tonight," the hostess said.

For as many times I had to speak to Drew's assistant before the date, I was surprised Drew didn't have a reservation.

"My assistant will call you and tell you where to meet me," "My assistant will arrange to have you picked up," "My assistant will be hiding in a dark alley stalking you all day."

In retrospect, I knew more about his assistant than I ever knew about Drew.

"I usually only eat places where they know me," he said, after we got shut down for a table.

I decide Drew is a bit eccentric and quite possibly egocentric. Being that we were in Columbus Circle there weren't very many choices.

"Let's go to *Jean Georges*," he said.

We ducked into *Jean Georges* as though it were McDonald's and asked if they had a table. They sized up my date.

"You can't come in here dressed like that sir. You need a jacket."

They offered to "lend" him one. Poor guy, I thought, though he wasn't poor at all, in fact, quite the contrary, so I didn't feel that bad for him.

Drew and I sat down in the stuffy fancy restaurant as though we had been married for years and we were there to celebrate a platinum anniversary. I looked at Drew with his borrowed clothes. Drew was used to being one of the most fashionable guys in the room. Now he sat there awkwardly in an ill-fitting borrowed coat.

Fat guy in a little coat, I chanted in my head.

Though Drew wasn't fat. In fact, Drew was handsome...for an older man.

So this is what it was like dating an older man, I thought to myself. I was that younger girl dating an older man. Huh. I was the cliché. Although Drew wasn't known as an older man. Drew, in fact, had been placed on New York City's most eligible bachelor list by many top publications. It was just me and one of New York City's most eligible bachelors, out to dinner, borrowed blazer and all.

As Drew and I spoke I found it refreshing. He was smart. Raised his kids on his own. He had very nice eyelashes. So long and dark, I thought. I looked a little closer and began to examine his face. Was Drew wearing makeup? Possibly mascara? I think he was. Drew was wearing *manscara*! I blinked rapidly trying to clear my vision. I think there was foundation too!

I quickly texted Alexis: "Does Drew wear make-up???"

"It's possible. Some people think that."

WHAT???

"They think that because he *does*." I shot back.

After dinner we hopped in Drew's car. He told me he would have the driver drop him off at home first and then the driver would take me to my house. Breaking news: chivalry IS dead. I'm not so much a rules and manners girl, but for a guy that just asked me out on a second date, was he really letting ME drop HIM off, in HIS car, with HIS driver? I found it funny that he couldn't ride in the car the extra ten blocks out of his way to be chivalrous.

After a few more dates, I decided Drew was used to having the entire world revolve around him. Drew and I would go to his favorite restaurant. I am not complaining because it's one of my favorites as well. Drew would order for us and never ask me input of what I wanted. The waiter would come by.

"Can I take this for you?" he would ask.

"Ok" Drew would say, without asking me if i was finished, and the waiter would basically pull the fork right out of my mouth. At one point the bus boy and I wrestled with each other over my salad plate.

"DREW SAID IT WAS OKAY!" he hissed.

As I had guessed earlier, Drew was in fact, a bit eccentric.

"I don't use public bathrooms," he had announced one night at dinner.

I laughed.

"No, I really don't," he continued, "the idea is so disgusting to me, I just can't do it."

He was serious.

"What if you have to go to the bathroom?" I ask.

"I just don't."

Huh. Whatever works, for your bladder, which I am surprised

hasn't exploded into 4 million pieces. I suddenly had to use the bathroom and used the one in the restaurant.

That Darcy, such a plebeian, I pictured him to be thinking.

I really liked Drew. He was a warm man who clearly loved his kids and was practically raising them on his own. I respected that. You could tell he was a good friend to those he cared about. He was smart and often self-deprecating, which I found to be endearing. But when push came to shove, and after Drew and I had been on a few dates, I couldn't do it. I couldn't bring myself to go home with Drew. In the end, I felt like Drew was too old for me.

For what it's worth, I ran into Drew this past summer. He has been dating a 40-year-old very seriously for a long time and he looked very hot. I guess in the time since I had seen Drew last we had both matured and evolved as people. I am a big believer that timing is everything and for Drew and I we met at the wrong time.

84

AULD LANG SYNE

December 31, 2010

Should auld acquaintance be forgot and never brought to mind? Should auld acquaintance be forgot, and auld lang syne?

Without old acquaintances, I would not be who I am today. Without *GayDate, Andre, Chef Hottie, Robbie* and all of the other crazies I have met along the way, I would not be Darcy Dates. So as the clock strikes midnight, bringing us into a brand New Year I will not forget you. I will remember you fondly and thank you for making this all possible.

I did hear from a bunch of old suitors as the New Year approached. Maybe they figured as I jumped into the new year I would bang my head on the ceiling so hard I would forget why I didn't want to date them in 2010? I won't forget. While I don't know what this new year brings, I do know this: If I didn't want to date you in 2010, I won't want to date you in 2011.

2010 was actually a great year full of some wonderful surprises, but I know 2011 will be even better. Wishing you all peace, love and happiness in the New Year.

With Love,
Darcy

85

WHAT'S IN A NAME?

JANUARY 3, 2011

When I was out with Leo the other night we ran into some old friends of his.

"This is Darcy. My girlfriend Darcy," he said, without skipping a beat.

Wow. Did he introduce me as his girlfriend? Wow. Okay. Sure. *Wow.* Major.

After a quick chat his friends walked away.

"Girlfriend?" I asked playfully.

"I didn't know if you heard that," he smiled.

"I did. I liked it." We locked eyes and I smiled back.

"*Who needs titles?*" I used to say. An old mantra I developed years ago while waiting on the corner of fear and disinterest.

Well, apparently this is a title I want. Who knew?

86

WISHFUL WAXING

January 5, 2011

Guys, I bet you don't know this...but girls do something called wishful waxing. It's similar to the "If you build it, he will come" philosophy from the movie, *Field of Dreams*, but different.

87

ROBBIE ON HOUSEKEEPING

JANUARY 11, 2011

THE OTHER DAY Robbie e-mailed me a picture he had taken of himself with his new phone. Luckily, this time, the picture was not of his penis.

As the image loads I notice something peculiar. Just then the phone rings. It's him.

"Did you dye the front of your hair?" I ask.

"No."

"Yes. I'm looking at the picture. Did you highlight it?"

"No. Why? It looks lighter?"

"Yes."

"UGH. I have been bleaching my teeth and I think it gets in the front of my hair."

Crickets. How would that possibly happen? Unless he does it standing on his head while drooling down the front of his face. *Yuck.*

"Darcy, I have this new ironing technique I learned. You soak your shirts, and then you hang them in your shower until they dry. It's amazing."

"You know that isn't ironing right?"

"It is. They end up not having any wrinkles."

Sure. If you are blind. And you like to wear hard shirts that have turned into shrinky dinks.

"Darcy, all I can think about is you and your boyfriend. I just keep thinking about you having sex with him."

"I don't think I want you thinking that. It feels invasive."

"I can't control myself."

"Can you prescribe yourself some anti-anxiety meds for that?" I shudder at the idea of Robbie being able to write prescriptions.

"Please be my girlfriend. Please."

"Robbie, that ship has sailed. Or sunk. At this point it may even be some type of diving attraction complete with barnacles."

"That's rude Darcy. How can you say that to someone who loves you as much as I do."

"The real question is how am I still in your calling rotation?"

"I have a shortcut for you now."

"What does that mean? Is there a slide you can use to fall directly through my ceiling? If so I need to know. Right now."

He laughs.

"You're a moron. My new phone has this thing, where you can make someone a shortcut. You are on my top five speed dial list."

"What does that mean?"

"I can call you quicker."

"Is that even possible? How did I get on that list exactly?"

"Cause you are my angel, and I call you the most out of anyone."

"Who else is on that list?"

"You, my mom, my brother, my best friend and my boss."

"That is a pretty important list for me to be on. Do you think that's appropriate?"

"Well, I love talking to you. You get my serotonin flowing."

"Are you dating people? Like, when you aren't stalking me?"

"Yea, but you are the mother of all girls, and I don't mean that

literally, because you are a mother, I mean it as a figure of speech because-"
"I get it."
"Can I come over?"
"NO!"
"Sunday is our night!"
"Our night? We don't have a *night*."
"Fine."

88

CROSSING THE LINES

January 18, 2011

After dropping Bear off at school the other day, I arrived home to quickly slip into my most comfortable clothing, not to be confused with *Pajama Jeans*, for a morning of ass kicking at a local spin class. My phone rings. It's a private number. I glance at the clock. Who on earth could be calling me at 8:34 am? From a private number?

"Hello?"

"Hello?" It's a guy's voice. I assumed it was Leo. I wasn't that awake yet. I am super slow in the morning.

"Hey." I change to my sweet voice. The sickeningly sweet phone voice that makes my friends gag.

"Hi. Is it too early?"

"No! Of course not. I have already been to school and back. Just getting ready to get my ass kicked at spin."

"I was going to leave you a message. I didn't think you'd pick up."

I suddenly realized. This *isn't* Leo. Who was I talking to?

"I'm sorry, who is this?" I ask.

"It's Jeff."

"Oh!!! Jeff! Hi! I thought you were someone else."

Okay. Got it now. I work with Jeff, or should I say, we recently started working together last week. I don't know him that well. I wait to hear what it is that Jeff wanted, or needed at 8:30 am on a Tuesday.

"Oh. Okay." He sounded disappointed. Did I offend him?

"So, what's up?" I ask. Still unsure of the purpose of this call. It had a very slow pace for a work call.

"I was going to leave you a message. I didn't think you'd pick up. So I am just going to tell you."

"Oh. Okay." Seriously? I never realized how socially awkward Jeff was.

""Do you want the PG version or the X-rated version?"

Crickets.

I sat with my mouth agape for a good 30 seconds before I could actually find the words to speak.

"I'm sorry?"

"Do you want the PG version or the X-rated version?"

Did Jeff just repeat the exact same sentence? Does Jeff not realize our entire work relationship just got uncomfortable. What is wrong with people?

I sat silently.

"Hello?" Jeff asked. Unaware of why I might be trying to disappear into thin air.

"Hi."

"Which one do you want?"

I couldn't believe this. I didn't expect this from Jeff. He seemed so professional!

"I'm sorry. Who did you say this was?" I had to double-check.

Silence.

Jeff asks awkwardly, "Wait, is this? Who is this? Oh my god. I think I have the wrong number."

I realize it is not Jeff from work. Just a horrible coincidence.

"Ohhhhhhh! I thought you were a Jeff I worked with."

"I am so embarrassed. I have the wrong number. Who is this?"

"It's not your girlfriend."

We said our goodbyes as though we were old friends at this point. I don't know who that Jeff was, but I do know he was having phone sex that particular Tuesday morning. Luckily, it wasn't going to be with me.

89

NIGHTMARE ON BOYFRIEND STREET

JANUARY 21, 2011

I CAN'T SLEEP. I have been having nightmares. Bad ones. About Leo. It of course has nothing to do with Leo and everything to do with the fact that I have a boyfriend. There. I said it. Out loud.

"Hi, my name is Darcy. And I have a boyfriend."

Hi Darcy.

It makes me sound like I am 14 years old doesn't it? I don't even recognize myself. Here is the thing: my life for the past few years has been very compartmentalized. Bear is the main compartment. Then there is work. There are friends. There have been dates or people I was seeing. They don't really overlap with friends. I keep them separate. But, I actually want my friends to meet Leo. So, I guess, the compartment spilleth over.

But the nightmares...are bad. They are heart stopping, wake up in the middle of the night, try to talk yourself awake so you get the dream out of your head completely, run into the other room to make sure Bear is safe and sound, lock the front door and consider deleting Leo from my phone bad. They are bad. Bad.

I called Alexis the morning after one particularly bad one.

"I had another Nightmare about Leo. it was so scary I don't even think I want to speak to him today."

"You're crazy. Gotta go."

"Okay."

I guess she was right. It is kind of crazy to hold a dream against someone. The problem is, it's not about Leo. It's about the *idea* of Leo.

The other night when Leo was sleeping next to me I examined his face looking for staples or a seam, maybe a zipper up his back so at any minute he could rip his face off and become a scary beast of some kind. But I found nothing. Only an ice hockey scar under his chin, which by the way, I think is super cute. It's one of my favorite things about his face.

The problem is, the idea of a boyfriend just feels unfamiliar. It makes me feel vulnerable and out of control. I protect myself like a pit bull protects other pit bulls from Michael Vick. But with Leo, all that protection goes right out the window. I do stupid things like download special ringtones for him. And he has one for me. I might as well be walking around with a T-mobile sidekick in a mall in middle america somewhere, smacking my gum and wearing sweatpants with the word "Pink" across my ass.

Over Christmas, I went to an island with Bear and my family. Leo and I downloaded Skype onto our respective computers so we could have some face time while I was away (see: a few lines up where I describe myself as a 14-year-old with a T-Mobile sidekick phone). But then I think about it, and think about all the things that can go terribly wrong. I think about all the *what ifs*. What if Leo is all wrong for me? What if I start wearing Pajama Jeans? What if I stop shaving my legs and I never get to wear a sequined mini again? What if I become frumpy and start to only wear flats? What if one day I can't stand the way he chews? What if we lived together and he wanted a Raymour and Flanigan bedroom set and a black leather sectional?

What if I want to start collecting figurines and start needlepointing and drinking tea? What if I start liking crafts? What if we stopped having sex and started using words like companion and life partner? What if, what if, what if...what if???! But then I have to remind myself that *what if's* can also be good sometimes. Right?

90

REAL PHONE CALLS FROM REAL MEN

January 24, 2011

A guy friend called me up the other day. He sounded totally distressed.

"I need to talk to you. I need advice. (*Insert dramatic sigh here*). I was talking to this girl I have gone on three dates with and I really like her. But as I was talking to her, I accidentally hit a button on my computer and porn started playing. Really loud. She got upset and said she would text me later and that she doesn't really know what to say. What should I do? Did I do anything wrong?"

Huh. I'm stumped. What would Ron Jeremy do?

Paging Ron Jeremy, paging Ron Jeremy. We have a question for you on the white courtesy phone.

A RING ON IT

JANUARY 27, 2011

I WAS MEETING a friend for dinner the other night. While waiting for her, I grabbed a seat at the bar. I was sitting next to a couple who appeared to be on a first date. I couldn't help but eavesdrop, as I love a good dating story. The following is the conversation I overheard:

"Is your divorce finalized yet?" The man asked timidly.

"No. It's still in the courts. I still wear my wedding ring. We made a pact to not take them off until it was all finished."

She held up her left hand to display her ring finger, replete with both engagement ring and wedding band.

Awk-ward. I can only imagine how he felt. Probably a sense of relief that he wouldn't have to put a ring on it. You know, since she already had one on.

I have decided I prefer to be on other people's first dates rather than my own.

A VISIT FROM ROBBIE

February 3, 2011

Robbie found Leo. On Facebook. He sent him a friend request, and challenged him to a duel. I wish I was kidding, but sadly, I am not. A *duel*. I never realized Robbie's close resemblance to *Dwight Schrute*. He also wrote "Stare into the face of your competition." But who is keeping tabs? After that I had to unfriend Robbie. He was now disrupting my relationship and bothering Leo and it had to stop.

A day after the aforementioned duel invitation, I was driving with my mother and my cell phone rang. It was Robbie. In true Robbie fashion he called about 6 times. Between the ringing, and the GPS lady, my nerves were wearing thin. I asked my mother to answer it (she doesn't let me use the phone in the car. See: *Driving With My Mom*). I asked her to talk to him and to tell him to please leave me alone.

She picks up the phone and they quickly exchange pleasantries like they have known each other for years. She has sat through many awkward phone calls from Robbie on speakerphone in the car.

"Robbie, I am so sorry, but Darcy has a boyfriend now and you have to respect that."

"With all due respect Ellen, Darcy is fair game and I will fight for your daughter."

"I understand what you are saying, but maybe it's time you give her some space Robbie."

"No. I love your daughter, and I am never going to give up. It's game on!" he hung up.

"What does 'game on' mean?" my mother asked. I just shook my head. As far as I was concerned, there were no words.

A few weeks, a few hundred phone calls and a few hundred texts later, I am home and I receive yet another text from Robbie.

"I am coming to your house."

"Don't you dare. I will not let you upstairs," I replied.

I had thought that was the end of it.

Less than an hour later I get a call from my doorman.

"Robbie is here?"

"He cannot come upstairs under any circumstances."

"Okay." my doorman says, and hangs up.

I am glad he is now privy to this unfolding unhealthy mini-drama.

My cell phone rings. It's Robbie. His voice is echoing, which means he is now causing a scene in my lobby.

"How can you not let me up! I came all the way here!"

"I told you NOT to."

"Darcy, this is bullshit! I have to talk to you. I have to tell you something!!!"

"Tell me over the phone then."

"I want to tell you in person."

"Why? So you can chop me up into little pieces and keep me in your freezer."

"Real nice Darcy. Come on! Let me up!"

The screaming was escalating. I had no choice but to go downstairs to escort him out of my lobby.

I came downstairs and he is smiling like this is a normal meeting. Like he wasn't stalking me or causing a scene with my doorman. If the police had him in cuffs he may not have even noticed.

"Oh Darcy you look so cute. Come here. Give me a hug."

"Leave. Right now."

I looked at Robbie. While he was adorable (in a crazy, restraining order kind of way,) I suddenly remembered how young he was. It was like the scene in the movie *Big*, where his clothes get bigger and bigger as he walks away from her car and she realizes the whole time, he was just a little boy.

"I'm sorry. You have to go. I have a boyfriend. We tried it. It didn't work Robbie. It's time to move on."

"I love you Darcy. I want to spend the rest of my life with you."

"You don't know me Robbie."

"I have known you for almost a year."

"You mean, you have *stalked* me for almost a year. That doesn't count. Look it up! On Wikipedia. Stalking does not a relationship make."

He laughed.

"Can we just go to couples counseling together? Just once. Try it."

This is sick, but I immediately thought what a good blog entry that would make. I picture the shrink to be sitting on the couch,

"So, what is the biggest issue in your relationship?" she would ask.

"I don't know. Maybe that we aren't actually in a relationship?" I would say. Robbie would be staring at himself in the mirror.

"Good night Robbie. I am going."

"Please, just grab coffee with me on the corner."

"Goodnight."

I turned and walked back into my building. I avoided looking my doorman in the eye. Now, not only did my doorman know I had a healthy vagina (see: *Don't Ask, Don't Tell*), but he knew I had terrible taste in men.

ADVICE FROM MY DOORMAN

FEBRUARY 7, 2011

YOU KNOW how I have discussed the awkward, often dysfunctional relationship I have with my doormen. Where I picture them to judge me silently and keep tabs on my personal life. Well, this just in: They actually *do*.

One day after the unannounced visit from Robbie, I walked into my building after a long exhausting day of work. The same doorman who had watched the Robbie drama unfold, was on duty and made eye contact with me as I walked through the front doors. He shook his head.

"Is that guy nuts?" he asked.

"Pretty much."

"He came in and asked for you, and I got his name wrong. I asked if his name was Robert. He started yelling 'Robbie, Robbie!' The way he was talking to me started to piss me off. I was so happy when you said he couldn't come upstairs and I got to kick him out of the building."

"Yeah. You know, we dated nearly a year ago, for a minute and he hasn't left me alone since."

I realize I was probably giving too much information.

"Yeah, I remember him."

"Yeah."

Awesome that he remembers the chronology of the men I have dated. That's not uncomfortable.

"You know who I liked the best? That really tall guy. With the son."

"Ah. Colby. (See: Yankees Vs. Red Sox) Yeah, that was a few years ago."

"Yeah. I liked him the best. He was really cool."

Is this appropriate? I wonder. Is this what other people talk to their doormen about? Or only me? Probably only me.

"I thought you were gonna get married to him," he tosses in quickly.

"Really?" I fake smiled through my teeth and wanted to die. I wondered if there was some dry cleaning behind his desk. I am pretty sure I could suffocate myself in the plastic.

Beat.

"The other one was cool. The tall guy that you dated after Colby. The guy with the glasses. He was cool. He was nice."

Huh. Well this was unwelcome awkward advice. I felt like I was in the movie, *A Christmas Carol,* only it was *The Boyfriend Carol,* where my doorman was the ghost of boyfriends past, taking me on an unsolicited journey back in time. I may or may not have heard metal chains dragging behind his ankles. If I had to go through this, the least he could do was bring me to my future for a bit so I can see how things end up.

"Am I dating anyone in 12 years?"

"Excuse me?" he asked.

"Nothing." It was worth a try.

So you know when you ask yourself, is my doorman paying attention to my private life? Is my doorman judging me? Judging my actions? Now you know. The answer is yes.

94

SURVEY SAYS...

F EBRUARY 22, 2011

A FEW YEARS EARLIER...

Once upon a time I walked into a bar on the Upper West Side to meet one of my J-day-tay dates. I was looking forward to this date with this very tall, very handsome stranger. He was from Kentucky and Jewish. The *chupacabra* as Patti Stanger would say. Over the phone he had a southern twang of some kind. Or so I thought. More on that twang later.

As I made my way through the bar I saw him sitting at a table, which was awkwardly close to the table next to him.

These two girls are going to love listening to our first date unfold, I thought, as I approached. But he was handsome. Five star handsome. He looked just like his pictures, which is not always common. We were off to a good start.

"Hi! Andy? Darcy." I extended my hand.

"Well hello Darcy!" he said as he pulled me in for a hug.

Ho. Ly. He was the gayest man I ever met. Well, maybe not as gay as the date who took me to the Indigo Girls concert and held my hand and wanted to skip. I turned green. That twang wasn't just southern, it was downright RuPaul.

I glanced at the two girls at the next table who glanced back at me. There was something in their look, an awkward disbelief, that I knew I was not alone in thinking this.

I dreaded grabbing the seat across from him at the table and cursed myself for having to play along with his charade. I always say, I love a gay man, but if you want to play for my team, you have to wear my uniform. And my uniform doesn't involve a beard of any kind.

I sat across from Andy, who might as well have been Andy Cohen on Bravo, who I live for, but don't want to date for obvious reasons. My eyes glazed over and I went into hibernation mode. There may or may not have been a screen saver slowly crawling across my face.

"Darcy, why don't I go grab us some beers?"

"Okay," I smiled through my teeth, cursing him for putting me through this.

As soon as he got up I turned to the girls at the next table who had their eyes fixated on us the entire time.

"Hi girls, level with me. Is my date gay?"

"Oh my g-d yes!!!! When we got here we thought he was cute, but then spoke to him and assumed he was gay. Then you showed up. We were wondering if you knew you had a gay boyfriend."

You know that girl who people look at and think, *"doesn't she know her date is gay?"* Okay. Got it. I'm her. Good times.

"This is our first date. I met him on *JDate*," I confided in these complete strangers.

"That is why I won't try internet dating. I'd rather be alone forever," one of the girls said as she looked at me with accusing eyes. She might as well have thrown a dart at me, not that it mattered much at this point. Who am I to judge? I was sitting there waiting for my gay date to return with my draft beer.

"Oh! Here he comes," she said in a hushed tone and left me alone to role-play two straight people out on a date on a Saturday night. I wondered if someone was handing out Playbills.

I watched him walk towards me. So hot. *The boys must love him*, I thought.

I decided to not fake it. I went for it.

"I'm sorry. I just can't. Are you...are you gay?"

"What?" he laughed, but didn't immediately say no.

"I mean, are you?"

"I need to tell my friends that right away," he said. He took out his phone, and started typing furiously. He showed it to me, a text that read:

"My date thinks I am gay."

A few moments later his phone buzzes.

"Aren't you?" his friend wrote back.

And suddenly the voice of Richard Dawson echoed through my head. *Survey says...you're gay.*

95

LESSONS FROM BOYS NIGHT

February 28, 2011

The other night I accepted an impromptu invite to boys night. What better way to gain insight into the inner workings of the male mind than to become one of them, if only for a couple of hours.

I learned of the great lengths one guy would go to in order to NOT have a lady friend spend the night. We will call him Pete Daniels. According to Pete, to prevent a lady caller from spending the night he does the following:

1) Hides the toilet paper. After all, a woman can't possibly be comfortable with no toilet paper.

2) Removes the additional pillows from the bed. Won't she get the hint she is not welcome for an overnight stay if she doesn't have her own pillow?

3) Keeps only a twin blanket on a queen size bed. Sorry, no room for you under the covers.

Pete, you are adorable. However ladies, my advice is to *not* go home with Pete Daniels anytime soon. If you must, remember to bring your own sleeping bag. Oh! And toilet paper too, of course.

96

DODGING BULLETS

MARCH 15, 2011

It's happened to all of us. We meet someone, we like them, it doesn't work out how we had hoped. You start to wonder…was it me? Did I do something? Was there someone else? "You deserve better," they'd say, but you don't think they really meant it. The thing is, sometimes they might. And you may never know. Or one day, you may find out, like I did, that they weren't lying.

A little over a year ago I met Vince. He was smokin' hot in a dark, brooding, sexy, sweaty drunk mess with a hint of genius type way. He worked in a field that required the brains of a rocket scientist. He was a few years younger than I was, and living in New York City temporarily for work. Relocated here for only two years, before he was to return home. Home being halfway across the country. On an early date, possibly our first, I told him I didn't think it could ever work with us. I lived here, where I had to remain until Bear was 18, a custody agreement I had with Jason, and there was zero chance I would be moving. From that moment on, Vince must have decided I was nothing more than a sexual conquest of some kind. We had chemistry, hot chemistry, which is *all* we had, and I knew it's all Vince wanted. I asked what it was Vince was after and he was honest. Sex. He even went as far as telling me he didn't want to date anyone. It was much more fun to hook up with different girls all the time. I figured it really meant he wasn't interested in dating *me*. I wasn't interested in casual sex. While it may be fun, it's a little too empty for me, and I don't think I could handle the morning after. He would try, and I refused to cave, so we parted ways. Which of course led to a penis text, his last ditch effort at one more shot.

Eventually, I stopped entertaining Vince's inquiries for any type of get together. Vince and I remained Facebook friends, but never spoke. Over time Vince seemed to find a girlfriend. A serious one. His profile picture was of the two of them, as was hers. He was now listed as being in a relationship, and they were constantly "checking in" together at his house. My Facebook newsfeed was filled with his status updates and her replies. This had been going on for nearly a year. They seemed to be progressing well. According to his status updates, she was moving back home with him. They seemed happy and very much in love from what I could gather. Good for Vince. He was all grown up.

Last week, mid-day I received a text from Vince.

"Hey."

I couldn't imagine what he wanted.

"Hey," I wrote back.

As far as I was concerned we had nothing to talk about.

He continued to ask me how things have been, chit-chat as though we were old friends and then asked the unthinkable.

"We should get together."

I was confused and bewildered. *Get together? Are you going to bring your live-in girlfriend? The one who checked in at your apartment an hour ago, according to my Facebook newsfeed.*

"Why?" I wrote.

I really didn't know why he would want that. Yes, at times I can be that naive, or maybe it's more hopeful of humanity.

"Because we always had a lot of fun."

"That was a long time ago," I replied.

"That type of thing never changes," he said.

Yep, he was officially crossing the line.

"Things are different now. You have a girlfriend, and I have a boyfriend," I said.

"Then we have to be extra careful," he wrote.

Crickets.

Are you KIDDING me?

"Sorry, you have the wrong girl," I responded quickly.

"I was always disappointed we never fucked," he said, as though he was saying he was disappointed he never ate in a neighborhood restaurant before it closed.

I had nothing to say back really. My jaw was on the floor. I was silent. My phone buzzed yet again.

"Want to see what you do to me?"

I knew what was coming. Another picture of his penis.

"No. Show your girlfriend."

"She already knows."

"What? What I do to you?"

"Hahahaha," he responded.

Ugh. He was more of a scumbag than I could have even imagined.

I sat in silence, shocked and saddened for his girlfriend. But then, stuck in my own self-absorption I realized I was having a once in a lifetime opportunity. I was able to literally look into what my future would have been like had I ended up dating this guy. I was starring in my very own episode of *Quantum Leap*. I would have been posting pictures of us hugging, status updates about how much I loved him, making plans to drop my life here and move with him cross-country and BAM, he would be texting one of his Facebook friends for a booty call and I would have *zero* idea. So I dodged a bullet. I didn't even mean to, but I did. Next time someone tells you that you deserve more, or that they can't give you what you want, listen to them. Do not try to jam a square peg into a round a hole, or your fat ass into skinny jeans, in other words; don't try to force something that just isn't right. Like I have said before, my favorite quote is, "When someone tells you who they really are, believe them the first time."

97

MOVING AND SHAKING

APRIL 13, 2011

I MOVED. Moving sucks. Not that I actually moved. That doesn't suck. I am excited about that. It's the *act* of moving that is terrible. The boxes, the manual labor, the not knowing which box your stuff is in, the piles of stuff that seem to line the hallways of your otherwise very neat apartment. In general I don't like to keep a lot of stuff around. I am not a piles person, I am not a hoarder type person what-so-ever. But during the move, I certainly looked like one. You never actually know how much stuff you have until you start to pull it all out of your closets at once. During the move, I enlisted the help of my mother to help me pack. She has a knack for keeping me focused, making things look neater, and actually getting things done, unlike myself.

A few days ago we were packing up my bedroom. I am not sure what happened but my mother, the otherwise focused packer, saw this as an opportunity for an extreme snoop-athon extravaganza. Not that my mom is not usually nosey, but she practically forgot her main purpose and got sidetracked by every small drawer and secret compartment in my room.

"Can't you go for big items like blankets and pillows? Why are you opening small zippered compartments in my handbag??" I asked.

She would come at me as though everything was suspect and had a slightly dirty, deviant, double use. Sure, some of the items in my room are private, who doesn't have some of those items buried deep in their sock drawer? But all in all, my drawers are the drawers of an otherwise healthy woman in her thirties.

"Darcy, what do you want to do with these?" she said, extending a pair of bunny ears on the edge of her finger as if I used them to play Hugh Hefner's mansion from time to time.

"Mom, I wore those trick-or-treating with Bear a few years in a row."

"Oh," she said, tossing them to the side with little expression, as though she didn't really believe me. She might have even covered herself in *Purell* after touching them.

I don't even know how she found those. They were literally thrown in the bottom of the closet, possibly stuffed into an old gym tote or random shopping bag in the back most desolate corner of my closet.

Then she got to the good stuff. A pack of condoms.

"What do you want to do with these?" she asked. Holding them up and pretending to look away as if she didn't really care.

"I don't know mom. Maybe blow them up like balloons and have a parade down Fifth Avenue. Did you have something better in mind?"

Why couldn't she look at them, and then look past them and grab something else, like a blazer or a pair of high heels. Why question me about something she knows the use for, and knows I do not care to discuss with her. Nor does she want to discuss it with me. She looked irritated.

I felt bad, but I couldn't control myself.

"Oh wait, I know! Maybe I will just put them on a penis. A really big one," I said.

"Nice," she sighed as though she had failed miserably.

"Well, if you aren't going to like the answer, don't ask the question."

At one point she came out of my closet with a pack of cigarettes. Left over from 10, if not 100 years ago from a night out with some girlfriends where the evidence of an unhealthy evening was left on my coffee table. Reverting back to my high school days, I had hidden the box of Parliaments so deep in my closet as to never be found again. Except, of course, by my mother. I am pretty sure to access those you needed to do some secret knock on the floor board, which opened up to a combination lock, which opened up to a burly bouncer, who only hands them over if you know the secret handshake. She came strolling out of my closet holding the bag at arm's length, opened to reveal the evidence. A box of cigarettes so stale, they could probably make it into the Smithsonian.

"Darcy, UGH! What do you want to do with *these*???"

"Oh! Definitely keep them," I plead. Just cause.

"That's disgusting," she said as she stomped back to the closet in search of the next scandalous item.

"You know mom, there are regular things you can pull out of my closet. Sweaters, pants...rain boots." *A latex gag mask,* I want to tease, but I keep it inside, because she may actually believe me.

From there she went right into my underwear drawer.

"Why do you have so many pairs of underwear? I have never seen so much underwear in my life!" she said in a judgemental tone, as she rifled through my drawer. Surely there must be a hidden treasure in there somewhere!

"Because I am *single* mom. That's what *single* people do. They have *tons* of underwear. Just *tons*. Lace, cotton, boy shorts, thongs, crotchless. You name it! Something for every occasion."

To that, both of us, exhausted and borderline dizzy from packing, laugh hysterically. She had a clear moment when she realized how ridiculous she was being.

After the packing was complete, and the movers had moved their last box out of my apartment, my mother and I hopped in a cab with my most valuable possessions to beat the movers to my new apartment. I was eager to get Bears' room set up as soon as possible so he wouldn't feel disrupted in any way.

As the taxi pulled away from my building I turned my head and watched it fade away through the rear window. I had a moment of sadness. I know it's hard to gauge from this blog, but I am an extremely sentimental person. I had a lot of memories in that apartment. Bear and I shared a lot of special moments there. He had several birthdays there. He learned to swim, he learned to ride a two-wheeler, he learned to read, he learned all the words to Lady Gaga and Neo, and every other top 40 song on the radio there. He grew out of *Little Einsteins* and into *ICarly* there. He went from loving *Thomas the Train* to *Star Wars* and the *Knicks* and *Rangers* there. He completed several grades of school in that apartment and I watched him transform from a toddler to a boy, all while we lived in that apartment. My divorce was finalized in that apartment. I learned to stand alone in that apartment. I had my heart-broken in that apartment. I learned my father had cancer in that apartment, and lost him six months later in that apartment. That apartment is where my life had taken place, and my most important memories were made over the past few years. I learned my strengths there, and many of my weaknesses there. *Darcy Dates* was created there, alone in my bed one night on my old laptop.

The cab turned onto my new street. One of the valuables that somehow made it in the taxi with us was my unworn wedding dress. (See: *Bridal Skeletons In My Closet*) Why it got special treatment of a taxi escort rather than a moving truck I can't be sure.

"I love that we have the wedding dress," my mom said.

We both laughed.

"Are you really going to wear this one day?" she asked.

"Why not?"

We pulled up and to the building and the doorman approached the taxi.

"I'll carry you over the threshold," my mom said, "Or at least I will carry your wedding dress over the threshold."

We laughed again.

New apartment, new memories to be made. The journey continues. Of course I will take you with me. Stay tuned.

98

I'M DIVORCED, YOU'RE DIVORCED… LET'S PARTY?

APRIL 25, 2011

I WAS on my nightly conference call with Max and Alexis. Max tells me he has just returned from a fabulous dinner party and there he met a really cool, pretty, divorced woman who is currently single who I *must* meet. He suggested the two of us could go out together and hit the town.

"You guys would have so much fun going out together. You are both divorced. And you'd really have a great time."

"Really? Oh. How old is she?"

"Sixty-One."

"Years old???!" I asked.

Alexis and I laugh hysterically. The conversation had taken a very sad turn.

"I don't understand Max. Just cause you're gay I don't suggest you go hang out and party with every gay person I meet."

Alexis and I laugh even harder.

Apparently, this is what happens when you are divorced. People want you to hang out with other unmarried people. I don't know if you know this, but if you are a single adult, you are put into the same category with all other single adults. It's like the economy class of relationship status.' I am used to this by now... My mother actually tried to set up a 28 year old gay male friend of mine, with her never married single friend who is 54. And a woman.

99

A DIAMOND IS FOREVER. AND SO IS ROBBIE

MAY 2, 2011

YOU THOUGHT he was gone right? Robbie? Well he isn't. He still calls several times a day. As you know, I don't answer much anymore but the other night I decided to see what the latest Robbie drama would bring.

"Hi Robbie."

"Where have you been? I call you hundreds of times and you don't answer."

When he says hundreds, by the way, it's a literal statement.

"Why did you call me at 2:37 am last night?"

"I wanted to talk to you."

"About?"

"Are you still hanging out with that loser boyfriend of yours?"

When Robbie refers to him as a loser, it's strictly because it is not him.

"Yes. And don't call him a loser ever again."

"Are you going to marry him?"

"I don't know that I am ever marrying anyone. But I am going to *date* him."

"Forever?"

Seriously? He makes this too easy.

"Maybe."

"So you're gonna date him forever?"

"It's possible."

"So you're telling me I will never have a shot at dating you ever again since you are dating him forever."

"Yes."

"Then why do I keep calling you?"

"You tell me. I often wonder the same thing."

"I screwed up Darcy. I love you. I am not giving up."

"You have been trying for a year. That is a year of your energy wasted."

"Over a year."

"If you want to admit that, sure."

Worried Robbie is gone for good? Don't. After that conversation he called an hour later, the next morning at 11, 11:45, 5 pm, 8:30pm, 12 midnight and 1:23 am. Oh, and he is still calling. I have one more good update, but I will save it for another post…

100

TIME TO GO

May 9, 2011

One of my dates once told me he doesn't like when women wear watches.

"Why not?" I asked as I glanced down awkwardly at the watch on my wrist.

"I don't like when women are concerned with time."

Crickets.

I am not sure what society he lives in. Apparently one where women float around aimlessly hoping they coincidently make it to their appointments.

"Where were you honey? Our reservation was at 8. It's 11 p.m." He would ask his oblivious lady friend.

"Wow. I'm sorry. I had no idea what time or day it was. You know I am not concerned with time. At least I made it here."

"True. I love you."

"I love you too honey."

Or maybe this aforementioned woman who is not concerned with time and unable to wear a timepiece of any kind would call for a doctor's appointment.

"We can fit you in at 11 on Tuesday."

"Oh. I don't keep track of time. I will come when it feels right."

At least she would be giving the doctor's office a taste of their own medicine. (See: *The Doctor Won't See You Now*.)

101

MY PENIS PEN PAL

MAY 12, 2011

I HAVE HAD ALL the penis one girl can take. *Sigh*.

Well...via text. Somehow, somewhere along the line I picked up a pen pal. A *penis* pen pal. Remember this guy? (See: *Dodging Bullets*) He will not stop texting me pictures of his penis. At this point, I can't even be sure that he has any other limbs or even a face. He may just be a penis stump with an Iphone. I get more penis texts from this guy than I do breaking news updates from CNN. At least *those* I can unsubscribe to. This is one subscription I can't get out of. The harder I try to shut him down, the *harder* he tries. Literally. I have the pictures to prove it. I can't even change my number. Cause then how would Robbie call me? What's a girl to do? It seems I'm stuck between a cock and a hard place.

Guys, let me explain, in the simplest form. Texting penis pictures isn't hot. It isn't sexy. Let me walk you through what happens when you text a girl you *aren't* dating a picture of your genitals. We immediately call our best friend. We forward her the picture. We will laugh. At you. Then, said best friend will show it to her husband. Who will comment on your size. Then we all laugh together. For weeks, if not months or years, you will only be referred to as the guy who texted the penis picture.

At no point are we turned on or longing for you in any way. So just stop. Right now. Trust me.

102

MATCHMAKER, MATCHMAKER MAKE ME A MATCH...THAT IS ALIVE

May 16, 2011

I was with my mother at an estate art sale. The collection belonged to a woman who had passed away at age 94.

"Darcy! *Pssst*," I hear my mother whisper screaming from the next room.

"Yea?" I said as I walked in to see what she wanted.

"This guy is cute!"

"Huh?"

"This guy. In the picture," she says, pointing to a shelf of framed photos, "Maybe he is single."

"Maybe he is *dead*. We are at an estate sale and you want to set me up with someone in a picture from 40 years ago?"

"But look. In the picture he is with a girl. Look at the way he is looking at her. It looks like you. You may be his type."

Crickets.

103

TAXI CAB CONFESSIONS

M*AY 23, 2011*

3 MONTHS EARLIER...

It was freezing in New York City. Just, unbearably, bone breaking cold. The type of chill that stays in your bones, and doesn't leave even when you are inside.

I had just gone to a fabulous birthday party on Bowery and needed to get back up town to relieve my sitter. Standing in front of the swank hotel I spotted a sea of loud fashionistas waiting for cabs as well. It was Saturday night and everyone was out. I was about to turn from a sequined hottie in skinny black pants and Louboutins, into a dirty old pumpkin. Not only were there no cabs, but there were people waiting in front of me for cabs.

One in particular seemed rather cute and approachable. We had already made small talk over a livery cab that wanted to charge way too much to get him to his destination, so at this point, I couldn't do the signature New York City taxi flagging move, where you just walk ahead of the person a half a block. We were old friends at this point. He was definitely going to get one before me, and my fingers and cheeks were about to freeze off.

"Where are you headed?" I asked, turning myself from savvy new yorker to creepy hitchhiker on a dime.

"Midtown."

"Hey, I will drop you off if you let me share your cab."

Was this safe? I certainly hoped so. He didn't look scary, not that scary people actually do. Look at Ted Bundy and Robert Chambers. They were handsome, yet I am sure we all agree, very very scary.

I hopped in the car with the stranger and we quickly chatted about what we each did for a living.

He told me he was a chef, to which I told him my best and only recipe. Not that he really needed a recipe for salmon that calls for duck sauce packets left over from chinese take-out. He was a professional chef. He could probably make his own duck sauce. Can you even make your own duck sauce? Huh. Never really thought about it. He told me he would like to give me cooking lessons. Over dinner sometime.

Freeze.

I had already had an experience with a younger chef and it didn't end well (See: *Darcy Plus Party, Ghost of Risotto Past* and *It's Complicated*). Not to mention, I was already spoken for. I told him that the offer was sweet, but not only was I dating someone, but I was older, and a mom.

"Get out. I would have pegged you for 27. But I don't mind. Who cares about your age. And that's cool that you're a mom," he said with confidence.

This was a nice change of pace from my best friend Alexis, who likes to tell me I am old. I fell in love for a minute and then I came back to reality.

"That's sweet, but it's kind of a non-starter."

We pulled up to his destination and he had to hop out. He asked for my contact info. I didn't give it to him, but I did tell him to read my blog, as I assured him this exchange would be in it.

"I'm going to find you. And we are definitely going on a date one day," he said as he handed the driver a 20, "Take her wherever she needs to go."

It wasn't for me, but it was a great New York story and it just goes to show you that you actually *can* meet people everywhere. Even in your taxi. Now, I am not encouraging any of you to get in random cars with strangers. In fact, I advise against it. But keep your head up and your eyes open. Strangers are everywhere. And some…are single.

104

MY WINGMIDGET

June 6, 2011

It was Memorial Day weekend in the Hamptons. As always, New Yorkers crammed themselves into the most eastern shores of New York. By the way, I don't even know if that is geographically correct, but for the sake of this story, let's pretend. Bear and I were sitting on the beach, relaxing in some much-needed sun after a truly heinous winter in New York City. We were de-frosting with both friends and family.

Bear was alternating between digging in the sand and running toward the ocean. He has finally reached an age where he jumps in the waves and bodysurfs. No one ever tells you this, but motherhood is essentially a series of mini-heart attacks. With each wave Bear jumped, I would hold my breath as I stood knee-deep in the freezing ocean. After using up our last dry towel, I left Bear with my family and walked back toward the car to see if I could scrounge up one more.

As I am walking back onto the beach, I spot a man. A handsome man walked in my direction. It took me a second, because he was wearing sunglasses, until I realized...I knew this man. Not only because he was a pro-athlete, but because we were friends at one point. A couple of years ago when we had met over something random, it seems the aforementioned pro-athlete took a liking to me. But we remained just friends. Because he was married.

"Grayden?"

He stopped and turned slowly toward me. Such a hottie. Always was and always will be.

"Darcy? Hey. What's going on?"

We made the usual small talk, chit-chat, the 'I could really care less what we are even saying because I can't wait to tell Alexis I actually saw you here' conversation that means practically nothing. Unbeknownst to me, during said conversation, some members of my family and friends had seen us talking and they knew exactly who he was. One of them had announced to the group,

"Now THAT is Darcy's type," but I had no idea that was going on, because I was here. On the stairs. Talking to Grayden.

Suddenly I see Bear running up to us.

"Hey, Bear. You know what sport he plays? You know what team he used to play for?"

"I know. They told me."

They, meaning my family and friends who were watching from afar. Awkward that Bear just said this.

"Hey! You are my moms type!" Bear yells to Grayden.

Grayden is a gentleman and pretends not to hear. I, on the other hand, was planning on darting into a hole that some children were digging on the beach and never crawling back out.

"*Cover me. Quickly. No, no, don't worry, it doesn't matter that I can't breathe,*" I imagined myself screaming to the children.

But I stood and acted like Bear never said a word.

Bear sensed no one was responding.

"Hey. You. You are my moms type. Mom, he is your type right?"

HO-LY. Just kill me. I glanced quickly into the ocean to see if a tsunami was about to swell. Nothing. It was peaceful and beautiful. Damn you nature. You never work when we need you to.

Suddenly Bear and I went from cute mother son duo, to creepy gypsy grifters. I imagined Bear pulling out a porridge bowl, "*please sir, may I have some more?*" he would ask. UGH.

"Oh! Look at that! Is that a mermaid? Look at the kite! Bear! Let's go see it. Grayden, it was great seeing you. Gotta run. Kite!" I may have even tripped in the sand as I was trotting away, Bear in tow.

When the coast was clear, because I had actually dragged Bear to another coast, I asked him,

"Sweetie, what was that about?"

"What?" he asked innocently.

"That whole thing, about being mommy's type."

"Aunt Lucy told everyone the guy you were talking to was your type."

"And what do you think that means?"

"Um…I don't know."

"Got it."

I was a little relieved he had no idea what it meant. For all he knew, it meant I wanted to draft this pro-athlete onto a fantasy sports league of some kind. Bear doesn't see me as a single person. He sees me as his mother. And for a long while, at least until he is 28, I would like to keep it that way.

105

ROBBIE.COM

JUNE 13, 2011

THE FOLLOWING IS 100% true. I know what you are thinking, there is NO WAY it's true, but I swear. Each and every last detail is true. And that is why...I can even write this blog.

Robbie gets better and better with time like a vintage wine, or mid-century furniture. Robbie called me frantically. Seven times in a 20 minute span. I decided to pick up because I had a hunch something was up. Luckily for all of you, I did.

"Darcy. Thank gd you answered. I need a favor."

"What?"

"*(Insert name of massive dating site here)* is interviewing me via Skype next week to put me in one of their commercials. I need you to Skype with me and tell me if I look good and what I need to do. Like if I need to dye my hair, go tanning, whatever."

Huh?

"Dye your hair?" I finally got the words out.

"Yea. Whatever."

Silence.

Folks, this could be the new spokesperson for a particular dating site. Use it with caution.

"Okay." I said. Because wouldn't you?

A few minutes later Robbie called me on Gmail video chat. He asked how he looked. I said he looked good but he could use a bit of eyeliner.

"Eyeliner?"

"Yes."

"Why?"

"To give your eyes some definition so they don't look so washed out."

"Really? So just eyeliner?"

Oh boy.

Robbie tells me he has the perfect answers prepared for his interview. I told him I would play interviewer. (I mean, obviously this would make for excellent material.)

"Why do you like internet dating?" I asked, pretending to be the interviewer. The interviewer oblivious to the fact that they were allowing a complete crazy person to represent their public company. Although I was officially crazy too, as I was role-playing with Robbie on GChat.

"Being a doctor," he begins, "I have limited time to meet people. This allows me to work crazy hours, and still meet interesting people."

Wow. He was prepared. He sounded so normal I kind of wanted to date him. But the crazy cloud lifted.

"So, we done here?" I asked, rushing him off of the video chat before Bear could enter my bedroom.

"I also want to add to my answer, that I wouldn't have to do internet dating if the girl I loved, Darcy, would just marry me."

"I'd leave that part out. It shows the...you know," as I motioned the international symbol for crazy with a finger pointing and twirling to the side of my head.

I said goodbye and clicked off the chat.

The days following were filled with emails, texts and phone calls filled with questions from what color shirt he should wear to does he need a tan, and other questions that made me wonder how I ever got to this place. The one where I wonder if I am actually more insane than Robbie since I continue to let this go on.

The next night I was lying in bed, so utterly exhausted I actually thought I saw a unicorn gallop out of the corner of my eye. I see an unknown number on my phone and decide to answer. Obviously a mistake.

"Hello?"

"Darcy, it's important. I just texted you a picture. I dyed my hair. Can you look at the picture and tell me how it looks? I did it myself. Out of a box."

I could only sit with my mouth half-open. Too exhausted to speak but dying to see what Robbie looked like with a home hair dye job.

"Why? What color? What the fuck?"

"Just look. Tell me if it's too dark. If it is, I can bleach it."

"Bleach it? What?"

"Yea, whatever."

"Do you even know what 'bleach it' means?"

"Of course I know. I just want to know if the color looks good."

"Just…just stop."

I look at my phone to find the picture. It is Robbie, in the hospital, wearing scrubs. Taking a picture of himself in what appeared to be some type of doctor locker room you only get to see on Grey's Anatomy. Or, if you are an actual doctor. Or, apparently, if you have a doctor stalking you.

"Did you…did you dye your hair in the hospital?"

"No. How does it look."

"I don't understand."

"What don't you understand? How does it look?"

"I just can't even answer, because I just don't understand."

106

DOG DAYS OF SUMMER

JULY 11, 2011

I LIVE FOR DOGS. Well, at least I live for *my* dog. That being said, I am not a dog run person per se.

Judge if you must, but the whole chit chatting about your dog with strangers isn't my thing. When I am walking my dog, I don't want to talk to you about your dog. Sure, your dog is cute. My dog likes your dog. But I don't want to talk dog with you. Is that mean? Does it make me a bad person? Possibly. I never really thought about it.

It was a beautiful summer morning in New York City. I decided to take Batman, our dog, to the local dog run. On this particular morning the dog run had a rather large, aggressive dog who was walking around humping every dog in sight. I don't know what the etiquette is, since I am not a frequent dog run visitor, but I would like to think if your dog is humping all the dogs in the vicinity you might put them in time out. Or hire them some doggie type hooker. Maybe there is some middle ground…like a leash.

This particular morning was painfully hot. I stood there, dressed inappropriately warm for such hot weather, coffee in hand, Adidas track pants on, sweating my brains out, wondering just how much time one is to spend standing in a dog run to be considered a good dog mom. My main goal that morning was to protect Batman from being molested by the aforementioned dog who had decided to go wilding.

I am standing next to a man watching the humpfest unfold when he turns to me.

"Ugh. Doesn't that look good to you? Wouldn't you love to try that right about now?"

Crickets

"What? Hump?" I said, as I furrowed my brow.

"No. That. Dive in that water," he said, pointing to some dogs taking a refreshing dip in a tub of water.

No. That wasn't awkward. Of course not. Maybe I should become a cat person

107

HOW TO PICK UP A GUY

July 19, 2011

There are so many cheesy pickup lines. And then there are mine.

It wasn't a pick up line exactly. In fact, I don't think there was a line at all. Here follows my simple strategy on how to pick up a guy.

I had just spent the night with a group of friends. After dinner in one restaurant, and drinks in another we had made one last attempt to visit yet one more spot.

Never let them bring you to another location, I think silently. This is advice from a criminal profiler I once heard speaking on the topic of homicide, not drinks with friends. But the same feelings applied that night.

I hopped begrudgingly into a taxi and rode across town to deliver one of my friends to a party she wanted to attend. Upon arrival, there was an issue with the door policy that I wasn't paying attention to. Maybe the list had been closed for the night, maybe we weren't on it, maybe we were just losers...whatever the case, we had, as a group, decided to not go upstairs, and instead hit the bar downstairs. I was relieved to not have to attend. My buzz was wearing off and my bed was calling my name. We grabbed a few seats at the bar and started to wind down our evening. One by one, my friends were dropping out, but for reasons I can't explain, most likely laziness, I just couldn't get my ass out of there. I was losing steam quickly when the bartender delivered me a glass of champagne.

"This is from the gentleman at the end of the bar."

Scared to look up as I knew it could go either way I finally peeked up through the front wisps of my hair and caught a glimpse of a man who waved quickly and shot me a smile. He was cute enough so I motioned him over to thank him for the drink.

"How come he got you a drink and not me?" one of my straight male friends asked me.

"Probably because I have a vagina," I smiled and the stranger approached.

"Thank you," I said, extending my hand, "I'm Darcy."

"Hi Darcy."

"Why the drink?" I asked coyly.

"I thought you were pretty."

I smiled and picked up the glass and said cheers before taking a sip. I knew it was safe to drink it as it came straight from the bartender, and not roofied as my mother had drilled into my head a million times before about taking drinks from strangers.

Said stranger was visiting from Connecticut. It didn't take long to decide he wasn't for me but I continued to make small talk as I calculated my escape plan in my mind.

A few moments later my friends who had gotten a second wind, or maybe by this point it was considered a fifth wind, suggested we pop into the party upstairs. I went along, for no good reason. I didn't want to, but my feet followed and before you know it we were riding the elevator to the top floor with the Connecticut entourage we had acquired at the bar in awkward silence. The second the door opened, I saw an old friend. I walked up to him and gave him a quick peck on the cheek.

"Hey Darcy."

"What's going on?" I asked, scanning the room for familiar faces.

"Not much. Hide me, I am trying to ditch these strangers from the elevator."

"Which isn't very nice since one of them sent her a drink," my friend chimes in facetiously.

"What ever happened with Richie?" my friend asked.

Richie is a friend of his that he had set me up with at a dinner party once years ago.

"Come on. You know Richie wasn't for me."

"How about this guy?" he says, pointing to a guy who was rapidly approaching, unsuspecting that his friend was about to pimp him out.

I look over. He was cute. Very very cute. My friend gave me a brief run down.

"Okay," I shrug.

Suddenly confidence, or should I say craziness swept over my body. I was tipsy, tired, bored, and looking for a little entertainment. At this point my social filters were just about shot.

"Hi," I said, as he approached.

"Hello."

"Paul thinks we should meet," I said.

"He does?"

"Yes."

"Why?"

"To date."

"Really?"

"Yes."

"Oh."

"Think we should go on a date?" Fuck it, I thought. It was beyond late, maybe midnight, and I just felt like messing with him for fun. And he was cute. And a date with him probably wouldn't be terrible.

"I don't know. Do you think we should?"

"Maybe. Do you think we have chemistry?"

"Not sure. Why don't you give me a little kiss and we will see."

With that, I did. Softly on the lips. I have zero idea what I was thinking, and I knew the entire exchange was ridiculous. But I didn't really care. I had nothing to lose. Other than my pride. Which I had probably lost about 5 minutes earlier when I initially started the conversation with the sentence: "Paul thinks we should meet."

"That was pretty good," he said.

"It wasn't bad. Maybe you should take my number?"

Who are you Darcy? And what are you doing?

"Okay."

Really? That easy? I mean, why wouldn't be. I have known him for less than 2 minutes and I have already kissed him on the lips. Something I actually swear I have never done. Except once, a New Years kiss with a stranger on a dance floor in college. Right after the countdown to midnight. But New Years is fair game isn't it? Or am I a ho?

He reached for his phone and asked for my name. Which he didn't even know. Even though we had already kissed. That, by the way, is definitely NOT playing by The Rules on my part. I am no stranger to that. Remember? (See: *Breaking The Rules*.)

"Darcy. What's your name?" Yeah. I didn't know his either.

"Sam."

"Really? That's my brother's name!"

"Really…"

"Sam what?"

"Silver."

Crickets.

I knew Sam. Well, not personally. But a while back someone wanted to set us up. We have a bunch of friends in common. Awkward. Shit.

"Huh. I think I know you. I think we have friends in common," I said casually.

"Really?"

"Yep."

Sam and I talked. Then we talked some more. We closed out the bar. Went to find another one, then another, then another. We were fast friends. Our night involved taxis all over town, and eventually me falling asleep in a gay bar while he ran to get me a grilled cheese sandwich next door. I liked him so much I didn't even hold the gay bar against him like I did *GayDate* guy. In this case, the gay bar was the only thing open. And I chose it. We then walked. For a long time. We tried to get our palms read by a psychic but got turned away at 5 am.

"We're closed," she mouthed through the window.

"But you're awake?" I mouthed back. She didn't seem to care.

"I think everything in the city is closed," I said to Sam. "Sadly, our night is officially over."

"Let me drop you off in a taxi at your place."

"Come on. Not necessary. It's so out-of-the-way."

"Are you kidding? Of course I am dropping you off."

"You aren't coming upstairs!"

"I won't!"

With that we flagged down a taxi and hopped in.

"I'm hungry. Want to grab breakfast?" I said as I saw the sun rising in the distance.

"Sure! Where to?"

"Nah, I think I should get home. Get a little sleep."

I figured I wouldn't look nearly as hot as the sun was rising and my mascara was probably strewn all over my face by this point. It would probably be best if I left while it was still a little dark. Even though it wasn't really dark anymore.

"You sure?"

"Yea."

As promised, he dropped me off and didn't even try to come upstairs. He was a total gentleman. He even texted me the next day telling me it wasn't a dream. Oh. And we ended up falling for each other. Pretty damn hard.

I thought that was a good New York story. And a good lesson on how to pick up a guy.

108

SUGAR AND SPICE AND ALL THINGS…TECHNOLOGICAL

JULY 26, 2011

THE FOLLOWING IS an actual conversation that took place in my car this weekend.

"Bear, tell Grandma what you put on your apple this morning that you LOVED."

"Cinnamon," Bear says proudly.

"He put cinnamon on his apple and *loved* it." I repeat proudly, as any mother might when their child tries something new.

"I don't know what that is," my mother says quizzically.

"What? Cinnamon?"

"Yea. What is that?"

"Cinnamon? Cinnamon!"

"What is cinnamon?"

"I don't understand," I say. Bewildered.

"I have no idea what that is. I have no idea what you're talking about."

It's as though somewhere along the drive we had swapped my mom out for Borat.

"Seriously mom? Cinnamon? The spice? That you eat?"

"Oh!! Cinnamon. When you said apple, I thought you were talking about an Apple computer. I thought it was some new app."

Dear Steve Jobs, If you happen to be hiring at the genius bar, please contact my mother.

109

I DON'T HAVE TO SAY I'M SORRY…'CAUSE I LOVE YOU?

August 9, 2011

Ah, Love Story. We all loved that movie. We all cried. Hard. And the most famous line…we all know it. And we all love it. When Ryan O'Neal, or should I call him Oliver Barrett? Or maybe just "preppy" apologizes and Jenny, played by a very hot, young Ali MacGraw says, "Love means never having to say you're sorry."

Yes! Yes! We all cheered and smiled through our tears and our swollen eyes. That is what love means.

WHAT? No.

Um, clearly the person who wrote that line has never actually been in love. Or in a relationship for that matter. Because love doesn't mean that. Let's see how we would apply that to everyday living:

"I don't understand. You hurt me. Why can't you just say sorry?"

"Because I love you?"

Folks, don't try this at home. You heard it here first.

I find with love, you have to say sorry more than usual. It's a friggin' sorry marathon. When are you more inclined to say sorry than when you actually care about someone and love them? And when you are in an actual relationship...sometimes...it can be one big sorry extravaganza. Not always. But sometimes. Just sayin'.

110

YOUR MAMA

SEPTEMBER 6, 2011

Jerry Maguire. One of my favorite movies of all time. I loved the movie. I loved the soundtrack. I even loved that kid who talked about the human head weighing 8 pounds. Or maybe he annoyed me? I'm not sure now. It was a long time ago. But basically, what I do remember, like almost everyone else, it completed me. It came out in 1996. I was only dating my ex-husband at the time. I was not a mother yet, and certainly never imagined I would be a single mother, at that. Life was easy, uncomplicated, and I...was in college.

A while back I had gone out with a friend. We went on one or two dates maybe a year ago. Whatever the reason, timing, life, chemistry, Robbie dragging from my leg...we never went out again. But we remained friends. Especially when he once sent me a text that said,

"You are the only girl that makes me laugh."

Guys take note. We like those texts.

While we were out, he regaled me with his dating stories. Girls gone right, girls gone wrong, and girls gone downright wild. As I watched him speak, I realized, I didn't know this side of him. When we had gone out he was quiet, conservative. I thought he was possibly a virgin. Turns out he, and I mean this in the nicest way possible as he is a loyal Darcy reader...is kind of a slut. Sometimes several girls in a week.

"Who are you? I didn't know this is what you are all about. Making out with girls on stoops every night? Who would have guessed?" I said. Intrigued that he had such a wild side.

Later that evening, when I was home, tucked into my bed, watching 90 minutes of Andy Cohen genius otherwise known as the *Real Housewives Of New York City* Reunion, I received a text from him.

"On our first date I kept thinking about the movie Jerry Maguire- where the guy was like "the single mom is sacred.""

I smiled. I thought it was cute. This was Dr. Heart's way of explaining why he was so measured with me. This wasn't the first time I had heard this. Although, the first time I had heard it was in another form. On a date a few years ago, the guy had told me that his friend asked him if he was going to "Jerry Maguire that shit." I thought it was funny. I still do. I always have an inclination towards the inappropriate. Besides, I like the idea of turning Jerry Maguire into a verb.

The Darcy Dictionary:

Jerry Maguire:

noun: A movie and or leading character in a movie.

verb: To date a single mom.: *I am so gonna Jerry Maguire that shit.*

adjective: 1.To be so completely passionate about your job to the point where you write a mission statement that makes you the laughing stock of the office. : *That e-mail you cc'd me, the one to our boss that was a little creepy and over the top? It was a little Jerry Maguire-esque.*

2. To be man enough to date a single mom.

But here is the thing guys: dating a mom is cool. Moms are the best. If you get thirsty they will always have a juice box in their bag, and a matchbox car in their coat pocket if you get bored. They understand responsibility and unconditional love. And most importantly, they know who they are. Which is pretty darn sexy. Maybe Rod Tidwell was right. The single mom *is* sacred. It takes a real man to date a single mom. The ones I know and the ones I have dated have been great at this, which goes without saying as we wouldn't have made it very far otherwise. So to all you Jerry Maguires out there. You rock. And you… complete me.

111

THE GREEN THUMBS DOWN

SEPTEMBER 26, 2011

FLOWERS...ARE awkward. No. Wait. Let me rephrase. I *love* flowers. I love getting them. I love having them. I love seeing them. I love smelling them. I am beyond grateful when someone sends them. I love when my doorman lets me know someone has sent me flowers. This is a very exciting moment. I don't even wait until I get into the elevator to rip open the card. I once had a boyfriend who would send me flowers from one of the best flower shops in New York City a few times a month for over a year. I never tired of the delivery and would *oooh* and *ahhh* with Bear's babysitter as they arrived. Each arrangement nicer than the one before.

I love when my mailroom at work alerts me that I have flowers and I proudly carry them through my office, to my desk, as though I have just won an oscar. An oscar from FTD. Which then takes up 3/4 of my desk and I have to spend the rest of the week having to entertain annoying chit-chat as to who sent me the flowers and why. So maybe I'm actually undecided on the work flowers. There is always the one woman in the office who likes to remind me that I don't have enough natural light at my desk and that my orchid will die.

"It's fine," I'd say, as I'd watch my orchid die a slow death with each passing day, hanging my head in shame as I glanced at the high ratio of fluorescent overhead light in my corner.

That's when I'd curse myself for not being more successful. If I were I'd have natural light at my desk from the window overlooking the park and my orchids would live. Plus I wouldn't have to sit near Miss Evil Eye in the tight wrap dress.

You know what, now that I talked it out, just scratch the work flowers. They are too stressful now that I think about it.

But back to the awkwardness of flowers. There are several types of awkward flowers and today I will address three of them. While I am not writing much about my dating life lately, I am watching lots of reality TV. What I have noticed is that when people on dating shows go out to dinner, particularly if it's a reality show, for reasons I can not explain the man will often bring the woman a bouquet of flowers along on the date. I advise against it.

"But it's romantic!" some of you may cry.

Is it though? Is it romantic to get dressed up, put on a pair of your favorite heels, and then have to carry what is basically an awkward bush, wrapped in loud crinkly cellophane as you walk around? Is it convenient to place said floral extravaganza on the table while you eat? Staring at them, watching them wilt, wondering if they are going to die, as they will not see water for at least 5 hours? Is there any way a girl can walk with a bouquet, other than at her wedding and not look like a sherpa? No. There isn't. It's cumbersome and trust me guys, just send them to her door when you are not around. Only, of course, if she has given you her address. It will make her day and you will spare her those moments when she doesn't know just how many times she is supposed to say thank you as she carries them from venue to venue throughout the evening.

The next type of awkward flower is the single rose. Okay. In general, I am not a rose girl. I like ranunculus, peonies, and snapdragons. Back to the roses for a second, if you are sending them, I am loving them. But a single red rose, in an awkward plastic container...I just don't get it. It's usually coupled with a cheap white carney teddy bear of some kind. Teddy bear or not, the single rose is just...well, what is it? Then you have to walk in the street holding the single rose. It screams *"we were harassed by a street carney and forced into buying an awkward rose."* By the way, if it's coupled with baby's breath, that's even worse. For the record guys, if a flower is descriptive of anyone's breath, even a baby, and I happen to love babies, steer clear. Just a tip. A random one, but a good one at that.

Finally, we conclude this rant with the corsage. A girl spends her time trying to find the perfect prom dress. She wants a specific color, she wants to wear the perfect shoes. She will most likely have her hair done, sometimes her makeup, unless you were me. She is standing there looking the best she probably thinks she has looked since the day she was born and then you present her with a branch to strap on her arm. It sometimes goes from the wrist to the elbow adorned with ribbon. She wants to strut to the car, but the branch... it's weighing her down. Sometimes you pin them to the dress. But they don't want a hole in their dress. By the way, I haven't been to a prom in almost 20 years. Well, in 3 years it will be 20 years. I don't even know if people wear a corsage anymore. If they don't, discard this last paragraph completely and feel free to comment that I am old and outdated. I know Alexis will.

To summarize: Flowers yes, *send* being the operative word, skip the office unless she is successful enough to have her own window, definitely not at a restaurant, corsages are for old people who haven't been to a prom in 20 years.

112

FAMILY, PARTY OF 2

O CTOBER 3, 2011

FOR SPRING BREAK I took Bear to Disney World. As far as I am concerned, it's a right of passage for any child. I always loved Disney World as a kid, and I knew he would too. I was surprised how many parents would *tsk* at me, as though Disney were the devil.

"Ugh. I'd never do Disney unless my children insisted," they would say with their noses in the air, as if their children were asking for an afternoon in a shanty town. A shanty town filled with princesses and pirates… and general happiness.

It's the most magical place on earth for christ sake. Why the haters?

From the second we got off the plane, I was already amazed by Disney's ability to make the vacation seem seamless and special, as though they were waiting specifically for us. When we arrived at the hotel, I stood with Bear, luggage in hand (or on the ground…it's amazing how much a bag can weigh when packed for two people) and tipped the man who had carried it to the door for me.

"Thank you!" he said and then looked perplexed. "It's just the two of you?"

"Yes," I replied"

"Are you meeting your family here?"

We are a family, I wanted to say. But I just said, "No."

Instead, I imagined a Disney phone chain of some kind to begin as we entered the hotel.

"Mother and child approaching. Do not ask where the rest of the family is. No. There is none. No. Shhh. Here she comes. She is walking towards you."

I suddenly felt like a 16-year-old who gave birth to Bear in a high school locker room. Was this 1969? For all the diversity on the *It's A Small World* ride, they certainly weren't up to date on the modern family. I would like to see some male puppets on that ride. One white and one Indian. Kissing. And holding their black baby in Bjorn as the music plays on, *"There's so much that we share and it's time you're aware, it's a small world after all."*

After a full morning in the park I realized an incomplete family was a rarity in the Magic Kingdom, similar to unicorns or skinny people. People all around us, including families we chit chatted with on line would ask,

"Is it just the two of you?"

I started taking advantage of the pity that followed.

"Would you like us to take a picture of you two?"

"Sure" I'd say, putting my arm around Bear, both of us flashing our biggest smiles. It's as though we had our own private photog wherever we went.

"What great pictures of you guys! How did you get so many pictures of the two of you?" A friend asked upon our return.

"Oh, we had the greatest photographer. Yes. Her name was *pity*."

But wait. It gets better. One very cute ride operator in his twenties was making small talk with us when we asked for directions outside the exit of Bear's favorite ride. He kept referring to me as Bear's sister. He was good. Was he flirting?

"Are you having a good time?" he asked, with some kind of southern accent, which as you readers know, I have a soft spot for.

"We are having a great time," I said.

"I am about to make it even better."

With that, he opened up the exit and told us we could cut the *entire* 50 minute line. Bear and I looked at each other and squealed with delight. The greatest thing about hanging with Bear at this age is he gets it. He understood how cool this privilege was. We skipped up to the front and rode the ride without a care in the world. As we exited we thanked him.

"Is it just the two of you?" he asked.

"Yep," I said.

"You are too pretty to be alone," he said. Then he bent down to Bear's level, "You are lucky I think your sister is so pretty. I am going to let you cut the line again."

"Really??" Bear and I said in unison. Our eyes wide. We rode the ride again and again. Never once waiting in that long line.

On the ride Bear turned to me.

"He said you were pretty."

"Is that funny?"

"Yes."

The perks continued on through the rest of the week. From letting us enter the Indiana Jones stunt show 5 minutes after it started.

"Is it just the two of you?"

To random park employees offering up their fast passes.

"If it's just the two of you, you can have these."

In the end we had a great, magical trip, just as Disney had promised. And guess what? We shared it as a family. Just the two of us.

113

MY MOTHER, MY PIMP

OCTOBER 11, 2011

A WHILE AGO, my mother took me to a show for my birthday. Something we really enjoy doing together. As I sat quietly waiting for the theater to fill up, I got lost in my Playbill. Suddenly, I heard my mother's voice. She seemed to be deeply engaged in a conversation with the family next to us. I didn't pay much attention, as small talk with strangers isn't really my thing. I was too busy learning that the understudy for the lead had been doing summer stock in the Berkshires. Suddenly, over the hum of the crowd, I hear the words my mother is saying. They were becoming more distinct with each passing sentence.

"This is my daughter Darcy. It's her birthday."

I didn't hear what the strangers had said, but I did hear what my mother said next.

"She is single. If you know anyone?"

I could only sit with my mouth agape and my eyes wide, praying for some type of overhead light to come crashing down on my head.

"This is her picture," she continued, as she held up her IPhone for them to see.

The strangers were nodding and smiling politely.

"She is beautiful," one of them said. To be nice.

"She is beautiful. She needs a really nice guy. So if you know anyone."

I needed to make this nightmare end. That very minute.

"Mom?' I said, leaning forward in my seat, waving politely to the strangers.

"Yes?"

"Can I speak to you for a second?"

"Yes?"

She sat back in her seat.

"What are you doing?" I asked in a harsh whisper.

"I'm showing them your picture. Maybe they know a nice guy?"

"Really?"

"Sorry. They told me they were visiting from St. Louis."

"So now you're reaching out to the midwest to find me a man? And why are you giving them so much information? And why are you showing them my picture?? I'm sitting right here!"

"You look beautiful in that picture."

I could only stare at her blankly. We may have even had a staring contest. I can't be sure because I was too busy planning my escape in my mind. Was the stage too far to swing out of there via curtain?

"Please stop showing everyone my picture. And please stop trying to get me dates. Particularly in the midwest. Unless of course they are with women. Cause I am a lesbian now."

"Darcy. Ugh. No you're not."

Suddenly concern washed over her face.

I looked down at my Playbill to look for something. Anything.

"If you are a lesbian, I just want to say that you and your girl-friend are always welcome in my home."

"That's very after school special of you to come around like that."

Beat.

"Don't worry. I'm not a lesbian. That too would involve dating."

She smiled and kissed me on the head. Relieved I wasn't a lesbian, and anxious to get back to the midwestern contingent to her right.

Three things in which my mother will always be consistent: She will always show people my picture when I am sitting right there, she will make sure I know that if I do become a lesbian, my girlfriend is always welcome in her home, and she will always look out for me and have my back 100 percent. Love you mom!

114

THERE WERE TWO IN THE BED AND THE LITTLE ONE SAID...

O CTOBER 17, 2011

I RECENTLY DECIDED to upgrade my bedroom replete with new bedside tables. Bear came in to assess the new setup.

"Mommy, I am so glad you got a table for my side of the bed."

"That's not your side of the bed."

THE THING ABOUT CRUSHES

O CTOBER 24, 2011

I REMEMBER when I was a newlywed, I had an old camp flame coming into the city. The one that always made my heart beat a little faster. The one I would kiss every time we got together. I was newly married and *he* was coming to the city. It's not that I wanted to kiss him, but it was then that I realized. Oh...marriage is... *everyday*.

One night, while sitting at home, *not* using the Cuisinart we had registered for for our wedding, I started to think about all the people I never quite got around to making out with, who I would have liked to make out with. One in particular came to mind. Brady Reardon.

I met Brady when I was younger. Way younger. Way too young for Brady. I was 16 years old the last time I had seen him. He was 26. He spent his summers right down the street from me. My relationship with Brady was similar to that of Natalie Portman and Timothy Hutton's relationship in *Beautiful Girls*, only I didn't wear overalls at 16. I was guilty of wearing inappropriate dresses and tops from Betsy

Johnson. Truth be told I was 16 going on 26. It was a sweet, innocent relationship that felt like more to me. Maybe because I had wanted it to be. But I was sure, in some way Brady liked me too, even though he ever acted on it (except for the one time he grabbed my cheek and kissed it softly, to which I vowed never to wash my face again. At least until later that evening. I mean, come on. I was a teenager and obsessed with *Sea Breeze*).

Brady and I would flirt. Or rather, I would flirt with Brady. I know it sounds odd but it always felt like Brady flirted back. He treated me like a little sister but I always had a hunch, even then, that there was more to it. He was never inappropriate and always treated me with respect. Brady was from the south and had a hot southern accent that I didn't get to hear much of in the Northeast. He was big and strong and just...dreamy. I hearted him completely.

The summer had ended, and it was my last summer with Brady.

Brady moved to Texas, or Atlanta. Possibly Alabama. Even though I lost him, I never forgot him. From time to time I would look him up. But never found him. Until one day, after my divorce, I found his parents. On the internet. Like a crazy stalker. Or like my mother. I called them and asked for Brady's contact information. Including his email. I didn't think I had the nerve to call, but I emailed him right away.

When I saw his name in my inbox I was psyched. It turned out, Brady was living down south still, he was divorced and had two children. We caught up quickly and I told him to let me know if he was ever in town. He promised to, but life got in our way and took us in different directions. Brady never came to town, that I knew of, and once again we lost touch...until Facebook.

Brady and I became Facebook friends, and exchanged a few emails back and forth. He was settled in his life down south, and I was in New York City. We talked about a visit soon, but it never came to fruition. Over time I would see his updates, though there weren't many, and it appeared he had a girlfriend. Good for Brady. Bad for me. But enough about me...let's talk about me.

I woke up one morning to find an email in my Facebook inbox from him.

"Darcy, I am in the city. If you want to meet up, give me a call," complete with his cell phone number.

My stomach dropped. It didn't take one minute before I shot him a text, "Absolutely!"

Later that evening we picked a place to meet up for a drink.

I was standing outside waiting for Brady when I suddenly saw him walking toward me. From a distance he still had the same walk. I think I squealed like a pig from excitement, but kept it all inside. As he got closer I realized he wasn't as tall as I remembered, but back then I didn't wear 4 inch heels. He was still taller than me and that's all that really mattered.

He approached and gave me a big hug and a kiss on the cheek. He still felt the same. He had gone a bit grey and his stomach was a bit rounder than it used to be, but his smile was the same and so were his eyes. He let out a little laugh. Yep. It was Brady.

"Look at you, all tall," he said.

"It's the heels," I said, as I flashed my foot at him.

We walked into the restaurant and grabbed a seat at the bar. I couldn't believe I was sitting with Brady. His thick southern accent took me right back to my 16-year-old self. We talked about everything from our kids (his were teens now), our divorces, our careers, where we had been, and where we were going. He told me about his relationship that had been going on for 2 ½ years.

"You are older than my girlfriend," he said.

"Wow. That's cool." I guess? Or are you calling me old? Not sure.

Brady seemed pretty distant. Like he was out for drinks with a business associate.

"Brady, do you remember me?" I finally asked.

"Yea I remember you," he said.

It didn't sound convincing.

I mean, of course he remembered me. Enough to be my Facebook friend, and meet for drinks when he was in town. But that's not what I meant.

"But do you *remember* me?" I asked again.

"Darcy, yes of course I do," but there was no feeling in his answer.

"Do I look different?? Other than being 20 years older than the last time you saw me. Do you recognize me?"

Okay, I was fishing. For something. Anything.

I realized at that moment, while as a teenager, I thought my crush on Brady was reciprocated in some way or another, it wasn't. I was surprised. I could have *sworn* it was. Really, truly. Even my closest friends who watched our interactions would have guessed otherwise. But I could tell by his indifference he just thought of me as any other kid. Regardless, I was excited to see Brady and it was nice to catch up and talk about old summer memories we shared. Even if he hadn't been wondering about me all these years and we had completely different memories of what our relationship was.

Feeling slightly deflated, fatigue was starting to set in. I had a really long day and had a very early meeting the following morning. I let out a yawn. I tried to hide it but failed miserably.

"Am I boring you?" he asked.

"No. I just had a long day, and I have an early meeting tomorrow."

"I can't believe you are yawning."

"It's not you. My brain is tired, but I'm not tired," *I carried a watermelon.*

"You have the tiniest hands," he said, placing his hand next to mine on the bar.

"I guess I'd prefer that to man hands," I said and smiled.

"They are half the size of mine," he said, pressing his hand to mine. The thing about Brady is he was always so rugged and strong. Still was. Even though he was looking a little softer around the edges.

"Want to get out of here and go somewhere else? Want to grab something to eat? Head to another place?"

"Whatever you want. You are the tourist in this town tonight." I said.

The truth is, while I was so excited to see Brady, and his smile made me feel about 20 years younger, I was bummed that my crush wasn't reciprocated, and my adrenalin about seeing him started to wear off since it seemed I was just another random friend to him. I figured it was time to call it a night. Plus, we had already covered the fact that he was probably going to marry his longtime girlfriend.

"Let's head out of here and find another place."

He tipped the bartender one last time and put his hand on the small of my back (for a millisecond, not that I was counting) to escort me out of the restaurant.

We walked out of the bar onto the quieter city street.

"Where to?" he asked.

"Let's just walk and figure it out," I said.

Suddenly, I felt a strong arm around my waist. It was so sudden I wasn't even sure it was Brady. But it was. He whisked me to the side of the sidewalk and pulled me close. He kissed me. Hard. Good hard. Not bad hard or creepy hard. Just...passionately. It was so quick I could barely balance myself.

"Um... What was that?" I asked.

"Oh shit," he said.

With that he kissed me again. Harder this time.

"FUCK," he said, as he took a few steps back running his hands nervously through his hair.

"What?"

"Darcy. Damn you are beautiful."

"What??"

Brady suddenly clenched his fists tight. He put his hands behind his head as though he were literally trying to hold himself back.

"UGHHHHHHH. Damn it."

Great. Did Brady have Tourettes? Had I missed that?

"What's going on here? About 20 minutes ago I was wondering if you even knew who I was or that I was even a woman," I said.

He covered his face with his hands and slid them back through his hair.

"Of course I know who you are. I was just trying to be a gentleman, but then I couldn't let this night go by without letting you know there was attraction. Man Darcy, you are sexy and you are beautiful. Look at you."

I looked at him. Stunned. It was the moment I had always waited for and it was finally here.

"I kept asking you, all night, if you remembered me, because it seemed like you didn't."

"Darcy, of course I remember you. I thought you were beautiful then, I knew when you grew up you'd be *this*. But you were so young, and I would have never crossed that line. But of course I thought about it, you know, about when you were *older*. From the minute I showed up and saw what you look like now I knew I was screwed."

I knew it!

"I thought about it too. A lot." I felt like a teenager making this disclosure. Not a grown woman with a child.

He leaned in to kiss me again. He held my face with his hands and looked into my eyes. Then he took a step back and started pacing around. He might have even walked away and came back. Here was this strong, tough guy who had lived in Iraq and fought in Desert Storm. And *I* was making *him* nervous.

I laughed nervously, "What's wrong?"

He let out a deep sigh.

I knew what was wrong. He didn't need to tell me. For as great as this moment was, he had a girlfriend. A long-term girlfriend. Who was *everyday*.

"Don't make this mistake. You will regret it. And I don't want to ruin us, and your memories of me, with feelings of guilt or regrets." I said and took a healthy step backward.

"In two and a half years I have never come close to crossing the line. I don't know what is going on Darcy. I just...." clenching his fists again.

I got it. We had been waiting for a moment like this for 20 years, literally, but life got in the way. First I was too young, then he was married, then I was married, now he has a girlfriend. Sometimes timing is everything.

"It really says something about chemistry," he said.

"What do you mean?"

"We had it 20 years ago. And we have it now."

"I know. But this isn't our time. Again," I smiled.

"When I saw you, you blew me away, and then you said you were 35, and I realized you were older than my girlfriend. You were a woman now. And I realized, you weren't a kid anymore."

"Sadly."

In that moment I realized what was so amazing about Brady was that he would remain my crush. Crushes were perfect. They were flawless. Because they aren't real. You don't get to see people's flaws. They are insulated in bubble wrap made of wishes and fantasies. You don't know if they leave dishes in the sink, or don't call when they say they will. You don't know if they don't handle conflict well or make terrible boyfriends. You do know that you think they are good-looking, funny and you are attracted to them in several ways. But a crush is a picture that you take, a snapshot that stays with you unmarred by reality. Sometimes a crush... is better than the real thing.

"I'm going to go before you make a big mistake," I said, kissing him on the forehead.

"You're killing me Darcy."

He wanted to say he would call me, I wanted to tell him to. But for now, there was nowhere to go from here. He called me the next day to tell me how special he thinks I am.

"Likewise, Brady," I said, and silently thanked the universe he lived many states away.

And just like that, Brady was re-shelved in the crush archives of my mind. Maybe I would check him out of the library one day and take him for a spin. Life is unpredictable. You never know...

116

SOMETIMES…I STALK TOO

OCTOBER 31, 2011

AFTER BEING MARRIED for 7 1/2 years, and living with my husband a few years before that, I had gotten used to a man around the house. A man who screws things, nails things, you know…good with his hands. No, no. Not *that*. I mean actually screw and nail. With tools. Manly tasks, involving dangerous things like drills, hammers and the like. Okay, well maybe my Jewish husband wasn't *that* great at those things. There was that one time he assured me he could run the cable into the next room by drilling through the wall, only to drill through the actual cable itself, leaving us cable-less over a long holiday weekend. Needless to say, after that, I hid the drill. In the garbage.

When I began living on my own with Bear, I realized I needed a man around the house to do things like hang heavy mirrors, change lights in fixtures I couldn't reach, mount tv's on the wall and cook for me. Well, that last part is just a bonus. I guess that's what *Seamless* is for, no?

That is when *he* came into my life. Fernando. He was the head handyman in my building who I would pay a little extra on the side to do such odd jobs. I got used to having Fernando around the house. Well, at least in my building. I would shop with ease buying furniture that needed to be assembled, extra-large pictures that needed to be hung...really, whatever my heart desired because I had Fernando to do it for me. Until... he found another job being the super at a building a couple of blocks away.

When I received this news from my doorman one day I didn't take it well. It was as though my husband was being deployed.

"Noooooooooooooo!" I envisioned myself screaming, clinging to Fernando's leg as he walked off into the sunset, or at least into the subway with his tool kit.

"Why are you leaving?" I asked, after I took the elevator to the basement and found him (or stalked him) in the boiler room.

"It's a better job."

"But you've been here for years!"

"Exactly. Now I am going to be the super. It's a lot more money Darcy."

"I understand." I said.

I may have even copped an attitude. Which I realize wasn't fair. It's not that I didn't want Fernando to have a better job. I did. Really. But I also didn't want to lose my house husband.

"You'll be fine Darcy. John can take care of the same things for you."

John was the *other* handyman. And by other, I mean the one I didn't like. He wasn't as good. He was also smaller than me, so if I couldn't lift something, why would I ask *him* to?

I rode back up in the elevator to my apartment, sulking. I sat on the couch looking at everything Fernando had done for me. Freshly painted hallway, check. Perfectly mounted flat screen TV in my apartment, check. I would never have such a well maintained home again.

Suddenly everything in my apartment seemed like something that needed fixing and there was no one there to do it.

A week later Fernando was at his new job. I knew it was a couple of blocks away. I had decided to have new shades installed in my bathroom and there was no way I was asking skinny John.

"Hey, Frankie?" I asked my doorman as I was leaving to take Bear to school, "What building did Fernando go to?"

This is sad, but I had visions of walking there, boom box in hand, and standing outside the front door holding it over my head like LLoyd Dobler in *Say Anything*. Frankie blessed me with the coveted information, but I never went over there. Even though I wanted to.

A year later I moved. My new apartment needed everything. And I needed help. With nowhere to turn I picked up my phone and quickly pulled up Fernando's number. It rang a few times before he picked up.

"Hello?"

"Hi! Fernando? It's me. Darcy. From your old building? A couple of years ago? *Awkward*. Yes. Hi! Oh, everything's fine. It's just that, well, I moved. Yes. Into a new building. And there are a lot of things I need done and I am looking to hire someone. Would you be interested?"

I let the question linger and it was met with semi-silence on the other end. Like one of the Bachelorettes waiting for their rose at the most dramatic rose ceremony yet, I silently begged in my head. *Please, say yes. Please choose me.* I may have even made that awkward squinty smile.

"Oh. I have a friend who would probably do it. Should I give him your number?" Fernando said, completely uninterested.

What? Passing me off to his *friend*? Was Fernando turning me down?

"Oh. You mean, you can't do it?"

At this point it was becoming embarrassing for all parties involved. I was basically pleading. Music may or may not have started to play. You know, the kind where they try to get people off the stage when their speeches are too long.

"Darcy, I am just so busy with this new job. I don't have any time."

"Oh. Okay. Well if you change your mind, just let me know."

Just like Robbie, I wasn't really taking no for an answer.

I hung up the phone and realized: Fernando had moved on. And I had to as well. I did what I always do with guys I stopped dating so I don't ever feel tempted to contact them again. I deleted his number from my phone. I had to come to the realization that there were other men, with other drills in the sea.

Oh, and guess what? Coincidentally, in my new building, the supers name is also Fernando. He may not be the same as my old Fernando, but they have the same name. So for now…it will do, or at least, it will have to.

117

FRIDAY NIGHT LIGHTS

D<small>ECEMBER 7, 2011</small>

B<small>EAR PLAYS A SPORT</small>. He has a few coaches for this sport. One in particular, the best coach in my opinion, spent some time talking to Jason and I one day after Bear's practice. As it turns out, he too grew up in the city and we all shared a ton of knowledge about the city as it used to be. Jason and I decided Bear should take a few extra lessons with said coach. We will call him Lex.

"You call to schedule the lesson. He likes you," Jason said as we walked out of practice with Bear.

"What do you mean? He likes both of us."

"No, but he *likes* you."

"Really?" I asked as we all loaded into a taxi, "How do you know?"

"Don't worry, I know."

Jason loves to offer me advice, albeit inappropriate (See: *Advice From My Ex-Husband* and *Take My Ex-Wife, Please*), but on occasion he is right. In this instance, I felt he wasn't.

As the weeks passed and I did notice Lex becoming friendlier. I would often catch him looking for me and I thought Jason might be onto something. Over time it began to feel as though he was actually flirting with me. Teasing me about a goofy winter hat that I much adored last season replete with giant pom-pom on top. When he told me I had mischievous eyes, I was pretty sure he had officially stuck a toe into inappropriate waters.

I sent him a text one afternoon asking if he was available to give Bear a lesson the following Saturday.

"Bummer. I thought you were asking me out," he replied.

I looked at the text and slouched in my seat. I peered over my shoulder to see if anyone was looking. Hopefully they weren't, as I was in my house, alone... and that would be beyond creepy, but it felt a little wrong and incredibly awkward.

I didn't know how to respond. So I did the lamest thing possible. I responded. With "lol." *Ugh.* "lol" is worse than "I carried a watermelon." Let me tell you something about lol. It's overused, and often used when people have nothing else to say. When people write it, I don't imagine them to actually be laughing out loud. Unless they write it in all caps: "LOL." Then, I can imagine I got *at least* a giggle. That is neither here nor there, and has nothing to do with the story, but I felt while we were on the topic I should address it.

I can't believe I am going to say this. But Jason was *right*. The coach was hot for me. I had mixed emotions about this.

I have to admit, it felt good being adored in my worst moments: Arguing with Bear over putting on his equipment, having Bear *not* listen to the coach and having to sit through a lecture about it afterward as though I was being scolded by the principal. Trying to juggle Bear's pizza while getting him suited up, resulting in tomato sauce being smeared all over my face and clothing. Having the coach see me coming in late to practice, a sweaty mess, after not being able to find a parking spot nearby, therefore having to park on the other side of the earth and haul heavy equipment and a 7-year-old through the streets of New York City...only to find out...he thinks I look pretty darn cute doing it? That's flattering. But on the other hand, is it really a good idea to date someone I rely on to make my son a pro athlete? I know, I know…but a mother can dream no?

On the other hand, of course, there is the *Friday Night Lights* factor. I LOVE *Friday Night Lights*, and everything about it. How much do you love the coach? Coach Taylor is the best. And so is his wife. I could be her if I dated the coach. Kids would knock on our door all day and odd hours of the night.

"Darcy? Lex? I need to talk to you both. My parents kicked me out of the house because my step father is a drunk and I'm in love with a girl from the wrong side of the tracks."

Lex and I would fix the entire problem and have the family reunited in under an hour. That or the kid would live with us, and join our ever-growing family. We would convert all young strippers into honors students, and any and all drug problems of any teen living on the edge would be a thing of the past. Then I have to remind myself: We are not talking about football. And this is not Texas. Oh yea, and I am not a principal. *Sigh*.

Maybe dating Bear's coach isn't a great idea. So…I didn't date him.

118

KICK OFF YOUR SUNDAY SHOES

DECEMBER 12, 2011

HAVE you ever thought someone was *so* boring, they were like a one man Footloose town?

Me too.

119

THE MOST DRAMATIC ROSE CEREMONY YET

DECEMBER 21, 2011

It's holiday time in New York City. Holiday time means holiday parties, and lots of them. After an impromptu change of Thursday night plans, I headed out with a few friends to an old friends party. One of the friends I was with, I had dubbed my lucky charm. You see, he is one of my best wingmen and I always have the best dating luck when he is with me. So I put on my highest heels, my skinniest black pants and my finest embellished top and headed out for the holiday festivities with my crew.

After spending two hours at the first party, we ventured to our next location which is currently one of the hottest spots in New York City nightlife. We got a table and piled onto the banquette, when suddenly, I locked eyes with one of the most handsome men I have seen live.

Now here is the thing: He wasn't *my* kind of handsome. He was Tom Brady handsome, which is obviously very handsome, but a little too pretty. *For me.* I like guys that look like they have been through it a bit. A scar or two, possibly a crooked nose, you know, signs of life. I'm not really the pretty boy type, but he was cute with a smile that could light up the entire room. He planted himself in front of me and we continued to make serious eye contact for a good 40 minutes, constantly checking back.

"Do you know this guy?" I said to my lucky charm. "Is he your friend? The one with the brother? You know…that guy you once introduced me to?"

"Who? Ian? No. But he *is* staring at you Darce."

"I thought so."

I continue to lock eyes with the handsome stranger and then turn my attention to my friends. After a quick walk around the room and a location change I spot said handsome stranger and notice he is wearing the same shoes my ex-husband always wears. They are from LL Bean. Those Boat shoes. The ones that people stopped wearing in 7th grade. People who aren't my ex-husband. Or this guy.

He inches closer to me in the crowd. He is finally close enough to talk. He stands with his chest close to mine. He is about 6'1" and general heaven.

"You know, those shoes come with a special policy. You can send them back to LL Bean when they are worn out and they will send you a brand new pair. Forever." I said, as I smiled my most Darcy smile and gazed directly into his eyes.

"Are you making fun of my shoes?"

"No. I like them."

"Good. I like you. Who are you? You are the most beautiful thing I've ever seen."

"Me?" smiling coyly. *Is this for real? And why is he laying it on so thick?*

"Can I steal you away? Let's sit down," he says, shuffling me to a sofa.

We are now sitting alone on a sofa in a dark corner. I ask how old he was as he definitely looked younger than me.

"31."

"Ah. I am too old for you. I'm *36*."

"That's not too old. And you are beautiful. Who cares."

When is it too early to tell someone you love them? Can I tell him now? Now? What about now? Maybe now? How about now?

I was looking at his flawless face, his perfect teeth, his piercing blue eyes. I thought he was way too handsome to be picking *me* up out of the crowd. It was a pretty hot crowd that night, and I've got to admit, the competition was stiff.

"Where are you from?" I asked, trying to figure out this handsome boy's story.

"Grew up in the city until 8th grade, then moved to Connecticut."

Explains the shoes.

"I like a Connecticut boy. What do you do?"

"Finance."

He was sweet. He looked like he stepped right out of an episode of *Friday Night Lights* as the hot new ball player. And for this moment, he was mine.

Within a few minutes of chatting he grabs my face and tries to go in for a *major* kiss. With tongue. A real *real* kiss.

"Whoa. Sorry, I wasn't ready for that," I said, pulling back my face and making it my own again.

That was awkward. My friends were watching from across the room. Their mouths agape.

Suddenly, my friend approaches.

"Aren't you that guy? That guy from TV?"

"Yes," he says, with an embarrassed smirk.

"Really? What show are you on???" I asked. I definitely didn't see that one coming.

"I was on the Bachelor, and the Bachelor Pad."

Crickets.

Now, if you are a Darcy reader you KNOW how much I love reality TV, and those are shows I watch. But I have missed a few seasons lately. *Damn you Darcy. Why did you have to take up writing and spend less time focusing on your DVR. UGH. Such an overachiever.* But at least kissing me in the first few minutes made sense. He was used to having to vie for one woman's attention against 20 some odd other bachelors, all in a 45 minute time frame. He thought he was working under the wire. Makes sense now.

"Yeah. You are Bachelor X (real name omitted)," she says accusingly.

"Yep."

Okay, now please. Please walk away cock block. I chant silently in my head. But she doesn't. She goes in for more.

"I met you. At a party."

Oh boy.

"You dated my friend."

Not good.

She stared at him with intense crazy eyes.

Please make this stop.

"I'll leave you two alone now."

"Thanks," I said. I may have murmured it from under the sofa I was now hiding beneath.

"This is really awkward with all your friends staring at us," Bachelor boy said.

I look over to see my friends, also known as my cock block crew, staring at us like we were on stage. My lucky charm was dancing in my fur vest in our direction, my other friend giving him the look of death, and the other two just staring in awe like they were witnessing an orgy with animals and carneys.

I tried to wave them away without him noticing.

"Come with me, let's go somewhere else," he said.

"I can't right now."

"But they really aren't leaving us alone. It's kind of weird."

"I couldn't agree more."

"Then come with me."

"I...just can't."

The truth is, I didn't really want to. I wasn't in the right mind-set to follow a cute boy gd knows where. Not tonight.

"Well, I can't do this with all of them right there."

I didn't blame him. I said goodbye to my Bachelor. No rose for me at this ceremony. I could almost hear Chris Harrison in my head "*Say your goodbyes now Darcy.*" It's okay though. I didn't want to be *that girl*, dating *that guy* from TV.

Given that I have never had an actual rose ceremony, this certainly was my most dramatic rose ceremony yet. We will always have that.

But it is nice to know, this mama has still got it. Oh, and note to self, next time, I will leave the cock block crew at home. (Sorry guys).

120

BREAKING BAD

DECEMBER 27, 2011

GUYS, I am not quite sure how to say this...so I am just going to come right out and say it.

(Insert sound of throat clearing here)

"My penis would break you in half" is *not* an okay pickup line. It's just not.

Are we clear?

GENERAL HOSPITAL

JANUARY 2, 2012

I WAS SICK. Really sick. I had a virus. The flu. Whatever it was, I was ill. So ill in fact, It landed me in the hospital to get rehydrated.

I was lying in a bed in the ER, an IV of fluid dangling from my arm, my hair tied into one gigantic rat's nest and I may have been any number of shades of green. My mother stood by my side nervously.

The Doctor on call spoke to me for a bit about my symptoms and ordered a few tests. When he walked away my mother asked me,

"Why didn't you ask him if he knew anyone?"

"What?" I said, barely able to respond.

"Like any single friends for you?"

"I did."

"I didn't hear you."

"That's because of course I didn't. I am lying here looking the worst I have looked in I don't know long. He was asking me how many times I vomited over the past 24 hours and I had to describe what it *looked* like. Should I have thrown in that I also like *Pearl Jam*, long walks on the beach, and candle-lit dinners?"

She laughed, "Well, you never know."

"Do you think there was any shot he was going to run home to his friends and say I saw the hottest chick today. She was listless. She almost threw up on me. I don't know if she has showered for days. Don't miss out on this incredible opportunity."

Beat.

"Come on Mom. Really?"

She laughed. We both did. Hysterically. But out of the corner of my eye I saw her trolling the emergency room for other *single* doctors.

When I got home that night she stayed in my apartment to help me out. I was awoken at 6 am to a very faint sound. It sounded like paper. Being ripped. Slowly. Wait. That sound was…familiar. But no, it couldn't be. But it had to be.

"Mom? Are you opening my mail?" I called from my bed.

"I am organizing it," she called back from the living room.

Crickets.

Mom, I know you are reading this. Thanks for everything! Thanks for helping me out and being the best mother ever. And of course, giving me the best material!

122

HAVING WHAT IT TAKES

January 9, 2012

One of the reasons I married my ex-husband is because I saw how he took care of his mother when she was sick. He not only quit his first major job out of college to move to the Mayo Clinic in Rochester, Minnesota, with her for three months to take care of her (he was an only child, and she was a single mom), but he visited her every single day in the hospital for nearly a year until the day she died. That's when I decided he was a good man and had what it took to be a good husband. It was exactly what I would have done for one of my parents had they fallen ill. And it's exactly what I did for my father 11 years later when he was diagnosed suddenly with stage 4 Pancreatic cancer. When I sat with my father for the 6 months of his courageous battle I realized it's not what you had, but it's who you had by your side.

I had been broken up with Colby (see: *Yankees vs. Red Sox*) for nearly two years when my father died. But he was by my side every step of the way. I knew that Colby loved me. Real, real, deep love. The kind that Nicholas Sparks books are made of. Colby rode in the car with me to my father's grave after his funeral. He didn't say a word but I knew he was there for me and I felt totally comfortable falling apart, as I knew he would be there to catch me. When the service was finished, there is a Jewish tradition, where each person has the opportunity to shovel dirt on the grave. Helping fill the grave means you have left nothing undone and it is the ultimate final respect for the deceased. After everyone had their turn I looked over at the men who worked in the cemetery who would have the job of filling the grave when we left, and then I looked at Colby.

"I want you to do it," I said, through my tears.

"Do what?"

"Fill the grave. I don't want strangers to do it."

I knew Colby could handle it. All 6'4" of him. Colby said nothing. He was standing there in 98 degree weather at the end of June in a dark suit and began to cover my fathers coffin. I looked on believing that Colby was a superhero. He could do anything. And would for me. I felt much better knowing that my dad would be covered with care.

After I was released from the ER I was still incredibly sick, and guess who showed up to help me? Leo. (See: *Deal Breakers* & *Songs About Darcy*). Not surprising. We had always remained friends and as far as I am concerned, he was always the ultimate mensch (if you aren't familiar with Yiddish, it means "a person of integrity and honor." Thank you, Wikipedia). When he checked in for the holidays and heard I was sick he *insisted* he come right over and take care of me. I didn't even have to ask. I hadn't dated Leo in 10 months, yet I could still count on him. He knew I was alone. Bear was on vacation with his dad, my mom had put in overtime and needed some sleep before she was to leave for her own trip, and I...was alone. Really sick, and alone. I couldn't even get up to walk to the kitchen. By the fifth day, I had a fever. A high one. And I was scared. Leo wanted to help and wouldn't take no for an answer. He came with flowers, two kinds of soup, and a ton of Gatorade. He sat with me and for the first time in two days I was able to eat. He even assembled a Hanukkah present I had gotten for Bear and he walked my dog in the freezing cold. When he came back, seeing that I had eaten he asked if I wanted anything else.

"A brownie maybe?" I think it's the first time in days I had asked for food.

Guess what he did? He went back out into the cold and got me a brownie. He even sat through two hours, two different states of the real housewives, a show he can barely stand. He left when I was falling asleep. My fever was breaking and I was ready for bed. Like a gentleman, he left and checked on me periodically through the evening and late into the next week, stopping by a few days later to bring me even more food, making sure I was getting enough.

"I can't believe you would do all of this for me."

"Of course I would. I care so much about you. I would never want you to be so sick alone."

Last year in my New Year's Entry (See: *Auld Lang Syne*) I asked the question: Should auld acquaintance be forgot and never brought to mind? I had an answer then, and I have the same answer today. No, old acquaintances should *not* be forgot. Without old acquaintances, without the lessons people have taught you along the way, you would not be who you are today. I have had men set the bar incredibly *low*, but today, I am measuring the standard to those who have set it incredibly *high*. Because that is what we all deserve.

I do not know what this New Year brings but this is what I do know: Surround yourself with people who have your back. With people like that in your life, you can do anything, because you know they are right behind you to catch you if you fall. And there may be times you fall. But feeling safe to take the risk is half the battle.

I don't know who I will date in 2012, but I do know this: They better be by my bedside if I get sick or by my side if I need them there. I want someone I can rely on. Someone to take care of me when I need the help. And someone I can count on. The same way they would be able to count on me. I don't want a *guy*. I want a *man*.

Someone who will fight to the death in the gauntlet for me if the need should arise, just as I would for them.

When the going get tough, the *weak* get going. But the strong... they stay by your side.

Wishing you all love, light and all the best in 2012.

Darcy

123

ON BEING DISCOVERED

JANUARY 17, 2012

I WAS DISCOVERED! Really! You know when models or actresses get discovered? Great talents of one kind or another? Yeah. It was nothing like that.

I was standing in Starbucks when all of a sudden I was approached. By a woman. She was rather attractive.

"Hi," she says, grabbing my shoulder gently and whipping me around so we were now having some type of private conversation.

"Hi," I say, quickly scanning my brain wondering if I have ever met her before.

I never forget a face, but apparently had forgotten hers.

"I notice you aren't wearing a wedding ring," she said in a low tone whisper, glancing down at my hand.

"No. No, I'm not."

Hi, my name is Darcy. And I'm divorced. I want to say, but realize that would probably be too much information for this stranger.

"Are you single?" she asked.

I thought for a second. I wondered if she was hitting on me and suddenly realized I was not ready for my foray into lesbianism, even though I often tell my mother that I am.

"Yes," I said, scared for what was coming next.

"Well, I think you are gorgeous. And you are perfect."

"For?"

"Setting up. I have a lot of great men."

I half smiled, not sure of what was going on. I quickly wondered if my mother had slipped her a hundred bucks and a bottle of tequila. I stood cautiously.

"I deal with only the best," she continued.

I let out a nervous laugh, unsure what to say.

"You see, I am a matchmaker. A very very high-end matchmaker."

"Oh? Wow. Well-"

"I have men pay *a lot* for my services. Well, our company's services. But for the women, it's free." Somehow through small talk, she discloses these men can pay anywhere up to 50k for their services.

I furrowed my brow and my jaw dropped a bit. I quickly wondered if matchmaker was code for Madam. I mean, 50k sounded steep. For a date? You could get those for free.

"I, I don't-"

With that she slipped me her card.

"Call me," she said.

She might have even handed me a bottle of Love Potion number 9, but that part is blurry now. Her email address and company website were engraved on the front of the heavy stock card.

"Oh...okay...I'll check it out. The website. You know..."

"Trust me," she said, as she walked up to grab her coffee.

"You just go to dinner. That's it. And if you like them, great, if not, we set you up with someone else," she said over her shoulder and she walked out on her very high Jimmy Choo heels.

I went home and immediately pulled up the website on my computer as though I was looking up some type of deviant porn act.

This…was a secret. A dirty one. Well, a secret I will share with all of my readers…which are a lot of people.

The website was filled with flashy pictures of gorgeous women and the site boasted their high-profile clientele.

I immediately called Alexis.

"Hello?"

"I am becoming an escort."

"What?"

"I was approached by this woman. She claims to be working for a "matchmaker," but I am on the site, and it looks like, well, it looks like an escort service. Even the name is uncomfortable to say."

"That. Is. Amazing."

"I know. Maybe Jason was right. Maybe I should be an escort." (See: *Take My Ex-Wife. Please*)

I googled the company and came up with a wealth of information. Apparently, they were pretty legit as far as matchmakers are concerned. But it still seemed a little escort-esque to me. In a bored moment, and realizing it would make for the best Darcy entry ever, I emailed my new friend, Heidi Fleiss, I mean Jackie the matchmaker, and made my appointment.

That night I turned on a red light in my bedroom and practiced dancing in my lingerie in front of my window, like any good escort would do. Oh wait, that's a hooker. In Amsterdam. What do high-end escorts in New York City do? Wear stilettos and mini skirts to Rangers games. Yeah. That couldn't be me. I like a lot of layers when I go watch them play.

The day of my "meeting" came. I wasn't quite sure how to dress for it. It was mid-day, in midtown, in a real office building. Do I wear fishnets? Or just jeans? A pants suit? Who was I kidding? I never ever owned a pants suit. It was particularly cold that day, and by the time I showed up my cheeks and nose were red, like the neighborhood drunk. Or a nice jewish girl about to make the jump to high-class hooker.

I approached the doorman (in this case, the *doorwoman*) in the lobby and told her what floor I was going to. She asked for my ID. My name was in the system so she could see where I was going. *Awkward.* She had bluetooth in her ear. I was pretty sure she was whispering to the person on the other end that a brand new concubine was arriving. She laughed. I cringed.

I walked to the elevator banks. I got lost. There were so many damn elevator banks. I have lived in this city since the day I was born. How did I get lost in a lobby full of elevators? Oh wait, I know how; my moral compass was clearly broken, as I was on my way to meet a Madam.

"What floor are you going to Miss?" one random lobby dweller asked.

"36?"

"Right this way," he said, leading me to the proper hallway.

He looked me up and down and I saw his head turn out of the corner of my eye as I walked past him. Ugh. Did he know where I was going too? Was he checking me out? Maybe he'd want to be my first client?

When I got to the offices they were beautiful. Really top-notch. I had to sit and fill out paperwork, just like at the doctor's office. Except instead of medical history I had to fill out things like relationship history. What were my hobbies? My interests? What was my type? Was this really happening?

I entered the room to meet with the matchmaker. Not the original one I had met in Starbucks, but her cohort. After answering a series of questions as to what I was looking for and what my type was, and what some of my deal breakers were, I asked her...as politely as possible:

"This isn't an escort service right? I mean...it's not...is it? I mean, I am not judging, That would be fine. Not for *me* but for other people-"

She laughed.

"No! Of course not. We just deal with very busy men, who are looking for something specific. And we find and screen the candidates for them. We will contact you if you meet their criteria, and you can always decline."

"Okay," I smiled, still not convinced.

The matchmaker was lovely though. Really. She seemed so normal.

I said my goodbyes and made my way back into the streets of New York City, putting on my sunglasses and pulling the hood of my coat over my head as I left the lobby of course.

By the time I got home, there was an email from the matchmaker telling me how great it was to meet me, and how she already had two people in mind for me with their brief bios attached. One was a surgeon and one was a hedge funder. The men sounded great. Truly. Successful, and kind, with very good life stories detailing acts of kindness and examples of how family oriented they were.

But I couldn't do it. I didn't feel comfortable with the process. I figured any man paying a service that much to have dinner with me, would expect a *very* special dessert. And it's just not how I roll. I also didn't love the story.

"Mommy, how did you meet daddy?"

"Oh, he paid a fortune to take me to dinner."

It was a little too *Pretty Woman* for me. And not the opera scene that we all love. More the Hollywood boulevard scene with the bad wig and the knee-high boots and the sofa in the elevator for two.

So I politely declined the dates. I want to find men *my* way. The old-fashioned way. Finding dates isn't my problem, but finding *the one* is. But I will let fate take its course. A serendipitous event that no one can predict. And I don't mind waiting. I have so many hours of trashy TV stored on my DVR I could stay content for a long time really.

Wait. Did I just say I didn't need to find a good man because I had so much DVR to catch up on? Where the HELL is that lady's card?

124

MILDLY MY TYPE

January 23, 2012

I had a date on a very very cold night in New York City. Very cold. He called me to plan it and we were discussing where to meet when I said,

"Can you believe how cold it is outside? It's *freezing*."

There was silence at the other end of the phone.

"Well. It's not...not so bad."

What? I lost four fingers from frostbite when I left my apartment this morning. What do you mean it's not so bad?

I tried to push my doubt aside that we would have very little in common and got ready for my date. I was wearing so many layers. I wore two jackets, and might have even put on Bear's snow pants. I didn't care how I looked. I was going for warmth. I remember showing up for a date recently and when I went to get my coat from the coat rack as we were leaving, my date said to me,

"You wore a puffy coat on this date?"

"Yes. It's freezing."

"Then you couldn't possibly think it was going to be good."

"Why not?" I asked.

"Cause puffy coats aren't sexy."

"But they are warm."

"I am wearing a Rag and Bone coat, and I am freezing. You know why? I wanted to look good for you," he whined.

It's not my fault you are the woman in this relationship. I thought, as I pulled my very warm Moncler fur hood over my head and hoofed it out of the restaurant like a clumsy Clydesdale.

But back to my date...

I was standing in the restaurant, layered in puffiness and GORE-TEX when my very tall dark and handsome date arrived in his suit. No coat.

"Where's your coat?"

"This is it."

"It's freezing. It's about 20 degrees."

"This keeps me warm."

"Wow." I said, as I spent the next 20 minutes peeling off layers of clothing. I may have even had glove warmers in. And a hot water bottle shoved up the back of my sweater.

"You see, I am a very positive person, I like to look at things in a very positive manner. So instead of saying "cold" which is a *negative* word, I like to think it's mildly refreshing," he explained.

"Ah. I would like to mildly de-thaw in the kitchen. Next to the oven."

We sat down and my date began to regale me with his adventurous tales. He had *actually* climbed Mt. Everest. It would have probably been a bad time to tell him I am too lazy to walk up the stairs at my local *Staples* so I take the elevator one flight. I was impressed with all that he had accomplished. He was also working on some other crazy expedition where he was walking to the North Pole. Ten days of no sleep. Only "rest."

"If you notice I have some scruff on my face. I usually shave everyday. But I have to grow a beard for the expedition or my face will freeze."

"Right. Of course. Wow," I started to picture what he would look like with a long creepy beard.

"When is that?"

"April."

"Wow. That will be quite a beard."

"Yea. It has to be."

Right now, with only the scruff he looked cute.

The thing is, I was impressed by his incredible motivation and his insatiable lust for accomplishment.

We ordered a bottle of wine and a couple of dishes. We were sharing stories about our background, our upbringing, our hobbies. Even though he was amazing, incredibly sweet and very accomplished, I could just tell we weren't going to be a good personality match. But the dinner was lovely and I enjoyed his company.

"Hey, you are a writer, you will appreciate this story."

I nodded, excited for what was to come next. It was a 45 minute story involving the writings of a priest. And something about a goat. I can't say for sure since I fell asleep halfway through the story. I had a dream that I got into a taxi that was driving by outside the window. I guess it was more like a nightmare, because I knew it wasn't real. In reality he had just ordered another bottle of wine.

Help. A tiny voice cried from within. *I'm trapped.*

He was trying and seemed like a really good guy. When all of a sudden he said it. Out loud. I don't recall what we were talking about, but I heard it clear as day.

"I don't have a television."

I literally heard the music in the restaurant screech to a halt. At that moment, the date was over. *RIP this date.*

"What do you mean?"

"Well, I don't have that much time. And the time I do have, I'd rather be doing something more important than watching TV."

Ah. So we didn't agree that the Real Housewives of Beverly Hills are important. I see. Well, we tried. We did our best. We sat through this lovely dinner and you are handsome, and incredibly kind. Obviously well read and very very good at your job. But I am trashy. I love reality TV. And like *InTouch* magazine. A lot.

When it was time for dessert, he asked if I had a sweet tooth.

"Yes." I said. Figuring he didn't. I don't think any of my dates had ever preferred dessert.

"Me too. What would you like for dessert?"

"Hmmmm." I said, looking over the menu, planning my attack.

"How about we get one of each?"

In that moment. In that single, solitary moment, he went from guy that doesn't have a TV, to the best date ever. One of each? *One of each?* He loved desert as much as I did. Maybe we could love each other.

After the meal, the very dessert heavy meal, I suited back up in my winter gear and we walked out into the mildly refreshing night. No. I can't. It was still fucking freezing. Is that not positive? Oh well. It's true.

"Good luck with all of your adventures," I said as I watched him freeze in nothing but a suit.

"Why good luck? Aren't I going to see you again? I had a great time."

"Oh. Yeah. Yes. I guess so. Sure."

The truth is, I wasn't sure. Well...I was. But for now, I didn't have it in me to say no. He was a nice guy. Very sweet and meant well. When he followed up and asked me for another date, I told him the truth. I didn't see it being a match. And I love TV too much.

125

ALL HIS CHILDREN

January 30, 2012

Once went on a date with a guy who had so many children he *actually* lived in a shoe. Or maybe it was a huge house in Greenwich. I forget now.

ELEVEN MISSED CALLS

February 8, 2012

The other day I logged onto Facebook to see a guy I dated post divorce just had a baby. He had 3 kids from his first marriage. This was his fourth. *Way to hog all the children,* I think to myself right before writing "Congratulations!" underneath the picture. The truth is I was happy for him. Afterall, *I* didn't want to date him. But I was happy someone else did. He was super nice, super funny…but just not for me.

This is not the first person I have dated post divorce who went on to get married and have children. In fact, several people I have gone on dates with have gone on to get married. At the time, they had told me they were looking for that. I was honest when I told them I just wasn't sure.

I would be lying if I said seeing the men I have dated, and passed on, go on to get married and have more children didn't register on some level. I am the first to admit I don't necessarily pick the right men to fall for. Although I am getting better. Kind of?

But there was one man. One man in particular that really threw me. Are you ready? Because I was not. Yup. Robbie. Even *Robbie*...had a girlfriend. A real one. His facebook relationship status is now set to "In a relationship with" and has the girls actual name. Which means she agreed to the relationship and went as far as confirming it on Facebook, which as you know gives it major credibility. He had been telling me he had a girlfriend for quite some time, but I didn't believe him. Afterall, how could it possibly be true? I thought it was a woman he paid, or locked in his basement. Maybe he was referring to his mother. But the other day when I was on Facebook a picture of Robbie came up in my newsfeed. A picture of him...and his girlfriend. For the first time ever I was curious about Robbie's life and clicked onto his actual page. There it was. Robbie was listed as being in a relationship with said girl. I...was speechless. I hadn't been hearing from him at all. Well I had. I would see his name come up on my phone from time to time. But it would only happen once, I wouldn't answer. And then he would vanish. This isn't the Robbie we all knew. Who called me upwards of 9 times a day for a year and a half.

About a month ago he called me and I decided to answer it. I told him I was really proud of him for being in a relationship with a girl that looked, at least from the outside, completely normal. Pretty even. He told me he loved her and she was the best. I was shocked, but proud. Slightly confused, but proud.

"I make love to her Darcy."

"That's. Awesome."

"She wants to marry me and have babies with me. I don't know what to do."

"Do it! You are a man now, and you seem to love her. And she loves you too."

"I don't know. I do make hot, sweet love to her." (I will spare you the details of what he really said)

"That's great. I am very happy for you."

"You want to be in a threesome with us?"

"What?"

"A threesome? You want in? Cause i'd like to make hot sweet love to you too."

"No. I'm good. Thanks."

He hung up on me, angry as always. He didn't resurface for at least a week. Checking in, of course, to see whether or not I wanted to have a threesome. He even offered up "making sweet love" to just him.

"But don't you have a girlfriend?"

"Fine. Goodbye."

The calls grew more frequent. And, I can't even believe I am going to admit this, but when I was very sick…I…called Robbie. *Oh gd. Hanging my head in shame.* for medical advice. There. I said it. I know. Yikes. He was surprisingly sweet and sensitive. Checking on me regularly. Telling me that if I wanted to get better I needed to drink mass amounts of Gatorade…and masturbate. I know, I know. My own fault for asking him.

The other night I was in bed and I looked at my phone. I had eleven missed calls. That could only mean one thing. Yep. I was right. Robbie. Feeling exceptionally bored, Bear was asleep and there was nothing on TV as all my regular run of the mill trashy shows were on winter break, so I called him back.

"I'm bored with fucking my girlfriend," he said as he answered the phone.

"No. No. Don't say that."

"I am. I gotta fuck Darcy. Lots of women."

"You listen to me. You somehow found a very attractive girl and tricked her into thinking you are sane. You be good to her. You understand?"

"I can't. I can't be with her anymore."

"Why?"

"I just can't. I need to be with *tons* of women."

"But *tons* of women don't want to be with you."

"Darcy. I can't. I don't think we are sexually compatible. She doesn't like the things I like in bed."

Oh boy. He started to go into details of what that meant. I wanted to mute the phone, but it wouldn't help me much, cause I would still be able to hear him.

"Robbie. Please. Trust me. You found a good girl. Who you care about. I think. Please hang in there. Maybe it will pass."

"Do you want to date me?"

"No."

"Fine."

And just like that, he hung up on me. As always. But don't worry. He called back.

127

THE PIMP AWARD

MARCH 12, 2012

I WAS SITTING with my date one evening and I had quickly decided the only redeeming factor was that it was a few blocks from my house at a place I had always wanted to try. He was handsome in a not-my-type kind of way. I wondered how long I would have to stay without it being considered rude. He spent the first 20 minutes lecturing me about tax reform. I spent the first 20 minutes playing jax in my head. I am sure he meant well, but he was a bit rigid, and at some point told me my child must be spoiled because he goes to private school.

"Not to judge your parenting."

"Of course not."

I hate you.

When the waiter approached, and asked if we wanted another glass of wine I looked at my date, hoping he too wasn't enjoying our date and he would say no. But no such luck. He suggested another round.

"Would you like some food? Are you hungry?" my date said, offering me the menu.

Maybe a bowl of soup. If you promise to drown me in it. You know, just hold my face in there. Until I stop breathing.

"No. I'm good. Thanks."

When our second glass of wine arrived I looked up only to make eye contact with the *most* handsome man. He was on the other end of the restaurant. We locked eyes, and both smiled at the same time. The entire restaurant fell away and that was all I could see. But I was trapped on terror island with my date. There had to be a way to slip said handsome stranger my number. After all, people have done it to me. But how? The restaurant was tiny. There was no way. Except... one.

"I'll be right back. I just need to use the bathroom," I said, slipping off the bar stool and walking into the bathroom.

When I got up, the handsome stranger smiled at me again. My date wasn't looking. So I smiled back.

When I got into the bathroom I quickly texted Alexis:

"Hi! Help! I am at (*insert name of restaurant here*). Please call the restaurant and ask to speak to the hot guy with dark hair and a black sweater who is sitting by the door with another man who is wearing a plaid shirt. Tell him your best friend is on a terrible date and give him my number. He will know who it is."

I hit send, prayed for the best and walked out of the bathroom, back to my date.

Not two minutes later the phone on the bar lit up. I saw the bartender speaking and passed the cordless to the waitress. Her eyes grew wide, she looked around the room. I saw a lot of commotion and whispering among the manager and staff. The waitress began to walk aimlessly around the restaurant with the cordless phone.

THAT'S MY GIRL! It could have been the most genius idea I have ever had. Well, at least my most genius idea that week. I couldn't follow the events that were unfolding as I had to follow the conversation that was going on on my actual date.

"And anyway that's why McCain had to go with Palin as a running mate," he said.

"Right. Of course."

Now the entire restaurant staff was in on it. Yes, this is a terrible story, and makes me a very bad date. I realize. But I was on a bad date, so don't I get some type of pass here?

I watched the waitress approach said stranger with the cordless phone. I see said stranger and the waitress talking. He looks up at me and smiles. He takes the phone. This was AMAZING. I watched him on the phone. I don't know what they were talking about, but they talked for a couple of minutes. I knew Alexis was getting the whole scoop for me. His friend kept turning and looking at me. So did the table next to them. We were all smiling. My poor date had zero idea this was unfolding.

Until he said,

"Those guys keep checking you out."

"Which guys?" I said, acting completely unaware.

"Those guys. Over there," he motioned in their direction.

Oh, that guy? You mean my next date? Oh. Yeah. Him. He's cute isn't he?

"I didn't see."

Ugh, I may have been going to hell, but it was *so* worth it.

I got another text from Alexis.

"His name is Matias. He is from Argentina. He is going to call you."

Finally, I was brave enough to end my date. I couldn't really take it for another minute.

"Well, we should get going."

"Really? Oh-"

I was kind of abrupt.

I walked him out of the restaurant and to the subway on the corner.

"It was really great meeting you," I said and gave him a one arm hug. You know the kind. When you add an insincere pat?

"You too."

In the spirit of full disclosure. I may have pushed him down the stairs to get him out of there faster.

When the coast was clear and my date was safely underground, I snuck back to the restaurant. *Who am I?*

"Hi!" I said to the Argentinian duo who was now waiting for me at the bar, "I'm Darcy."

"I know," he said with a thick accent.

He was even more handsome up close.

After some small chat I asked how old he was.

"25."

Wow. That was *really* young. I wasn't expecting that. It's as though I actually reached into a cradle and pulled him out.

"I'm 36. And a mom. And too old for you."

"You are perfect."

It was good enough for him, and apparently tonight, good enough for me.

Matias ordered a bottle of red wine and we talked for hours. He was sitting so close he would whisper in my ear as we spoke. And I liked it.

One of the waiters came up and whispered to me.

"You know, we have all decided you get the pimp award. We have never seen such a smooth move."

The bartender gave me a knuckle punch. "Excellent job girl."

I smiled. I imagined accepting my pimp award. *I would like to thank Alexis, for helping make this possible.* I would say as I accepted the golden cane, or was it a pimp cup? Whatever it is that pimps carry.

When we were done with our wine, we walked out into the cold night air. He held my hand. Or maybe I held his...because he was a child. And I wanted him to be careful crossing the street. We walked, we talked. I practiced my Spanish. He was polite and told me it was good. He walked me all the way to my block. He kissed me. It was the kind of kiss you want. The kind where you melt into each other and your knees get weak. I was happy.

"Do you want to come to my apartment for a drink?" he asked.

I looked into his dark eyes. He was so handsome, unbelievably sexy...but I didn't need to go home with him. He was a stranger. A very young one.

Matias asked me to dinner the following night. I didn't accept. I realized I didn't need Matias. What I needed more was the lesson. The lesson that at any moment you can feel a spark with someone. When you least expect it. Even when you are on a bad date. With someone else.

ROBBIE GETS COCKY

APRIL 4, 2012

"Do you know that I have given a UTI to every girl I have dated?"

"Um...no. I actually did *not* know that."

"It's cause I have a such a powerful penis."

Crickets.

"Want me to give you a UTI?"

"No. I'm good."

At least he has a new angle. Promising things like infections and discomfort. Come to think of it, he's like an infection. That you just can't get rid of. Oh Robbie. We love you.

129

THE END

APRIL 19, 2012

I STARTED WRITING Darcy Dates nearly two years ago. It was born in my bed on my laptop one evening after I had my fill of experiences and wanted to start documenting them. It started as something I did for myself. I shared it with five friends, who shared it with their friends, and so on, and so forth...until I had real readers. Who were strangers. I couldn't have been more honored. To write publicly is to really put yourself out there and I couldn't have been more thrilled that people actually *liked* what I was writing. But I wasn't completely putting myself out there. After all, I was writing under a pen name. Darcy, some of you will be surprised to know, is not my real name.

When I started writing Darcy, no one knew I was Darcy, but over time some people began to catch on so what I wanted to write about became harder and harder to do.

What I did realize through writing Darcy was while I thought I was trying to find love, in the process, I was really finding myself. In the time since I started writing Darcy I have broken some hearts, and some have broken mine. I have learned what I want in a partner, and I have learned what I definitely *don't* want. It's a process. While sometimes exhilarating, it's often exhausting.

When I lost my father I learned many important lessons. But one of the most important things I learned is it's not what you have, it's who you have by your side. Through this process my friends, my family, and my number one man, my son have been my rock. They have been my everything. I was one of the lucky ones because I had love with me all along. Real, true unconditional love.

I have a ton of stories I have written for Darcy Dates that I haven't published. That is mainly because I don't feel the freedom to write what I want like I did when this project first began. And without me being able to be me and write what I truly want to write it won't be as authentic as it always was. For that reason I have decided to no longer write about my dates. Fear not, as I will continue writing. I will write about other things. Life, daily observations, experiences, my mother and of course Robbie (because how could I not). But not my dates. I promise to keep you entertained, or at least I promise to try.

Thank you so much for your support over these past two years. I can't have asked for a better group of readers and I am so honored when each of you shared it, liked it, wrote to me, commented and shared your stories with me. I hope you continue to do the same when I am writing about other things.

So...I know what you are all thinking. *Where does the story of Darcy Dates end?*

My first love after my divorce was Colby. Some of you may remember me writing about him in *Yankees vs. Red Sox & Having What It Takes*. Colby and I were in love. Real love. He was my best friend and everything I wanted in a partner. To me he was perfect. They say timing is everything, and that may be true. Colby and I met when we were each newly divorced. We were just learning the ropes of single parenthood. Colby broke up with me suddenly and unexpectedly after a year of dating. He broke my heart into 4000 tiny pieces. I thought I would never recover. Three months later he came back. He said he needed to make sure this was what he wanted, after all he was so newly divorced. But it was too late. He had hurt me too badly and I thought it would never be the same. So I broke his, and started dating someone else. He waited. He tried patiently for over a year. I don't think he even dated. He just waited. We would get together, and I would try, but I was worried it was too broken and couldn't be fixed. Even though I loved him and thought he was everything. No matter what we were doing, through the years we would always find our way back to each other. He would drop everything when I would call. This went on for four years.

The truth is, I wasn't ready. I had to go on this journey and find myself and find out what I was looking for and what I needed and what I wanted. Through this process, I have. I started to really question what it is I wanted and what it was I was searching for. I learned that all relationships are different. There are even different types of love. Some people feel like a home. And others...they feel like a tent.

I started to think about Colby. Colby felt like home. I started to think about what we had. I started to think about what an idiot I was. He was one of the best guys I knew. I started to lose sleep over it. I started to think about it obsessively. I reached out to him several times over the past few months but he refused to speak to me. And I didn't blame him. I had hurt him. The same way he had hurt me. I finally decided to write him a letter. I put my entire heart in there and waited. But once again our timing wasn't right. Colby informed me he had a girlfriend. I asked if he wanted me to leave him alone. To just say the word and I would. He said yes. Being that this whole thing was my fault, and given the level of respect I have for Colby, I did. I knew it was my own fault. You see, ten months ago, after spending a great few days with Colby I told him I couldn't be with him. Why? Because I knew being with Colby meant forever. And that scared the living shit out of me.

I didn't hear from Colby for two months. A week ago, after dropping Bear off at school, I was turning the corner into my building when I heard someone call out.

"Hey."

I turned to find Colby. All 6'4" of him standing there. He had been waiting for me. He was wearing a Patriots hat, but I will let it slide. Mainly because the Giants keep beating them in the super bowl.

"What are you doing here?"

"I knew you'd be dropping Bear off at school this morning so I waited for you to get home."

"Why?" I asked.

"I want to talk about that letter."

One of my favorite quotes by Orsen Welles is, "If you want a happy ending, that depends of course on where you stop your story."

I choose to stop the story Darcy Dates here. You, my friends, can write your own ending. What do you think happened with me and Colby?

Speak to you all soon. In another place.

All my love,

Jena (AKA Darcy)

ACKNOWLEDGMENTS

I was approached many times to turn Darcy Dates into a television show. It was comedic shorts and episodic by nature. After years of pitching Darcy as a show, being developed as a show, then being shelved once again, Darcy Dates has sat quietly and privately, out of the public eye. For my birthday I decided to publish it.

James, since this was originally written, I have watched you grow into a man. An amazing man. And I am so grateful for you. Every. Single. Day. To say I am proud of how you turned out is the understatement of a lifetime. Your dad and I continue to marvel at not only your accomplishments, but who you are as a person. Thank you for teaching me more about life than I could have ever learned on my own. And thank you for giving me the opportunity to love someone more than I could ever love myself.

When I look back and reflect on the journey of Darcy, I am amazed at how much I have learned about life and love since this was written. I am now engaged to the most wonderful man, who happens to not be one of the people in this book. I didn't want to ruin the ending for you by disclosing this, but I wanted to let you know that it did, in fact, work out. So much of life is timing. I realized I had to get to the point in my life when I had the bandwidth to truly incorporate a partner. The perfect partner. That happened when I became an empty nester. I would have never been able to dedicate myself to a relationship like this years ago. It was worth the wait, and I ended up finding a true gem whom I believe I was ultimately meant to find. It's a long story about fate and coincidence for another time. To my fiancé Steven, I love you. Thank you for supporting me in the publication of this book which I am sure, at times, was an uncomfortable read. But in the end, I found exactly what I was looking for.

Mom. Thank you, thank you, thank you. You have always supported both my good and bad decisions. You are always my biggest fan. I know this journey of me finding love was a stressful one for you, but ultimately, it worked out way better than we could have imagined. Raising me probably wasn't the easiest, but you were always supportive. Thank you for always, always believing in me. Thank you for never judging, well almost never, and letting me be authentically me. I love you and couldn't have done it without you. Thank you for providing me endless material, and sitting in the front row when I would do stand-up and laugh hysterically when the jokes were about you.

Dad, I miss you. Every single day. Six Months before I starting writing this, I will never forget you picking me up, specifically to tell me I was funny. Very funny. And one day the whole world would know. You will always be one of the funniest people I have known. You taught me how to pull off a good prank. Clearly, I was a good student. I constantly feel the loss of you. I love you always. Fuck Cancer.

David, thank you for remaining a best friend and part of my family. We essentially grew up together. Look what we created. We did good.

Brett, I love you. Sisters are forever and I'm so glad you're mine.

To the rest of my family, every single one of you. I love you all, and your support has meant the world. Thanks for letting me be slightly different than the rest of you and finding it endearing more often than not.

Kim and Jeni, thank you for being my best friends through it all, listening endlessly to way more Darcy entries than this book could ever hold. Kim, thank you for being my lifetime soulmate. July 8th is CIF forever. Jeni, thank you for letting me 3rd-wheel your marriage for the past 21 years. The two of you are my family and I am so grateful for the both of you. Thank you for being supporting characters in this story. You too Peter, you too. And thank you Jake.

Darren, thanks for believing in Darcy from the get go. We tried. Man did we try. But we will try again someday soon. So glad I could rip you from Wraith at the meadow in junior high and make you my partner on so many amazing projects. CGPS forever. I love you.

Jason, thank you for believing in me. And thank you for getting an iPhone so I don't have to read your green texts. Love you.

Danny Leiner, thank you for loving Darcy the way I did. You are so truly missed.

Ami, thank you for the original artwork for Darcy. When I think of Darcy, I will forever see that image.

Gary Belsky, thank you for your quote. Thank you for *everything*. Thank you for introducing me to David, he will always be my family. Look how much good has come from that. You're one of the most brilliant people I've ever known.

Wendy, thank you for believing so hard in Darcy and seeing its full potential. One day we will make something epic together. Glad to have you as one of my lifelong friends. Arturo's forever.

Robbie, every word out of your mouth was inspiration, even when I thought there was nothing left to write. When I told Robbie he was the main character in a project I was writing and he was everyone's favorite, he never asked what I was talking about. He only said, "Of course I am. I'm the best."

To my baby Blue, you taught me that you only think you are rescuing a dog, but they are actually rescuing you.

Matthew, you would have loved this. I miss you. Every single day.

And of course, to my readers. Without you, there would be no Darcy. Thank you for giving me your time and sharing the journey with me. Every single one of you meant something in this process. When you would write to me, tell me how you related, or laughed, or shared your stories, it always kept me going. Knowing some of you might have even purchased this book makes me happy.

You never know. There may be another book. Stay tuned.